More Prais

"From the roar of the S...
and solitary drive of miles and ...
again . . . *The Natural* reflects the life of the rodeo cowboy as it is and always will be."

—Danny Newland, seven-time announcer, International Finals Rodeo, and coannouncer, National Championship Chuckwagon Races

"It surely was good motel readin' while I waited on another rodeo performance. I can tell [the author has] been there and it seems like somewhere down my forty-seven-year rodeo road, I've met all of the characters in *The Natural*."

—Lecile Harris, legendary bullfighter and four-time Pro Rodeo Clown of the Year

"Dusty Richards is 'a natural' when it comes to telling Western stories. Told from the viewpoint of someone who knows the ins and outs of rodeo life, *The Natural* is a believable tale and a must-read for anyone who enjoys a good cowboy story."

—Dan and Peggy Eoff, Founders, National Championship Chuckwagon Race

"A real, honest-to-goodness factual book about rodeo, told from the inside out. . . . Dusty Richards spins a good yarn . . . a yarn told by an ex-bull rider turned rodeo announcer who is at the top of his game. The story of his cronies and their lives, their hopes and dreams, [is] a great read."

—Dr. Lynn Phillips, many-times announcer of the Dodge National Circuit Finals, the National Finals, the Circuit Finals, the WPRA Finals, NOTRA, AQHA, and many more in the United States and Canada

"What an exceptional book . . . a great rodeo story . . . very real and factual."

—Dave Eastlake, past President, The National Senior Pro Rodeo Association, and seven-time National Senior Pro Rodeo Association World Champion

Rodeo Riders #4

THE
NATURAL

Dusty Richards

A SIGNET BOOK

SIGNET
Published by New American Library, a division of
Penguin Putnam Inc., 375 Hudson Street,
New York, New York 10014, U.S.A.
Penguin Books Ltd, 80 Strand,
London WC2R 0RL, England
Penguin Books Australia Ltd, Ringwood,
Victoria, Australia
Penguin Books Canada Ltd, 10 Alcorn Avenue,
Toronto, Ontario, Canada M4V 3B2
Penguin Books (N.Z.) Ltd, 182–190 Wairau Road,
Auckland 10, New Zealand

Penguin Books Ltd, Registered Offices:
Harmondsworth, Middlesex, England

First published by Signet, an imprint of New American Library,
a division of Penguin Putnam Inc.

First Printing, June 2002
10 9 8 7 6 5 4 3 2 1

I dedicate this book to that hardy group of individuals whom I have rodeoed with in rain, snow, sleet, and hot sunshine. They know their own names—they kept time, worked as secretaries, served as committee directors and judges, flanked, picked-up, clowned, rode rough stock, steer wrestled, roped, barrel raced, loaded the stock, furnished livestock, rebuilt barriers, repaired chutes and corrals, fixed electrical outages, took tickets, parked cars, worked in the concession stands, worked as arena directors, tractor drivers, and gatemen, and helped hang my PA system and take it down. Some have gone to the big rodeo in the sky— my hat's off to them. To the rest, a big thanks for a job well done.

—Dusty Richards

Chapter 1

The PA speaker system bellowed directly over my head as I steadied my horse in the alleyway. "Ladies and gentlemen, let's give a great Jackson welcome to three-time Circuit Pro Finals announcer from Woodbury, Oklahoma, Brad Turner. Here's Brad!"

My intro, time to go to work. On cue, the eleven hundred pounds of palomino quarter horse between my knees bolted forward through the gate. I raised my 10X silver Resistol in my right hand and waved it to the thousands in the stands. The tumultuous applause meant we had a capacity crowd filling the seats for the first performance. In a long lope, Golden Boy rounded the arena wall with ease, both of us encased in the spotlight's circle, the light reflecting off the sequins on my new red shirt. Opening night, Jackson, Mississippi—and I was off going for the week's run. I turned on the wireless singer-style mic and checked Boy with the rein in my left hand.

"Good evening, ladies and gentlemen," I said. "And to the rodeo fans from across the great southeast, a big welcome to the greatest show on dirt. Is there anyone here who wants to rodeo tonight?"

The palomino shut down in a great sliding halt on his hindquarters in the center of the arena as the houselights came up. It was hard to find an empty seat on the west side. A near-sellout is always fun to work. The applause died down. The voice compressor on the PA system needed to be lowered some; I reminded myself to do it later.

"I'd like to welcome you to the first performance of this year's fair and rodeo. Let me introduce the reigning fair queen. Give a big warm round of applause to Miss Suzanne Whitt!"

The tall brunette, riding a good bay horse that cost her old daddy plenty, came bounding out to join me, followed by five pretty cowgirls whose names I read from an index card. Luckily, none fell off their horses. Next I introduced the rodeo board members, then Johnny Farmer, the stock contractor, plus an old Turtle Cowboy who lived ten miles down the road. After everyone settled in a line to my right, I brought in the sponsors' flags with lots of hype.

Upstairs at the controls, Swing Michaels, the music man, nailed his marks. Those new computer sound systems were sure sweet compared to a live band. In the past, whenever I needed a drumroll, the band director would always be looking off somewhere. Then by the time I got an outfit trained the hometown committee would hire a new bunch of musicians the next year.

We bowed our heads for the invocation given by a local minister, and one of the major sponsors' daughter sang the national anthem—off key. Johnny Farmer's wife, Dale, riding a big paint, carried Old Glory around the arena. It was going to be a lovely night to rodeo in Jackson.

The queen and the committee members rode out of the arena. During their exit, only two committee men lost their hats. The crew quickly rounded them up.

"Let's go to chute number two, and the Flying Star Rodeo Company's award-winning bareback bucking horse, Blue Velvet. From Wyndotte, North Dakota, here's Kenny Paulson!" Boy and I were settled in the opposite corner out of the way of the bucking horse's circuit. The arena director, Toby Hale, signaled to me that we'd go to chute three next.

The gray horse sailed out of chute two and into the arena. Paulson was a real veteran at barebacks. He marked Blue Velvet perfectly that first jump. I counted the hurls the big bronc made in the air: five, six, seven. The cowboy earned himself a seventy-four-point ride. That might win a little, but during the week ahead there would be plenty more good rides.

"How about it for Kenny Paulson?" I asked as the pickup man set Paulson down. The fans paid him off with a warm applause.

"You doing all right, Brad?" Paulson asked as he stalked by. I gave him a quick "you bet" away from the microphone.

"Let's go to chute number three! Geronimo, twice the pro final's rodeo top bareback horse of the year, is ready for this young man who hails from Texas. Shoat Krammer."

The gate opened and Geronimo, a sixteen-hands-high paint gelding out of Montana, exploded into the blinding light. My eye caught his mark out and I wondered for a split second if this rookie kid from nowhere could ride this stout bronc. Geronimo had loosened more bareback riders out of their rigging than any other horse Johnny Farmer owned. The crowd began to sense this might be the best bareback ride of the week. You could hear audible gasps. Despite spine-jarring jolts, the kid lay back and spurred

him like he was riding a fat man's recliner. I reined
Boy around to study the action, talking to the crowd
and personally impressed with how Krammer used the
big animal—one tough cowboy on a stout bronc going
as high as the arena lights, never losing his spurring
stride, never moving an inch from his seat. Perfect
control all the time. The paint's legs were on steel
springs, too.

The eight-second buzzer finally came.

"Shoat Krammer, ladies and gentlemen! Was that a
ride? Let's see what the judges say." I wheeled around
as the score came on the electronic board. "Eighty-
four points!"

Krammer sailed his hat off into space to the thunderous response, and I took a measure of his awfully
young face, flush with victory. That was the night I
met Shoat Krammer in Jackson, Mississippi.

The rest of the performance went smoothly. An old
pal of mine, Thad Brown, roped his calf in eight-six
and he immediately left the fair grounds for another
rodeo in Florida. I wanted to ask him about Gloria
Hines, but he was gone. Past the halfway mark,
Johnny Farmer, standing by the chutes, gave me his
bland okay nod, which meant he was satisfied with
how things were going.

Finally the barrels were hauled out and we were
down to bull riding. Johnny Farmer had enough tough
toros to put on three major rodeos in one night. He
fed them, he pampered them, and he expected them
to buck. His horse stock was super, but bull power
was his thing. We went entire performances when not
a single top cowboy rode one. The word on the circuit
from the contestants was, if you stayed on a Farmer
bull, you won money.

The first three flung cowboys, boots, and fringed chaps into orbit. I sat on Boy out in the center of the arena between the two pickup men, Glen and Chester. At this point in the performance, with the evening winding down, an announcer must double-check everything he's done thus far. Did he make all the announcements he was supposed to? Time to be certain that he didn't forget any of the sponsors or leave out mentioning an up-and-coming event tied to the rodeo.

"Getting ready in chute six is the rookie cowboy, Shoat Krammer, folks. Rodeo today is such a specialized sport, only a few cowboys try more than one event. Some, like the great legend, Ty Murray, have done it in recent years quite well, but the two-event cowboys in rough stock are few and far between in this grinding game. Shoat has sure drawn deep tonight in this herd of top bulls. In the past two years, no pro cowboy has ridden Iceberg. Turned out thirty-six times and no one, mind you, not one pro cowboy has stayed on his back for the eight-second whistle. And some of the best have tried him. Here's Shoat!"

The gate shot open and that charolais-cross bull burst out into the pen like a lit rocket, turned in midair, and ducked back hard to the left. Then he flew into a furious spin, switched out into a reverse which would have left half the good bull riders I know headed for a mouthful of dirt.

I wondered whether the buzzer would ever sound. Cold chills ran down my face. I'd ridden a few like Iceberg in my time. I knew that by this time the boy's brain had to be blurred like a whirling slot machine. Still, in the final seconds, when he reached out and began to spur that big bull's hide hard on the outside, I looked on in disbelief.

On a bull like Iceberg, you have to be screwed on tight to risk doing that or be a damned fool. The whistle blew, Shoat pulled the tail of his rope, and Bucky Starr, the bullfighter, took the bull away from his hand. Krammer landed on his feet, sailed his gray hat again, and headed away from the obviously furious bovine. Sure couldn't blame Iceberg. He'd tried his damndest, but trotting out of the alleygate, even he looked like he couldn't believe someone had ridden him.

The crowd stood on their feet, stomping and screaming so loud it hurt my ears. Johnny stepped out from where he stood beside the chutes, took off his felt hat and shook the boy's hand. A camera bulb snapped and I wanted that photo. In five years working for the man, I'd never seen that long, lanky stock contractor so formally congratulate a contestant. Speak to them, he did a lot of that. Bragged on them plenty and he was always friendly to the cowboys, but I'd never seen him so impressed as with that boy's skill in managing to stay on board his unridable beast.

"How about ninety-four points?" I asked the screaming crowd. Krammer would go away from Jackson a lot richer than when he arrived. He stood well enough in the barebacks to win a couple grand, but his bull ride paycheck would more than double that amount. Whew, I felt a shiver of jealousy. That boy could ride like a Texas sandbur.

After that ride, the rest of the evening went downhill. Even the fireworks at the end of the show lacked their usual sparkle. I bid the fans goodnight and invited them to come back to the rest of the performances, then I galloped Boy for the gate.

Swing, the sound man, leaned over the balcony above the alleyway exit.

"Everything go okay tonight?" he asked.

"You missed your music on one calf roper," I told him, checking Boy up with the reins.

"Yeah. Tomorrow night I won't watch all them tight pants going by me so close up there." Then he laughed.

"Do that!" I said, like I was mad—but he knew better, and I rode off to put up Boy for the night. Underneath the amphitheater in the alleyway between the rows of orange portable stalls, I unsaddled and began to brush him.

"It was a good show tonight. You did a super job," Johnny said, sauntering over to join me.

"Thanks. It went fairly smooth. That barrier in the steer wrestling needs to be overhauled." I bent over and combed Boy's front fetlocks. "Something's wrong up there, because it took them too long each time to get it on the steer's heads."

"I talked to Chester about it. He's up there with the judge fixing it right now."

"Figured so." I straightened and leaned my elbows over the horse's back, idly raking the blond hair out of the brush with the curry comb. "That Krammer made a whale of a ride tonight, didn't he?"

"Tough boy in both events. If he don't get hurt first, he'll win some big crowns."

"You know much about him?"

Johnny looked off and sucked on his eyetooth. "No. Funny thing, neither do the rest of the hands, at least not the ones I talked to. He must have crawled out from under a rock."

"Regional rodeos, high-school rodeo star somewhere?"

"Nope. No one knows much about him except he got his permit this year and started riding."

"Aw, Johnny, no one crawls out from under a rock and rides like that."

"A natural would."

"You're saying Krammer is natural?" I frowned at him. Johnny's face always looked fried by the sun, even when we worked indoors. Skin tight as a drum head, long jaw—he looked like the Marlboro man personified.

"Yeah, I think that boy's one of them."

I ducked under Boy's head and stuck the brushes back in the tack box. "How many of them have we seen in our lifetime?"

"Ty Murray—there's been a few more. Benny, Jim Shoulders. Listen, Brad, every once in a while God turns out a rodeo machine."

I closed the gate on the pen. Boy was busy chomping on the tender Bermuda hay in his holder. He had plenty of fresh water in his rubber bucket, and they kept good security on the fairgrounds. I was ready to go find myself a thick steak and a cold soda pop.

"I'll think on that machine business a while. You tell Miss Dale that I still feel sorry for her having to put up with you." I joshed him a little more about his fine wife, then headed for my RV out in the lot.

Yard lights—that's what my electric co-op back in Oklahoma calls pole lights—glared on the vehicle-crowded fairground's back lot. Off in the distance, the music and multicolored bulbs on the Ferris wheels went round and round, bringing back memories of sticky cotton candy and wasting a fortune trying to win a teddy bear for some girl in tight-fitting jeans whose name I couldn't recall.

Twenty yards from my RV, I could make out someone bent over at an awkward angle and leaning against the side of my rig. It caused me to take shorter steps and frown. Who was he? I glanced around, but no security was in sight. Bareheaded, he didn't look that big, anyway. Might even be some FFA kid.

"What's wrong?" I asked, drawing closer.

"I need—a ride," he said, still bent over holding himself with both arms.

This wasn't some kind of trick? I looked around to be certain. Were his buddies ready to hit me over the head from behind? Nothing in sight. I took him by the shoulder and raised him up. Blood ran down over his right eye. I recognized him immediately—Shoat Krammer.

"Help me—Turner—" he said, then he fainted in my arms.

Chapter 2

"Don't call the cops," he said, holding the wet washcloth to his forehead.

His response forced me to frown at the boy. He claimed he was eighteen, but he could have lied about that for all I knew. We faced each other over the dinette inside my rig. The twelve-volt bulbs gave off a weak glow that was never enough light for me. I reached up and turned on the 110-volt lamp on the wall. Maybe I could see deeper into this kid's face and learn something he would never tell me.

"Are you in some kind of trouble?" I asked. One thing I didn't need to be involved in was a dope deal gone wrong or some other sort of criminal activity. I had made a big enough mess of my life this far: a bitter divorce cost me the ranch my grandfather gave me. I sure didn't want to be a party to any goofy crime.

He shook his head but never looked up at me. "Naw, it's a personal deal."

"You need some medical attention." I hated that he wouldn't look me right in the eye. Damn it. The notion kept niggling me that he was lying the whole time, but still I wanted to give him the benefit of the doubt.

"Naw, I'll be fine."

"Sure you'll be—if that bleeding stops and those

ribs they kicked in didn't puncture one of your lungs, you may live."

"How did you know that? That they kicked me?" He blinked his good eye at me in disbelief and held the crimson-soaked cloth over the other one.

"You weren't holding your sides out there when I found you because your head hurt."

"I heard them say you were a straight shooter," he began, then stopped short like he expected me to answer him.

"I'm not no angel. But all right, I'm a straight shooter." I don't sniff coke or do drugs—and I'm trying to square up my life. Is that what you mean?"

"They said you were a good guy."

"Who's they?"

"The cowboys. Them, and the top hands from the finals. I don't know many of them by name."

"So what do you want from me?"

"I need a ride out of here."

"Hey, there's no crime here? You ain't murdered anyone, have you?" I held my hands up and waited for his reply.

At first, he looked bewildered, then he laughed once. "Naw, I just need a way back west when the show is over. I can pay you after tonight." A wide grin creased his smooth face, and he turned on all the charm.

He could pay me all right. But I wasn't satisfied that was the reason he wanted a ride in my rig. With my left hand, I squeezed my chin and considered him. Something kept stabbing at my conscience: Should I or shouldn't I offer him the cover of my rig and take him in? I could be asking for a lot of trouble; yet if he was just a kid in need, I hated worse to turn him

out. That damn ride on Iceberg and Johnny's words—
He's a natural—kept ringing in my ears.

I hadn't put a plaited rope around a bull's belly in
six years—no, seven. Yet I recalled the jealousy and
the cold shivers his ride gave me out there under those
lights. If you lived and believed like I did in the sport
of rodeo, you had to have a real gut feeling for the
stars, especially the up-and-coming ones. And if a
younger one on his flight up came in your direction,
in need of guidance, it was your duty to help him out.
That was the rodeo way.

"I've got strict damn rules," I finally spoke.

"Yeah?" He looked me in the eye.

"No dope in this rig, no funny business while you're
traveling with me."

He nodded sharply.

"I won't lie to you, you don't lie to me. I won't ask
you your business. Mine's my own. This is my house;
don't pilfer in it. Need something, I'll find it for you.
Secondly, I'm going to borrow one of Johnny's pick-
ups and take you to Jackson General. You can tell
them a bull did it. They love cowboys up there. But
I don't want you dying on me, either."

He gave me a quick bob of his head.

"Stay here and I'll be back. Johnny won't question
me. But I swear, Krammer, if you've lied to me, I'll
be one mad camper to deal with." I looked hard at
him for an answer.

"I ain't," he said in a husky voice.

To save my expensive sequined one, I changed
shirts, and hung the sequined number up, grateful it
didn't have much of his blood on it. The whole time
my empty stomach kept churning over whether I was
doing the right thing.

I found Johnny in his fifth wheel RV eating supper

with Dale, who came to the door when I knocked. A tall, willowy, attractive woman in her thirties, she could have been a movie star in my opinion.

"Hi, Dale," I said. "I need to holler at Johnny. Sorry to interrupt your meal. Hey, Johnny, I need to borrow one of your rigs to go to town in."

He tossed her the keys and she handed them to me with a smile.

"Want some supper? We've got plenty."

"No, I've got plans."

"Hey, don't do anything in town I wouldn't do," Johnny said and waved a piece of steak at me on his fork. Dale shook her head in disapproval at his words.

"Have a nice night," she said and I excused myself.

The keys were to number three, one of the big Dodge duallies. The cab smelled of stale tobacco smoke. I turned on the key and waited for the all-clear signal to start the diesel. It roared into action and I drove it slow through the dark lane between the rigs.

The kid loaded in the passenger seat, and we headed for the exit. He held the washcloth over his eye and slumped in the seat when I halted for the security guard in the gate shack who grinned and waved me on.

Jackson General Hospital was a couple of miles of nighttime city traffic away. I'd been there before with other banged-up cowboys and knew the route. When we drove up under the emergency room canopy, someone came out with a wheelchair. The kid stopped and frowned at the attendant holding his door open.

"I don't need that."

"You guys with the rodeo?" the white uniformed young man asked.

"Yes," I said.

"A bull do that?"

The kid nodded and the attendant, who was looking on in awe as he held the door open for him to pass.

"You ride bulls, too, mister?" the attendant asked me.

"I used to."

"Hey, I know you—you're the announcer, aren't you?"

"Yes."

"Man, how did you get hurt?" He looked me up and down.

"I didn't."

"Wow, I go to all the afternoon performances because I work here at night. Go to every one of them. Always wanted to be a bull rider."

"It's a tough business," I said to make small talk. Shoat had already gone inside and was standing at the admittance desk.

"Yeah, but I love it."

"Well, you keep coming," I said and managed to escape past him.

A tall, angular-faced desk nurse raised up, reached over the counter, and took the rag Krammer held away from his forehead. A look of disapproval swept her pretty face.

"You need to see a doctor and get stitches. A bull do that to you?"

"No," the kid said in his husky voice. "I fell off my horse." Then he shared a private look of devilment with me.

"Well, you've certainly taken a bad fall," she said. "Here fill out these forms. You have Pro insurance, don't you?"

"No ma'am, I'm a permit holder."

"I'll handle that," I said and tossed my credit card down on the counter.

Shoat turned and looked at me, then dropped his gaze. "Thanks, Turner. I'll pay you back."

"You better," I said, under my breath and meant it.

Another attendant brought a wheelchair. This time the kid had no choice but to take a ride. After the head nurse swiped my card through the slot and handed it back to me, she told me to take a seat. The doctor would be along shortly.

I flipped through the dog-eared sports magazines and kept checking down the sparkling hallway where they'd wheeled him off. I quickly dismissed my own regrets helping Shoat—he needed medical attention. But at a time like this, a man could wonder how he even got roped in the first place.

I was busy reading about the St. Louis Rams' coach when someone cleared his throat above me. I glanced up to see a face belonging to someone far younger than myself. He was a doctor. It said so on his badge. I'm used to sawbones like Doc Watson back in Oklahoma, gray-headed and ancient.

"We're taking your friend back to X-ray."

I blinked at him and then his words set in; he meant Shoat. It was late and the whole episode had me distracted.

"You're the man who brought him in?"

"Yes." I stood. "How serious are his injuries?"

"We won't know until we do the X-rays, but he has some damaged ribs. We sutured the gash in his forehead, but I can't guarantee he won't have a scar."

I agreed. A little scar never hurt anyone. Gave him character. "What about the ribs?"

"We'll know more in twenty minutes."

"Good, I'll be here. He need anything?"

"No. But he doesn't talk much, does he?"

"The kid? No, he isn't a talker."

"He couldn't remember ever having had a tetanus shot." The young MD frowned in disbelief at me. "And him around those horses and all that. It's a wonder he hasn't died of lockjaw by now."

"He's tough." Way I figured it, if the devil himself came after Shoat Krammer, he'd have to drag him screaming, kicking, and fighting the whole way out of this world.

"I'll let you know about his condition after X-rays."

"Thanks," I said, and watched the young man in his green scrubs walk back down the hall under the blue-white lights.

Well, Shoat, I hope the Good Lord's a-looking down and taking care of you tonight. Whoever gave you that beating had a meaning in it. From my experience, most misunderstanding between rodeo contestants never got past the fist-swinging stage. Besides, Krammer sure didn't act mouthy, not enough to make some old hands mad enough to beat the tar out of him, anyway.

I don't do well in hospitals, even visiting them. Damn, that boy's condition had begun to seriously worry me.

Chapter 3

Minutes passed like hours. The young attendant who'd met us at the door came by twice and asked me trivial questions about rodeo. I must have given him the right answers because he went off each time, acting pleased. At last, I saw the young doctor coming down the hall again.

"No punctured lungs," he said. I breathed a sigh of relief. "He'll be very sore for some time. He has several cracked ribs which should limit his physical activity for quite a while."

"He'll need a medical release from you—to get him out of other rodeos that he's already entered in," I said.

"Fine, I can do that." Then he frowned at me with some authority. "He doesn't need to get on another bucking animal for a minimum of six weeks."

"That's quite a long sentence for a rodeo cowboy."

"I know your kind. You think your bodies are indestructible. Anyway, I'm giving him two prescriptions, one for pain and the other an antibiotic to keep down any infection. Make certain he takes them—at least the antibiotic. Our pharmacy is open if you want to get it here. I don't suppose anyone else will follow up with him again. I mean, like his personal physician."

I shook my head; he wouldn't be seeing another as far as I knew. He probably didn't have one.

Thirty minutes later, with the pill bottles tucked in his shirt pocket, Shoat and I headed across Jackson for a meal at one of those twenty-four-hour chains. I was dreading their sorry chicken-fried steak that tasted like cardboard, but it was past two A.M. on the dash clock. Not much choice at this hour of the night. My empty stomach growled and moaned; I knew I needed to put some food inside it.

"That ninety-four score better hold up," the kid said, looking across the Formica table top at me. "Man, that total medical bill was high. Twelve hundred bucks!" He shook his head in dismay.

"Yeah, you need to get your Pro card."

"Tell me. Hey, thanks for paying. I'll get it back to you." Then he buried his nose in the plastic-coated menu.

A tall, anorexic waitress in her forties brought us water, and we reeled off our orders to her. Shoat ordered a burger, and I realized that would be on my bill, too. Broke, beat up, and forlorn, the kid looked done in.

"Take one of each of those pills," I directed.

"Yeah, the doc said for me to remember to take the antibiotics."

"You hurting?"

"Naw. A little sore is all."

"How in the Sam Hill did you get into town in the first place?"

"A buddy brought me down."

"He the one who beat you up?"

He nodded and looked away. That was the only answer I would get from him and I knew it. Whoever brought him to Jackson had beaten him up. All I could do was speculate about the reason: money, a woman, perhaps? When the waitress brought me the limp dinner salad, I hoped that whoever had worked him over had gone back home. I still had a week left in Jackson and a rodeo to announce at two p.m. staring me in the face, plus a night performance as well. It was how I made my living.

The chicken-fried steak came as no surprise. It had the exact same flavor as a fresh copy of *USA Today*. As I chewed on it, I decided the kid could talk to me whenever he wanted. If that ever came. My long day was about to draw to a close and this old boy was going to stretch his five-eleven frame out on the queen-size bed in that RV and get a few hours' shut-eye.

Someone was rapping on the side of the RV. I bolted out of bed, struggled to get on my Wranglers, and said loudly, "I'm coming," to stop the insistent knocking. My denim shirt half buttoned, I passed through and saw the kid was still asleep on the couch. Who in the devil was out there?

"Brad!" a woman shouted, as I stuck my sleep-rumpled face out in the bright Mississippi morning sun.

There she stood in a pair of tight red jeans, a frilly white shirt, her straw-blond hair in a ponytail, twirling a pair of expensive sunglasses. Zola Johns. Something about her pretty, long oval face and those sparkling deep blue eyes made the chicken-fried steak in my belly flop over like a big bass in a stock tank. I glanced back at the sleeping kid and held my finger to my mouth to silence her.

"What's wrong?" she whispered.

"Got a cowboy sleeping in here. He's had a rough night."

"More than likely some old girl, and you don't want me to see her."

"Get your fanny in here and look, then." I pulled back to let her pass.

"Well, I'll be damned, it is a guy. Can I use the rest room?" She pointed to the back.

"Sure—and there ain't no one in the back bed, either," I said.

"I knew you were saving yourself for little me." She kissed me on the cheek as she swept past. I admired the swing of her backside going down the hall, then I shoved in my shirttail and waddled barefooted back to my bedroom. I heard the throne flush and she popped out the door.

"Let's go get some breakfast and you can tell me all about him." She nodded toward the kid and frowned for an answer. I decided to let her stew a little about him. Seated on the side of the bed, I began to put on a fresh pair of socks, then reached for my ropers.

"Fine, I could eat a big one." I glanced over at her. Hyper as usual, she bounced up and down on the bed beside me like she was riding her barrel horse.

"He some friend or a stray—"

I silenced her with a finger to my mouth. She compressed her soft, full red lips tight like a little girl who'd been scolded by a teacher, and acted like she was deaf and dumb until I managed to get my boots on.

"Let's go," I said and we left Shoat to sleep in the RV. I wondered how anyone could have slept through Zola's pounding attack on the siding. I picked up a straw hat and followed her out the door.

"First, I have to check on Golden Boy at the barn,"

I told her and motioned to the Dodge with the gold sign on the door: FLYING STAR RODEO COMPANY.

"How come a horse always comes between a woman and her cowboy?" She slid in and sat in the middle. I followed her, resetting the straw hat on my head.

"What's his name?"

"Shoat Krammer."

"Sounds like a steer wrestler."

"You just got here?"

"Late last night. I came in from a small show in Georgia. I was sitting second there when I left."

"He's a permit holder out of Texas. He rides barebacks and bulls."

"I saw the bandage on his head. He get hurt last night?"

I nodded. "But a bull didn't do it. He rode Iceberg for ninety-four points."

She whistled through her white teeth. "No one rides that sucker."

"*He* sure did. Got into a fight afterwards with some guy who brought him down here. Broke some of his ribs, had to get several stitches."

"Sounds tough." She drew up her knees and hugged them. "He better find himself some new traveling buds."

"That's what I thought. So—how have you been?"

"Good. Can you believe I'm actually ahead in the money so far this season? I haven't told Daddy yet." She wrinkled her pert nose. "But he can afford me."

Chester was coming out of the building when we pulled up and he waved me down. "I fed Golden Boy. When you weren't up, I did it for you. Don't worry, he's fine."

"Thanks, Chester, you're a good man."

"No problem, Brad." Then he gave me a mean wink like he thought the reason I was so late was that Zola had been in my bed. Thank goodness, she missed his accusing look.

She and I drove across the fairgrounds to the Ramada and we ate a leisurely buffet breakfast. I always felt comfortable in her company. We'd had our times. But she wanted to win the world crown in barrel racing, and I had rodeos to announce. Our schedules were too different for anything more than tender flings and being frank with one another about the situation. Somewhere in the back of my mind, I wanted her to give up her pursuit of the title and just be mine— but in reality there were too many obstacles to my daydream. First, her father was a business tycoon and developer and had enough money to burn wet mules on a rainy day. She'd been married once before to an Argentinian polo player. And she was headstrong and beautiful.

"Where do you go next?" she asked, pulling her legs beneath her in the booth.

"Oklahoma. I have two weeks off. Going to help Gator Bledsoe and his brother Lonnie gather up some wild cattle on an old rough place that Gator rents."

"Ah, vacation time. I'll be coming back from a rodeo in Iowa about then . . ."

She looked at me out of those deep blue eyes. Bottomless pools that went on and on forever. I felt like a scuba diver in some tropical water plying my way down farther and farther. She wanted an answer. Would I be alone at my place? Zola was a very secretive person. She wanted to know if the kid would also be there, then.

"Come by my place. I'd be honored." Heck, Shoat should be gone by that time. I wasn't taking him to raise.

She nodded quickly and glanced at the clock on the wall. "You're up at two today aren't you?" It was already twelve-fifteen.

"Yeah, and I don't have much time do I?"

"Oh, I've seen you get ready faster than that." She wrinkled her nose at me as if to say, *Touché*, old boy.

I got the message. When I looked over at her again, she was staring off across the room. Then she waved at two other barrel racers who came in the restaurant to eat. I stood, dug in my Wranglers, and put some folded bills down on the table to pay for our brunch and the tip. We only managed to see a dozen more people we knew who wanted to stop and make small talk between the restaurant and the pickup in the parking lot.

Back at the RV rig, she piled in the door ahead of me, stopped halfway inside, and searched cautiously around, then announced over her shoulder, "Your patient's gone."

Where in the hell did Shoat go?

Chapter 4

"Yes, I should be there by Tuesday to help you." I had my cell phone to my ear. Gator Bledsoe, was on the other end, steer wrestler, cow trader, and a good guy to have on your side in a fight. Gator and I grew up together in Woodbury; we'd rodeoed and helped each other all of our lives. He looks after my stock when I'm out of town announcing; we've had a long-term ragged relationship. I was his best man and vice versa. 'Course, both marriages turned out so bad that we swore never to do that for each other again.

"Good, I'll get Lonnie to help us. Maybe we can get those cows gathered off them hills." Gator referred to his brother Lonnie, the number-two steer wrestler in the family, and he meant we'd try to round up some of his eared cattle out of the post oak thickets on the Sutter place.

"If it's raining we can put it off," I added, having no intention of being out in an icy winter storm chasing after wild cattle. "Oh—I've got a boy coming along. He's off on the injured list for a few weeks."

"Sure, bring him. Lonnie may be too busy to help us. I've got to go look at some more cattle right now. Been haying those over there so they might not be so spooky."

"Good. It will be spring soon," I said.

"Promises, promises. See you, hoss. Hey, I appreciate you offering to help. Can't get a damn soul to work anymore."

"I know. Bye."

The phone clicked and I folded it up. Chester was coming down the alley on a big stout sorrel and he swung down when he reached Boy's stall.

"Man, what're you up to?" the burly pickup man asked.

"Was up half the night getting a cowboy patched up."

"Who's that? Did I miss a fight?"

"We both did. Must have been right after the performance. Have you seen that kid Shoat Krammer?"

"Yeah, he's getting some feed right now." Chester nodded. "He looked a little battered up. He the one that you took to the sawbones?"

"Yes. What's he doing?" I looked around for him, but didn't see him underneath the coliseum.

"I put him to work on the crew. Something wrong?"

"No." The knowledge made me feel better—he hadn't simply run off.

"What happened to him?" Chester asked.

"Some guy brought him down here must have kicked the living daylights out of him."

"Oh. Say, you're announcing for us at the Crawdad Dance, ain't you?"

"In Beauregard, yes."

"Then I can take Golden Boy with me and you won't need to haul him back home."

For a long moment, I looked at Chester. There's not many men in this old world I would trust with the big yellow horse; Chester was one I would consider.

"What's the deal?"

"I'm going to buy this big peckerwood sorrel and

don't want to haul him with the other stock back to East Texas." He patted the stout red horse on the neck. "A guy I know brought him up here for me to try. I'll buy him and take both of them back to my place in your trailer."

"Your gas miles." I laughed and started into the stall with Boy.

"What do you know about Krammer?" Chester asked, being certain that we were alone.

"Not much." I squatted down and the pungent smell of the pine shavings ran up my nose as I brushed off Golden Boy's legs.

"They say it wasn't a guy he came with."

"Oh?"

"Yeah, she had one of them fancy sports cars. It was a Ghia something."

That was sure different. I paused in my brushing and pushed off my knee to stand. One of those cars cost a hundred grand. This rookie must have some rich friends. Thinking hard about the new information, I ran the brush over Boy's sides and withers.

"Then who beat him up?" I asked.

Chester lowered his voice. "He got into it a row with two thugs out back. I didn't think it would get that serious or I'd broken it up. Had other things to do about then and forgot all about it."

"I don't care who he gets into fights with," I said and ducked under Boy's head to do his other side. "Just so that he ain't into any funny deals."

Chester nodded. "You'll never believe this. That gal he was with? Had 'Honey-one' Missouri license plates on that fancy little car."

"Maybe her daddy don't like cowboys."

"Or her sugar daddy don't like cowboys diddling around with her."

"Yeah," I said, seeing Krammer bringing my saddle and bridle from the trailer.

"Hey, I can get that," I said, concerned he didn't need to carry it in his condition.

With a big smile on his face, two black eyes, and that sewn-up cut, he looked almost comical. "Aw, Mr. Turner, I owe you. Besides I've got to get well."

The saddle in my hands, I shook my head. "You need to mend. You've met Chester?"

"Oh, yes. Helped him feed the stock that ain't going out."

"I wondered where you went." Tossing on the pads and settling them on Boy's back, I cinched my good saddle and Shoat went on the other side to help.

"I was half awake when your lady friend came and figured that you two wanted to be alone. So I cleared out."

"Zola Johns," I said for Chester's sake. He nodded.

"You better not overdo it," I said and finished the cinch job.

"I won't," Shoat said. "Chester says I can earn my keep the rest of the week helping them with the stock."

"Fine with me." From my Wrangler front pocket, I dug out a spare key to the rig. "There's food and whatever in the refrig and pantry. Help yourself. Zola and I won't be needing any privacy—she is loading up after tonight and making two more shows."

"Besides that, she can't sit still long enough," Chester said to chide me.

"That's the truth," I agreed. I checked my watch—I needed to hurry and change into a fresh shirt.

"See you later," I said after Chester, who waved as he rode off down the alleyway.

"I'll bring the horse," Krammer said and I agreed.

"After I change I need to run up and see Miss Dale. Get the fastest times and high scores, plus any changes in the lineup."

"Don't worry, I'll have him at the gate for you."

Why did I hesitate? Unaccustomed to anyone taking care of my business, I guess.

"Thanks." And I smiled at him.

In the rodeo secretary's booth I did a mic check. Then on the two-way, I talked to Swing Michaels about lowering the voice compressor.

"Scratch Bobbie Lynch in the bareback," Dale said, while Swing complained in my other ear that unless he buried it, the compressor was low as it would go.

"What's wrong with Lynch?" I asked, as I drew a line through the competitor's name.

"Sick. Who knows? We have three turnouts in the bull riding."

"Why so many?"

"Krammer's score." She shook her head. "Those guys figure he's clinched first place and won't come get on the bulls they drew."

"Bunnette ain't coming? Man, he drew a good bull. Fifty-six?"

"Bunnette, Christy, and Donovan."

Bull riders had become primadonnas. Because of the high demand and large purses, every one of them had a computer, or access to one. Briggs Bunnette put bull Fifty-six in his program and probably deduced he'd come out with an eighty-five if the bull had a great day and he rode him. He probably cashed his "place" airline ticket to Jackson to ride someone else's ox to first place at another rodeo.

"We've got enough riders. The bounty bull is last," she pointed out on my mini program.

"Jeff Border got him."

She wrinkled her nose. "He's not got enough lead in his butt to ride him."

With a nod, I agreed. "You still there?" Swing shouted on the two-way in my ear.

"Yeah. Bury that compressor."

"Aw, Brad." The two-way went click, and I knew I had ticked him off. Still, Swing and I had a good relationship, he would do his dangdest to make it deeper.

"Good crowd out there," she said, absently sorting papers and checking in two ropers from Texas. I shook their hands and we spoke about the weather and cattle markets.

"There sure is a good price in our country," Larry Bogan said as I nodded to both of them and prepared to leave.

If cowboys couldn't complain about the drought, or giving away cattle at low prices, they'd soon run out of things to talk about. Hurrying down the narrow stairs, I said hello to several hands on their way to the secretary's desk. Ten minutes to kick-off, with a million things on my mind—sponsors, queens, announcements to remember about the special fair days—I collided into Zola and was brought around to full awareness.

"Oh!" she said and blinked at me. "Find your boy?"

"Yes, he's holding Golden Boy over in the alleyway."

"I saw him. Man, did he take a beating."

"Tough kid. I'd be in bed still bawling."

She drove a hard fist in my gut. "Naw, you're tougher than that. Anyway . . ."

"Anyway what?"

Shifting her weight from one Justin to the other, she wet her lips. With no lipstick, they looked on the pale side. "If he wasn't there . . . Aw, Brad, I really need to load up and drive."

"Hey, I understand."

Impulsive as usual, she kissed me on the mouth. Then she dropped her chin. "I promise—"

"Don't promise a thing," I said and raised her face up with the side of my hand. "If it works out between us, it will."

A wry set to her mouth, she shook her head. "I want it to."

"So do I." There—I had committed myself.

"You really do?"

"Hey. If I don't get on that horse down there—"

Her arms flew around me and she about smothered me with another kiss. Then she spun me around and shoved me on my way with a hoarse voice. "Go!"

"He's ready," Krammer said and showed me the reins as I fitted on the headset microphone. Hat in place, I put my boot toe in the stirrup and swung up. The house lights were already down. In the darkness, I slid the microphone in the holster, one of two wireless mics in addition to my headset. The holstered one was a spare, the other one would magnify Boy's action sounds as he ran the pattern. At the moment, I realized, I had not replaced the batteries in either of them. Surely both would not go out at the same time. I looked to the dark ceiling for celestial help. With my luck they would both quit.

"Ladies and gentlemen, rodeo fans, here is . . ."

The gateman was talking to Swing on this two-way; he threw it back and the palomino bolted forward. We began our circle around the wall under the spotlight. Another performance in Jackson on horseback and talking to a house filled with kids. They would enjoy the comic Skip Evers—he really could get the whole audience laughing with his horsing around.

Halfway through barebacks, the competitor couldn't get his rigging right and a silence filled the arena. Skip came to my rescue, in a high-stepping run.

"Bradberry!" he screamed in his high-pitched voice on the PA.

"Brad," I said softly to correct him.

"No," he said, doing a foot-in-front-of-foot walk toward me. "Your mamma never called you that on your birth certificate."

"You never saw my birth certificate," I said, playing the straight man.

"I did so."

"Did not."

"Hey, how many of you kids here believe I seen Bradberry's birth certificate? Shout, if you do."

He looked all around. The rider still was not ready. He was off the horse and standing on the back platform. Skip knew it and he dragged out the who-didn't-believe part, pleading and getting the youngsters into it.

"Well, I have it right here." Skip drew out a paper that unfolded until it was half the size of a bedsheet, then ran over and jumped on the wall and asked someone in the box seat if that didn't say Bradberry.

The woman agreed.

"See here?" Skip said and made a little circle like a confident rooster.

"That ain't my birth certificate."

"Is, too."

"Is not."

"They used this size paper because you were the biggest baby that was ever born in Oklahoma. Your mamma—"

My shoulders dropped like I was dejected and shaking my head, I said, "I'm going to cry."

"See there, kids! Ain't he the biggest baby from Oklahoma you ever saw?" That drew a big laugh from the crowd and the chute gate swung open. The cowboy marked the high-soaring pony out and made a good ride.

Skip held a red wagon boy-girl race for part of his act. The boy pulled the girl in the wagon a certain distance, then she pulled him back. Six teams. In the arena's soft ground it wasn't easy to pull them in it. Skip ran alongside chiding each team to hurry. When the boys climbed in, one girl must have been from the farm. She pulled that boy like a draft horse and won the trophy.

"Where are you from, sister?" Skip asked, bent over close after he gave them the trophy.

"Home," she said, and the crowd laughed.

In approval, Skip clapped her on the shoulder. "That's a mighty good place to be from. Isn't it, Bradberry?"

My turn again—I roused applause for Skip and the kids, then drew the fans' attention to the timed-event chute. I booted Boy for the other end of the arena to get ready for the steer wrestling. A couple of cowboys bit the dirt, no fast times. Next, the barrels were set up. Zola ran third in the order, so she was up on the "good ground"—cowgirls that run last have some deep tracks to put their horse into, so there is more of a chance for a fall or to get their horse off stride and knock down a barrel.

She made a good first turn and her horse, Thunder, headed for the second one smooth as velvet; around two and headed for the last one, the big chestnut horse took charge. The crowd and I were both into it, and her time of 15.21 seconds made her the new leader.

The barrels removed, I set the stage for bull riding and introduced the bullfighters, Chuck Wynn and Bucky Starr, two great cowboy savers who weren't afraid of the devil himself nor any bucking bull around. Skip came out in a green leprechaun outfit. He looked a little tall for that job, but he soon had the Irish jokes going and the crowd was having a good time. We bucked down two cowboys in short order, then Robert Yetts was getting his gloved hand ready, while I bragged about the veteran. Rope ready, Yetts's helper jumped clear of the gate and the big red bull blew out under the arena lights mad as I'd ever seen him.

Bulls have mad days, some more than others. Ought-Two dropped to the right and then he came back in a tornadolike turn that slung Yetts off. His hand got turned upside down and was caught in the bull rope. Hung up! My stomach turned sour as the bull tossed Wynn like a rag doll to one side; then head slinging, he gored Starr with the other horn. Both bull-fighters were down. From beside me, Chester spurred his big bay forward, grabbing loose his lariat to try to do something. Then out of nowhere, as Ought-Two slung Yetts like a rag doll around in circle, a hatless figure was beside the bull. He leaped on the bull's side, literally riding him on his elbows as the big animal continued to buck. The hatless cowboy jerked the tail of Yetts's rope loose; the rider was free. Yetts lay on the ground and the volunteer who saved him made two ducks and a dart while Chester swung his rope to distract Ought-Two away from Yetts.

The crowd was on their feet applauding. Both bull-fighters recovered and had the hatless figure standing between them, even before the still-angry Ought-Two exited the arena.

"Ladies and gentlemen," I announced in disbelief, "the young man who just saved that cowboy is Shoat Krammer!"

Chapter 5

Beer cans popped open. The crew was out back, all lounging around on hay bales. It was after eleven at night and I had already kissed Zola goodbye, told her to be sure to stop if she got sleepy driving.

"You done much bullfighting?" Wynn asked Krammer.

He nodded and dropped his gaze down to the aluminum can in his hand. "That's how I used to get the money to ride. My people were pretty poor. We did some sawmilling stuff. I caught chickens one whole summer to get money to buy my chaps, spurs, and a bull rope."

"Wow, you did live way back, sonny boy." Skip shook his head. "I bet you never got the Grand Ole Opry until Sunday morning where you lived, did ya?"

"We didn't have a radio," Shoat said.

They laughed and Skip nodded. He never liked being beaten at a joke; that was his business. I dug out a can of diet pop from the cooler and looked around. "Who bought the beer tonight?"

"Some sponsor sent it," Wynn said. "Give him an extra plug tomorrow night."

"I will if I ever learn his name. You boys in one piece?" I asked and dropped down on a bale of fresh-smelling Bermuda hay. Everyone knew that the bull rider Yetts had been taken to the hospital so I gave them the last report. "Yetts is going to be okay."

"Good."

"Tell us where you came from Krammer," Wynn asked.

"Murphy County."

"Where's that, in Texas?"

"Ain't Texas. I get my mail there at my sister's house. I lived in Arkansas."

"Been some tough hands come from Arkansas."

"I heard the reason them Arkies are so dang tough at riding," Skip said, "is 'cause they don't want to get bucked off on them boulders in the arena."

"You ain't lying there," Wynn said. "I use to do amateur shows and I did one in a stone quarry up there. I swear that place was all rocks."

Krammer simply smiled. They weren't about to drag him into their riding down his home state.

"How's your ribs?" I asked.

He wrinkled his nose and shrugged off my concern. It wouldn't have mattered if he'd been bleeding to death—at that moment, he was in his element. Accepted by his new found equals. Shoat wasn't a braggart, simply a guy to count on. Not for a moment had he ever thought about himself or his own safety when those two bull fighters went down. Someone needed to free Yetts, and he possessed those skills. No conscious decision, he acted out of instinct.

Three performances down and seven to go. Loitering underneath the coliseum seats with a bunch of good old boys, we exchanged rodeo and life stories to let the adrenaline ooze out. A man could have found plenty of fun in the Jackson nightlife, picked his choice from the many sexy buckle bunnies that always hung around, but this was more typical of the times after a show for me. A couple of cold sodas, maybe a meal, and then shut-eye.

"Anyone seen Swing around tonight?" Skip said, rising to his feet and searching around for the sound man. Skip's actions reminded me of a wild turkey looking for a coyote.

"Nope, he left a while ago with that skinny reporter."

"That girl from the TV station?" Wynn moaned as if that hurt him while he dove into the ice for another beer.

"Yeah. Little dark-headed one that interviewed Billy Redd before the show."

Ruefully, Wynne shook his head. "That guy is lucky with women."

"Yeah," Skip said and tossed his empty among a pile of others. "Oh, I would like to be a little mouse in Swing's pocket right now. I bet that will be an interesting date. Him and her can go talk all night about microphones and amps, huh?"

We all laughed.

Later at the rig, after talking about grilling a steak while we were with the guys, Shoat and I each settled for a ham sandwich apiece. Two performances always stretched into a long day. After a shower, I piled into bed. Shoat was still reading the latest rodeo tabloid when my head hit the pillow and I went out like a light. The last thing I thought about was the car with the HONEY-1 plates, but I was gone to sleep before I could ask him about it.

The curtain came down on the week in Jackson, and Shoat and I loaded saddles and other accessories in the underside compartment of the RV. Chester took my horse trailer and swore on his life that he'd be in Beauregard with Golden Boy in good shape.

It was early Sunday morning when I cranked up the diesel pusher and the two of us headed out of Jackson. A long ways home diagonally across the rest of Mississippi, all of Arkansas, and then a good two hundred miles up into the Oklahoma bluestem country from the state line. The weather report talked about cold temperatures but no storms in the next few days so we were soon rolling homebound on dry asphalt.

Shoat had his stocking feet on the dash and was lying back in the passenger-side captain's chair.

"Sure is a nice rig." Shoat looked around, impressed.

"I sure couldn't afford it, if the Big Stop RV Place in Tulsa hadn't made me a deal on it."

"I seen their sign on the side."

"They can put it all over as far as I'm concerned. It beats motel rooms to death."

"Or sleeping in pickup shells."

"Them, too. I did that, too, when I rodeoed."

"One time," Shoat said, "we rented a room for a single and seven guys slept in it."

"Yeah, and you had to wait for the towels to dry to take a bath."

"Naw, this guy, Shell, he flirted with this old gal who was a maid there and got all we needed."

"One in every crowd," I said and pushed the rig out onto the freeway traffic.

"I think she thought afterwards he was going to marry her."

"Must have had a line."

Shoat nodded, then didn't say anything more, like he had withdrawn into his own world.

"Something wrong?"

"Naw. Shell got killed last year driving a big rig. On the ice and snow. Crashed up there in Wyoming."

"Oh."

"Yeah, funny thing. Shell was always the one got us extra towels, got us invited to free meals everywhere we rodeoed, talked sponsors out of free beer, got us into clubs without paying a cover charge."

Shoat took his feet down and sat up. "Why, he's probably talked his way into heaven by now."

"I'll bet he has. How did you get started bull riding?" I asked as we flowed out of Jackson headed northwest in moderate traffic.

"You ever hear of Jasper Northcutt?"

"Small contractor up in Arkansas?"

"Yeah, well, he did some open rodeos up home. Took a liking to me. Let me ride his young bulls."

"So you said—you earned your rigging catching chickens."

"Hey, that isn't bad work, once your nose gets used to the ammonia."

"You never rodeoed with the Arkansas High School Rodeo Association? I know they have a good one."

"Naw, I never had that kind of money. I rode wild cows and steers at guys' roping arenas for practice."

I swung the rig around a slow car and frowned at the elderly driver. I could hear what my ex said all the time over similar experiences. "Some day you'll be old and you'll want people to respect you." I checked the rearview mirror, and once clear of him, I swung the rig back in front of the car and set the cruise control on seventy.

"I rode anywhere I could ride for free," Shoat continued.

"No one helped you—you never went to a rodeo school on riding?"

He shook his head. "You don't understand. Us Krammers are poor. We're them folk that set in line for the fairgrounds to open for the commodities they give out."

"I know something about that."

He stretched out and put his stockinged feet back on the dash again.

"Tell me more about this learning to ride business."

"I watched every tape I could get on rodeo riding. Over and over, I watched them, rewound and watched them again. I would sit in a chair and throw my arm back to be just like them. Get it out sideways when the bull spun, moved my butt, and put spurs in them every jump. Jasper, he always hollered from the chutes at me. 'Feet, boy, use your feet.' I'd remember I had to use my head, my arms and feet. Then pretty soon they began to work together. I didn't need to think about them no more, my left arm went up or out, my spurs went to looking for hooks in their hide. Kept my chin down and my butt in the middle of his back." He paused and then he nodded. "That's when Jasper said, 'Go get yourself a card, boy.'"

"You know that bull Red Mountain that they paid twenty grand for at Okie City?" he asked.

I glanced over. "Great bull."

"I rode him a full eight seconds at an open rodeo two weeks before they sold him. The judges gave me ninety points. That's a high score at an open rodeo."

"That is. How much did you win?" I asked impressed.

"Two hundred something. Paid for my permit."

"So you used a Texas address?"

"Oh, yeah, I ain't hiding nothing. My oldest sister

Jan gets my money and puts it in my account. She ain't like some of my kin. It will all go in the bank, and she keeps my books for me. That's why I use a Texas address."

"Some of the others might spend your money?"

He didn't answer, just studied the piney woods that lined the freeway. Then he cleared his throat. "We ain't only poor and crooked as a barrel of snakes, but there's Krammers who are damn out-and-out outlaws."

"This Jan's married?"

"Yes, she's got three kids and a good husband. They moved off down there because my family's got such a bad rep."

"And you became a bull rider. You aren't bad at barebacks, either."

"Jasper hated me riding them. Said I'd get busted up and wouldn't be able to ride bulls. Claimed some crazy bronc would crash in a fence and hurt me."

"But you rode them anyway."

"Yep. You know what I figured?"

"What?"

"I was already at the rodeo. If I won something in two events, it was better than only one."

"Good thinking."

"I love barebacks now. These pro horses soar out like a rocket and that's some kinda big high for me. At those amateur rodeos, you'd be lucky if they bucked at all; many were dirty, spoiled, and darted sideways. That horse I had back there at Jackson was like flying to the moon. You know what I mean?"

"Yeah, I've been there. Know all about it. Third money wasn't bad, either. I'll bet them boys up in Arkansas are glad you went pro."

"It's going to work out."

"What is?" I frowned at him then turned back to my driving.

" 'Cause at Jackson for the first time, I felt I belonged there."

"Belonged there? First in bulls and a third in barebacks."

"It ain't the money. You, Chester, Johnny, Skip, Starr, Wynn—well, you guys acted like . . . well, if I ever had a real one, like I was part of a family."

"Welcome aboard, son. You've joined a great family."

He nodded his head sharply. "I learned that—and something else. You all don't act like you need something from me for me to be a part of you."

"Heckfire, you jumped on that bull and saved a cowboy's life—"

"No, I was the one God chose to do that. Chester rode in, you'd done something. No, I haven't had such a good feeling in all my life as I have with you and them."

"Not even amateur rodeoing?"

"Oh, Jasper was good to me, and we had swell times, but I knew back in Jackson I'd never have to go back to Murphy County, be one of them Krammers that folks always watched out of the corner of the eye. Who the sheriff always figures we're the ones that stole the bed sheets off some widder woman's clothesline."

No wonder no one ever heard of him. Whew, he must have had some life growing up. I passed a slower yellow rental truck and then swung back in the right lane.

"You know when I was a senior in high school there were nice girls that their folks wouldn't let them go out with me, 'cause of who I was."

"Public enemy," I teased.

"I never touched anything wasn't mine." He dropped his chin. "I can't say that about them others."

"You know, you have to live your own life."

"I know, Brad, but thanks for giving me the chance. I figured that night I got beat up, if you didn't help me I might just give up this rodeo business."

"Changed your mind now, haven't you?"

"Yes, sir."

"You get healed. You need to get back on the road."

"I will. I promise, I won't look sideways till I get to Las Vegas."

"You'll probably get there before you know it."

"You ever ride at the finals?"

"No, got to eighteenth place one year. No one died or got hurt." I can recall how beat up and tired I felt at the end of that year. My last three months I got on too many bulls to do any good. Burned too many miles, took in too much of everything bad. Stormy left me in midsummer. We'd been married two years then. Somewhere in Wyoming, she took my pickup and left my stuff on the curb outside the motel-room door.

We didn't hook up again until I made a rodeo in Arizona that next spring. Oh, we'd talked—hell, we used up a couple hundred bucks in pay calls. Couldn't live with her. Couldn't live without her.

I tried to shake all my personal thoughts. What about the Karmann-Ghia with the HONEY-1 license plate. Where did she come in? Slowing down to fifty-five, my foot eased off the accelerator as we entered Winona, Mississippi's city limits. I decided the best thing was to let him tell me about her when he got around to it.

Time for a break. I pulled off into a truck stop and

we climbed out in the cool air to stretch our legs and use the restrooms. Armed with some snacks and fresh coffee in our thermal cups, we climbed back in and headed west.

With a George Strait CD in the player and the sound filling the rig, we rolled down the tree-lined freeway with the big tractor-trailer rigs. The condition of the pavement ran from smooth new surface to clunking over splits in the concrete for the next twenty miles. Then we dodged into slower two-line traffic for a bridge repair—they'd spend the next decade getting the interstates back in shape.

"She's sure a honey of a rig," Shoat said, stretching his arms out.

"A little too much like a big boat for rodeo competitors, but nice for an old man."

"Old man? How old are you?" he asked

"Thirty-six."

"That ain't old."

"Sometimes it feels like it."

"How did you ever get to announcing?" he asked, hoisting his coffee up.

"Happened in Arizona. I had broken my leg at Red Lake and was out for a while. Johnny Borders had amateur rodeos every weekend at his deal outside of Tucson. It was a dude ranch, Wild West shows, and he asked me to come down and announce for him."

"So you started that way?"

"Yeah, I guess I caught on pretty fast. And, buddy, if you can sell an amateur rodeo to a bunch of dudes, you can sure announce a real rodeo. I mean, well, I'm telling you, at one of them, you can go get a cup of coffee and not miss any action. It's a real challenge to announce one."

"Used to make Jasper so mad when the show drug. He'd tell me to get out there and say something funny."

"Wasn't anything funny to tell them, was there?" I responded.

"No. I didn't know anything funny. So he got a guy with a monkey to do it for a while. He was kinda funny."

"What did the monkey do?"

"Nothing much, but he sat on that guy's shoulder and that made folks laugh. He had a bear, too, but it always ran away when it was time to do his act."

I slowed up for some more construction. Fines-doubled-in-construction-zones are the national decor now on the interstates.

"I've seen that guy," I said, recalling the monkey and bear. "The committee at Weldon hired him once." I laughed, recalling the funny man and five other cowboys chasing a half-grown bear all over the fairgrounds. The local law with their .357s drawn to protect society, ran right on their heels. Those cops held their cannons in both hands and shouted, "Clear the way!" It was a merry chase that ended after the poor bruin scared the fat steer class out of their halters and they stampeded, crashing through those carney booths and tossing those stuffed bears everywhere. With all those fat steers bawling and charging about, and the entire county's FFA classes in hot pursuit, that bear got scared, turned tail, and ran back to his master to save his life. But the poor guy never did get the stupid bear to do his act in the arena.

"That's the same guy." Shoat slapped his legs and laughed with his head thrown back. "He never brought the tiger out, did he?"

"No, he didn't have it at Weldon. What did it do?"

"That cat was in a cage and it roared so loud all the

bucking horses bolted and crashed down the sorry fence at the Double Springs Rodeo grounds. Had to have a roundup before we could even start the rodeo—"

Still laughing so hard he could hardly talk, Shoat finally went on. "Boy, Jasper was burning mad when we finally got them back. He told that guy to take that damn cat home and don't you ever bring him to one of my rodeos again. Course by then them horses was so spooked all that cat had to do was purr and they got white-eyed."

"Been some doozies."

"He once hired this guy who was supposed to be like a *Montie Montana* with his trick ropes. He wasn't. Behind the chutes, we all was snickering because he was so bad at his act. He was standing on this horse, trying to swing a big loop, when his boots slipped and he did the splits on the saddle.

"He went, 'Oh!' and then fell off on his head. Jasper told us to go out there and carry him off. And far away. We did, with him moaning all the way. Crowd sure did laugh about that."

"I think I had him, too, once."

"Me, I could never announce." He shook his head at the impossibility of him ever working behind a mic.

"It isn't hard when it's announce or starve."

"Yeah, it would sure beat catching chickens."

"You're positive you want to go to my place?" I glanced over at him.

"Hey, I can work for my keep."

"Not necessary. I just figured you had a girl or something, you might want to go see while you were laid up."

"Hey, if I'm in the way—"

"Nope, but you can help us round up Gator's crazy cattle."

"What are you going to use for a horse?"

"Oh, I don't use Boy in that post oak brush to get up wild cattle. I've got some using horses at the house. Gator has some, too."

He hunched over in the chair. I could tell those ribs still hurt him. He never complained, and it amazed me how much work he did in his condition for Chester and Johnny Farmer while we were in Jackson. Shoat was sure enough no crybaby.

"Can't be no worse than them hills in north Arkansas," he said in a slow drawl.

"It won't be."

"I'll need to stop and buy some coveralls. It'll be cold as home up there."

I agreed with a nod. The crotch in one of my old pair of insulated ones would come to his knees. "We can find some place to shop between here and there."

Past midnight, we came down the long driveway with the starlight reflecting silver off the short grass stubble of my big meadow. The rig lights shone first on the open-ended barn, then on the single-wide mobile home under the yard light. There is something about being *home* that eases the muscles between your shoulders after eighteen hours of hard driving.

"What do we need to do?" he asked.

"Plug in the rig's electric cord to that box on the pole, and grab your things. This is my *casa*."

"Neat place."

"It will do." Then a memory knifed me in the gut. My grandfather's homestead. The one that had been in my family since the 1880s. The ranch that I lost through greed and stupidity. Grandpa Elliot, wherever you are up there—I'm sorry.

Chapter 6

The horses breathed out in great clouds of vapor. Gator Bledsoe handed out cotton team-ropers gloves to Shoat and me. Greatest invention since sliced bread for a cowboy. I can actually hold a hammer and drive nails with those gloves on. That burly Gator shook his head about the arctic-cold air that always moved in right when he wanted to ship cattle. He wore a leather cap with ear flaps; Shoat and I had on stocking caps. It had been ten degrees when we loaded my horses at the house, and the rising sun was too weak to do anything for the cold.

Shoat was kneeling down, roughing up the ears on Gator's mutt, a red heeler he called Dawg. The two had struck it off, and the heeler danced with excitement as Shoat petted and shook him.

"You warm enough?" I asked Shoat as I swung in the saddle.

"I'm fine."

Besides his new coveralls, he had bought some long-handles the day before, too. Gator wore his rust-colored insulated overalls and a few layers of heavy shirts. I had on coveralls, a wool shirt, and thermal underwear. Aside from my nose I was fine and I planned to use a kerchief mask if it didn't soon warm up.

"Call this the polar-bear roundup," Gator said and jumped in the stirrup. "You ever been on one of them before?" He swung his leg over in a style all his own, one I would recognize at a good distance, which must have been born in him.

"I was raised over in Arkansas," Shoat assured him, "so I ain't no stranger to cold."

"Good enough. We'll ride to the west fence and bring them back here. I've got hay bales in the pens, but they ain't much interested in it." Gator twisted around looking for the heeler. "Dawg, you stay with us."

"This your place?" Shoat asked as we rode the dim, grassy road.

"Naw, I rent it. Close to two sections. It's a good one."

Shoat agreed with a nod.

The Sutter place was broken by hills and some deep canyons—all covered in frosted bluestem and horse-high, scrubby blackjack oak. Cactus is bad, but blackjack oak is like stiff steel—even the branches don't bend or give when you run into them. Gator leased the place from a couple in Okie City. It had been in the Sutter family for years.

Shoat rode Benny, my short-coupled red dun using-horse who was sound and surefooted. I had Rooster, the big stout gray that I used for team roping. Both were nimble-footed in the cold, but we held them down so they took on no ideas about bucking. Plenty of prancing and twisting around, but so far, so good.

"How come you're getting them up this time of year?" Shoat asked, searching around as the three of us headed westward.

"The market's hot on springers. Most of these will

calve in sixty days. Got to strike when the iron's hot,"
Gator said and then quickly nodded.

"Gator's a cow trader," I said, to explain further.

"Why, Brad, you make it sound like I'm a cow
jockey." Gator frowned at me.

"Lord, Gator, you are."

"Ain't, either. I'm a livestock dealer."

"You trade cattle more often than I can count."

"Have to. You don't have to pay child support
every month."

"Yeah, they'll put you in the pen nowadays if you
don't pay," I added as we rode along.

"I damn sure ain't going there," Gator said and
shook his head. "Give her half a chance and she'd put
me there, too."

"Your ex-wife?" Shoat asked, reining Benny around.
The dun gelding wanted to outwalk our horses.

"Oh, man, I sure picked a mean one to marry,"
Gator lamented. "She's meaner than a bulldog and
twice as cross as a disturbed hornet's nest and that's
on her good days."

"She sounds bad," Shoat said.

"There's part of them." I pointed to an open ridge
to the south where a set of leery cows were making
their way to the southeast. Rooster began to act up
underneath me. He was ready for a chase. I checked
on the reins and he settled some.

"Yeah, there's a half dozen calves in that bunch,
ones we missed last fall," Gator said with a grim set
to his look.

"Gator's repaired the pens since that fiasco," I said
to Shoat.

"All right, they were a little flimsy."

"Flimsy? They were rotten."

"Those old sisters won't lay them down this time, I guarantee you. They're all welded pipe."

"We ain't wintering up here, either," I said to him as a reminder; our time on this job would be limited.

"We'll have them up there before you know it."

A red-tailed hawk came screaming overhead. He made large loops above us, looking for prey and screeching at the three steam-breathing cowboys and their ready mounts. The brush-lined road dropped off into a wide grassy creek-fed valley. Several bovines raised up their heads to look at us.

"We can start here," Gator said. "The others won't want to be left out. So they should come into the herd once we get the main bunch started for the pens."

"Shoat." I decided it was time to warn him. "There's a few banana-horned cows in here that will butt a horse broadside when they get mad. I wouldn't want Benny all skinned up."

"I'll keep an eye out for them."

"Shoat, you go right here. Brad, left. Me and Dawg will start for them. This bunch won't be bad."

"These are the good ones," I said to Shoat and then shook my head in warning.

"Mother-in-law cows," Gator said.

"He don't even have one of those, Shoat."

"Hey, she was nice to me. Should have married her, instead of Debbie," Gator said with a grin on his broad face. His flattened nose shone red. How many times had he broken it in a fight or scuffle? A pure wonder that he could even breath out of it.

I set spurs to Rooster and we cut south in a short lope. The wind began to come up, and my nose felt numb, though I knew the temperature had climbed some. Rooster made easy strides downhill, and the cattle acted ready to move out. I had them out-distanced if they broke that way.

Dawg had begun to bark, and I stood up in the stirrups to watch him. He was working like a dynamo around them, dodging flying heels and an occasional lowered head on the rainbow cows. A good-working heeler was worth a fortune, and Dawg belonged among the elite in his breed. Though he'd been mauled, rolled, horned, kicked, and run over by wild ones, it only made the red dog that much more enthused about lining up cattle.

In a position to head any wild ones that might come my way, I set Rooster down short of the spring-fed creek. A couple of crazies had broken to the north; Shoat and Benny had cut them off twice, but it looked like one or two of them might get by him when Gator shouted for Dawg to get them in.

A blur was all I could see, but he had hold of a tail and the cow slung him twenty feet, whirled, and prepared to fight him. Shoat, with the tail of a lariat in his hand, rode in hard and caught her off guard, busting her with the nylon. She bolted away and Dawg took to her heels, sending her back to the herd. Shoat bent over Benny's neck, flying low, but the red blur outdistanced horse and rider. Dawg turned the long-eared stock around and headed them back for the bunch.

"Got us a real hand," Gator said in approval of Shoat when I joined him. "That boy's about half a cowboy."

"He's stove-up now," I said. "You need to see him riding rough stock, when he's well."

"I'm looking forward to it." Gator twisted in the saddle and shouted at Dawg. "Get that hussy!"

An errant crossbred cow had broken for the blackjack. Mostly white with a brindle strip or two, she looked like a South Texas dandy to me. Shoat reined Benny around through the brush and went after her. His green stocking cap disappeared over the hillside on the left. In a short while, the bawling bovine came rushing back to join her cohorts, with Dawg nipping at her heels. The green stocking cap reappeared and waited for the herd to pass him.

"This Benny is sure a good cow horse," Shoat bragged on the dun, patting his neck. "I know some old boys in Arkansas would give a good price for him."

"He ain't for sale," Gator spoke up. "If Brad sells him, I'll have one less good horse to borrow for rounding up my stuff."

"I guess I better keep him. Hey, do you want Shoat and me to get that bunch over there?" I pointed to the leery ones still on the far ridge and looking ready to quit the country.

"See what you can do with them. I'll take these on to the main corral. Maybe we can get those wild ones in the small pasture and then work them in the pens."

"We'll try," I said and motioned for Shoat to turn off with me.

We headed our horses at a long trot. Standing in the stirrups, I knew the wild ones would soon figure our purpose and make a break for the thick brush. The thing I wanted to do with them was panic them toward the traps.

This dozen or so cows plus some yearling calves were the real spooks. My grandfather would have called them *haints*. That's an old expression for haunted, only worse. Shoat rode beside me, grinning despite the sharp wind. I knew his ribs had to be bothering him, but he never let on like he was discomforted.

"These the banana-horned ones?" he asked as we rode into a draw and could no longer see the bunch.

"Yeah, let's ride," I said, putting Rooster in a lope. My plan was to be around them and cut off their flight to the back of the spread. When we came to a trail feeding off the hogback, I told him to take it. He already had the lariat undone and charged up the steep hillside. I found a place I thought Rooster could climb up and sent him for the top.

Though I couldn't see him, I heard Shoat shout and yell to turn the group back. They had already broken to try and get past us. Spurs to his sides, I pressed Rooster harder up the steep hillside. Then above me, several mottled, long faces appeared. They were only checking and in a blink of an eye they broke away out of my sight.

The hard-breathing, big gray between my knees topped out and I saw the herd wringing their tails as they headed northeast. No Shoat. Then I heard an angry cow bawling and booted Rooster to the edge of the rise. There in the brush was a blue cow weighing a thousand pounds, tongue out and mad, on the end of Shoat's lariat. Benny was doing his best to keep the angry cow off both of them.

I jerked loose my rope and soon had a loop made, then forced Rooster down the hillside where they were mauling over brush, dried grass stems, and weeds. I missed on the first swing, and Rooster was forced to whip around on his hind legs to avoid the angry brute. Second try, I caught a horn and half a head, and I dallied off the rope and sent Rooster for the ridge.

Shoat put the spurs to Benny on the other side of her and he flew uphill. Rooster had no choice but to come with us. Growling like an angry dog and roaring when she got her breath on the end of both strings, the cow quickly proved she'd never been a 4-H calf and did not know how to lead. Both ponies got down and strained; the cow soon began to learn that it was come along or get drug.

Shoat, holding his dally, gave me a smile and spurred Benny on. The boy was eating this up. It was all right, but we still had half a mile of brush and tough country to reach the corral. The rope across my left leg was biting in. At last Rooster and Benny were moving the cow's stiff front legs even up hill. The progress was a few feet at a time, hanging onto our dally and our ponies charging hard until the cow finally came along. When we reached the flat on top, the cow, slobbers flashing and her tongue flying, lowered her head and charged. We allowed her to get between us and we set her down. Then with a nod, we headed for the pens. The brute really got mad, but chasing us was what we wanted it to do.

We bailed off the ridge through a bulldozer-scarred clear strip and hit the bottom at a hard lope. That cow stuck all four feet in the ground and managed to jerk our horses around, almost taking Benny off his feet. With a shift of the saddle horn, Shoat put the saddle back in place and with a nod, we both charged the hill. It was come on lady or get your head jerked off.

Three times, she got down on her side. Each time, when we rode back, she lurched to her feet, head down, ready to destroy us. Once I took up my rope and managed to turn her before she reached Shoat's right leg. It was drag and haul, but I could see the gate ahead. Then from the far pens came super Dawg. A hustling blue and here he flew. Both of our horses were straining on their load, breathing hard, their shoulders wet with sweat.

Dawg's ferocious charge at her heels sent the cow into orbit; it was a race for the pens for the two of us. The dog's sharp teeth must have activated her, for we were hard-pressed to go fast enough to keep our ropes tight. Once through the first gate, we never stopped until we were in the pens. Gator shut the gate and called off the heeler as the cow stood head down, tongue out, panting hard.

Without a moment's hesitation, Shoat rode over and jerked both of our ropes off her head. She was too exhausted to do more than toss her head at him; still, I'd have been lots more cautious than he was about removing them. He rode Benny off while coiling up his line.

Gator held the gate and nodded his approval when I rode through gathering my rope. "Hurrah, we got all of them this time."

"Give Shoat the credit for her."

"You team rope?" Gator asked.

"I can," Shoat replied.

"You don't steer wrestle, too, do you?"

"Naw," Shoat looked embarrassed as he shook his head.

"Good. If you decide to do that, you tell me. I won't enter that rodeo."

"What now?" I asked and dropped off Rooster, letting my legs catch up before I released the horn.

"Get on my cell phone and have them truckers get down here."

"We going to sort them before they get here?" I asked, undoing the cinch.

"Yeah, and I've got lunch at the truck."

"Jerky and beer?" I asked with a wink at Shoat, who I'd forewarned not to expect any great meal—if we got one at all, as far out as we were.

"I'm buying steaks tonight," Gator said and waded off for his pickup.

"Better be good ones. We don't care about good-looking waitresses," I said after him.

"Yeah, we'll go to the Barn."

I nodded to Shoat to assure him that we could find good vittles there. We could hear Gator talking loudly on the cell phone ordering trucks. We hitched the horses out of the wind to the side of my Gooseneck where the sun would hit them. They were settled down and would be fine. When we arrived at his dually, Gator was cleaning out the cab, tossing empties in the bed of his pickup, the one with the busted fiberglass wheel cover on the right side. He had done that one icy morning, and the gate wasn't as wide as he had thought. Shoat climbed in the back seat of the club cab. I took the front one.

"Truckers're coming," he said, handing Shoat a couple of packages of jerky from a brown sack.

"These are fresh," I said over my shoulder. "He got them this morning."

Shoat laughed. "I've eaten them after they aged nine months in the glove box."

"Ain't no beef jerky ever poisoned anyone," Gator said, indicating for me to get the beer out of the cooler between my legs. "There's your kind of pop in there, too."

We sat back as the heater began to blow out warm air. I unzipped my coveralls then chewed on the spicy beef sticks and washed them down with cold diet soda.

"How come you bought ice today?" Shoat asked, leaning over the seat to see it in the cooler.

"I don't want my beer frozen, just cold," Gator said, between gnaws of his jerky.

"I see."

"Gator buys a bag of ice with every case. Don't you?"

"Two bags in the summertime."

The cattle separation went easy. Big calves in one direction; eared cows by themselves in another pen; angus, limounsin, and charolais crosses in the third one. We were close to being finished when the dust of the first haulers trucks came into view.

"Got them eared mammas sold to a dude down at Tulsa. They're going there. After they calve, he's going to artificially inseminate them to some big high-powered bucking bull. Gave sixty bucks an ampule for the semen."

"He ever AI'ed anything before?" I asked, recalling some bad experiences of my own.

Gator grinned like a Cheshire cat. "I doubt it, but it would be fun to watch him try that on them wild sisters."

We all laughed at the notion.

"Back home, I seen this guy Wesley Lyons had his arm up this old cow inseminating her," Shoat began between chuckles. "The head gate fell down, she got loose and with his arm stuck inside her, she drug him a quarter mile. Old Wesley quit the AI business over her. Sold his tank and all them long plastic gloves."

"I might, too," Shoat said, going back to the pickup to grab another beer.

After the trailers were loaded and the drivers were instructed, Shoat went and called the guy in Tulsa to warn him the delivery was on its way.

"He ready for them?" Shoat asked, when he got back.

"He better be. His wife answered and she said okay."

"Maybe she's going to do the work?" I suggested.

Gator shook his head. "Naw, she's way too fancy for that. I've met her before. He's got lots of money, he'll figure it out."

We loaded the bawling calves on Gator's Gooseneck and then put his horse in back. The calves were to go to his house to be weaned.

The rest of the cows were going to two ranches owned by some guy who lived close to the Arkansas border. By the time we had them loaded, the sun was low in the west. February days could be almost too short. Gator gave each driver maps and conversed with them while we unsaddled and loaded my horses.

The Barn's a good place to be when the temperature drops to ten degrees at night. Big rock fireplaces under an elk or a buffalo head at either end of the dining room with four foot-log always ablaze in them. The warmth saturated the room with the strong smell of burning oak. My wind-burned face felt seared in the heat. Underage, Shoat had to sip Coke with me. Gator had a mixed drink while we sat on the stools at the bar.

"Hey, Gator, you haven't been here in a while," a thin waitress said, wagging by in her light blue uniform.

"You were off the last time," he said and raised a glass.

"You know where I live," she said. I shared a wink with Shoat.

"Man." Gator turned back to the bar. "I only took her home 'cause her car wouldn't start."

"Sound like that to you?" I asked Shoat.

Gator made a pensive face over his glass and then shrugged. "Aw, you two can go to hell. I was only being helpful."

"That gal that seats people is waving at us," I said.

"Her name's Joanie," Gator told me.

"You take her home, too? I mean, when her car wouldn't start?"

"And I thought you were my friends," Gator moaned.

"We are," I said, herding them along, getting anxious to eat.

The salad was crisp, the steaks mouth-watering and delicious. Big baked potatoes and heavenly fresh bread. We leaned back when we finished, and Gator's cell phone rang.

"Debbie?" he said into the flipped-open receiver. I saw indigestion set in on his pained face as he slouched in the captain's chair, nodded, and agreed aloud with whatever had been said on the other end.

"I'll get them after school on Friday," he announced. "I'll be there!" This time sharper than before. Then he hung up. He placed the small phone on the table.

"That witch."

"What's wrong?" I asked.

"This isn't my weekend to take the kids. It's hers. She says that she has to go to Tulsa on business and will be there for most of the weekend."

"So?"

"She found out that I had some plane tickets for Vegas is all."

"You still going?"

"Of course not. I love them kids. But she did that on purpose. I'll never buy tickets in Woodbury again—why that danged girl at the travel office never let her shirttail hit her backside before she called Debbie and told her about them."

"What'll you do with the tickets?"

"Give them to that girl I was going out there with and tell her to take a friend."

"Do I know who you were taking to Vegas?" I asked coyly.

"No," Gator said and looked toward the door. He wasn't telling me, either. Secrets, secrets.

It was some sort of miracle that we got out of the Barn without Gator getting into a fist fight. In his frame of mind, we very well might have had an altercation before we left. Business in the restaurant was slow because of the cold spell, so who he could have picked a fight with was not clear. But my steer-wrestling buddy had a tough reputation, a short fuse, and the ability to find an adversary in a heartbeat. Especially after his ex had whipped up on him like she had over the phone.

"Could I rent a car around here for a couple of days?" Shoat asked as we drove back in my rig to the ranch.

"Sure, they've got two agencies in town. No big choice. You going home?"

"Naw, I need to go up to Kansas City on business—unless you need me?"

"No, I'm going to catch up my bookkeeping, and pay some bills. Stays this cold, I'm not going anywhere or doing much. We have Gator fixed up."

"Good. I'll only be gone like three days."

"Tomorrow, we can call the car rental and I'll run you in town."

"Sure hate to put you out so."

"No problem." Then I recalled HONEY-1. Chester said it had a Missouri plate.

With Shoat off to KC in an impossibly small car, I went up toward the state line and ate lunch at the sale barn. Then I sat in the stands with Gator while he bought some cattle for various people.

"Kid's gone?"

"Yeah, he rented a car and went to Kansas City on business."

"He's a good one," Gator said.

"If he can get well and get back to riding, he could do all right."

"Yeah. Pen them with lot sixty-five," Gator said to the auctioneer. Gator scratched a note down on his buyer card, and the long-tailed charolias cross heifers headed out of the ring.

"Why Missouri?" he said to himself and turned back to me. "Thought he said he was from Arkansas?"

I explained the big fuss at Jackson and all about the sports car with the vanity plates.

"Hell, she's someone's mistress or wife. Some thugs probably beat him up over her."

"You may be right."

"Damn, Brad, he's going back for more, if that's the case."

"I don't even know where he's going up there."

Gator bid on some limousin steers, but soon quit and sat back—sold too high. "Man, that guy really wanted those suckers. Say, if you learn anything about Krammer needing help, you let me know."

"He's a big boy and he's got to learn."

"Yeah, but I like him."

"You're just spoiling for a fight."

"Me?" He rolled his eyes around in disbelief at me. "Hey, I'm serious. He ever needs two fists, have him call me."

"You're always the first one I'd call."

"Remember when we high-school rodeoed?"

"I remember back behind the chutes you KO'ing the bull-riding champ and us trying to revive him so he could ride his bull."

"Aw, that guy was a sissy. Bet he wore silk underwear. The pink kind."

"There's a good set of steer." I indicated the ones coming in the sale ring.

"Not bad, if that character over there lets up a little on his bidding."

"Don't punch him in the nose if he don't."

"Hey, I'm mellowing out. Dang his hide, there he goes. I better call my man."

"Don't hit him," I said with my hand firm on his arm.

"I won't, I promise."

It was already four o'clock so I said good-bye to Gator and left to go back to my place to do my chores and put my feet up. It was Tuesday, I reminded myself, facing the last vestiges of the day's red sun. Coming down the drive I could see someone's rig parked at my place, then I saw the low black camper on the pickup. Zola was there.

My spirits rose. With my company gone, we would be all alone. I parked before the porch and bounded up the stairs. She had a key, so the door was unlocked.

Something tackled me and I looked down into her baby blues, closing the front door.

"And where have you been all day?"

"Sale barn with Gator, ma'am," I reported.

"Likely story. You have been with some young playgirl all day. Tell me the truth." She began un-zipping my coveralls and I began to shed them. Bent over to undo the side zippers on the leg, I noticed she was barefooted. Then straightening up, I saw that the only thing that she was wearing was one of my tee shirts. Taking off the vest, I bent over and kissed her. Her fingers busy fumbling with my woolen shirt buttons.

My boots toed off and at last stripped down to my BVDs, I swept her up in my arms. Thoughts of her body made my stomach churn with emptiness. I wanted to kiss and hold her tight forever.

"Where is your boy?" she asked.

"Gone for three days. That long enough?"

She twisted her head to the side and looked hard at me. "For starters."

"Wonderful," I said, nudging the bedroom door open with my toe. "I'll turn on the electric blanket."

She winked and gave me a coy smile. "I already did."

Chapter 7

"So where is your bull rider?" she asked, pouring coffee in my cup. The early-morning sun spilled on the dinette table, and the whole kitchen filled with the aroma of her cooking.

"Kansas City, I guess. He rented a car. Well, I rented him a car with his money. You can't rent one unless you have a credit card."

Dressed in her jeans and a silky shirt, she looked like she belonged there. This breakfast-cooking deal was something new. I tried to act impressed. S he buttered toast, then delivered me a plate of scrambled eggs, ham, and potatoes with little chunks of green and red pepper. I shook my head in disbelief examining it.

"You fixing to go into a new business?" I asked, reaching for the salt and pepper.

"You better taste it first," she warned, bringing her plate over and sitting across from me.

I tried a forkful of the dish. "Yeah, it's good."

She shrugged and then laughed. "It came in a package. I picked it up yesterday before I drove out here."

"It's still good."

"I'm not sure this wifey business would work." She wrinkled her nose and made a face.

"They keep making ready-to-cook meals, you might just make it."

"You—" She shook her head in disapproval at me. "So, he just up and left, your boy?"

"No, first Shoat and I helped Gator to round up his cows off the Sutter place. Then he wanted to go to Kansas City for something."

"He's still a mystery?"

"No, I learned a lot about him coming home from Jackson. He says his family's all outlaws and welfare-takers. He worked hard to get into rodeo. Caught chickens to get his equipment."

"He healing?"

"He's tough. Yes, I think he'll be healed in no time."

"What will you do with him?"

"I don't know. I figure once he gets on his feet, he'll want to hit the trail again."

Her blue eyes peeked over the coffee cup at me. "Brad, you'd take in any stray that came along, wouldn't you?"

"Not any—"

"Me included." And she put her cup down and went back to eating, not looking at me.

"Hey, you being here is a big treat. I'm honored."

"Well, I ran out on you in Jackson."

"I didn't think you ran out. I knew you had places to be."

"I should have stayed there. I knocked down a barrel in Wabash and finished out of the money at the second show."

"How's Thunder?"

"Fine. He's in one of your box stalls. Where's Golden Boy? I didn't see him."

"Chester needed a horse trailer to take a horse he bought in Mississippi back home, so he's taking care of Boy until next weekend."

"That's the crawdad dance, right?"

"Yes."

"I circled it on my calendar." She winked at me.

"I'll be there."

"Will the bull rider?"

"Probably, but he's flexible. He can get a motel room for a night."

She squinched her blues into slits and I knew that the notion of rooting him out did not strike her as acceptable. It was her privacy thing. Either her conscience bothered her or she was embarrassed about being open over our affair—it got to her.

In a bound, she was up and refilling my cup. "Heavens, I'll get fired for not being a good waitress here."

My arm caught her around the waist and I drew her close. She bent over and kissed me. "You don't need to chase any cattle, go to a sale barn, or fix any fences today?"

"No. You disappointed?" Full and through eating, I pushed back from the table.

She piled on my lap. "Then we can do anything?"

"Sure, what have you got in mind?"

"After we feed Thunder . . ." She paused and made a face. "Gator won't come by, will he?"

I shook my head. "He's gone to check on some cattle he has on feed."

"We'll be all alone?"

"Yes. What do you want to do?"

She put her arms around my neck, looked me square in the eyes, and tilted her head to one side. "What do you think?"

"Good. So do I."

"Let's go feed him and get your chores done, then."

I slipped on a goose-down coat. She put on her bulky jacket, and pulled on her gloves as we went out into the sharp cold. The brown grass on the lawn crackled under our soles as we bumped hips and horsed around going to the barn. Our breath billowed in great vapors of steam.

In the hallway of the barn, I turned an ear to the sound of a dry cough.

Zola's face grew sober, and she ran to the box stall and looked over the board gate.

"Thunder, you sick?" she asked and slid the latch aside. In a flash, she was in the pen with the dark chestnut gelding, examining his eyes. Her hand found his ear as she paused to test him for a temperature. "I think he has some fever."

"Was he all right yesterday?" I asked.

"Oh, he gets fussy about eating." She let go of his ear and looked hard in his dark eyes. "But he sure didn't have that cough."

"We better bundle him up and take him to see a vet."

"Is there a good equine one around here?"

"No, but we can be at Stillwater in two hours. At Oklahoma State University they've got the best equine services in the nation."

"I hate to put you out—but he's my baby." Thunder punctuated her sentence with a low-headed cough.

"Hey, we'll get him looked at."

She came over and hugged me.

"Get him loaded in your trailer. Here, give me the keys."

She dug in her jeans pocket. "I don't have any makeup on—any my hair needs washing. Here." She dropped them in my hand.

"Hey, you look good enough for Thunder and me."

"I sure hope so." She clapped him on the neck and gave him a worried look.

"He'll be fine. I'll get the truck."

When I climbed into the cab, her sweet musk ran up my nose, a mixture of perfumed soaps and female scents that mingled in my sensors. For a long second I savored them, sitting on the cold leather seat, then I cranked the big V8 into action. If anything happened to her baby, she'd be a mental wreck. OSU's staff could cure Thunder if anyone could—then I recalled the electric coffeepot was still plugged in in the mobile home.

I left the engine to warm up, ran inside, filled two thermal cups, unplugged the coffeemaker, and made sure the stove was turned off. I then ran for the pickup, climbed in, put the cups in holders, and discovered the windshield was frosted over. Never be in a hurry. Under the seat I found a yellow spray can full of defroster.

"Sorry," I said, pulling up and hurrying around to open the trailer's back doors.

"It was so sunny out here, we were getting a tan." Then she forced a grin at me as Thunder stomped in the trailer. Once he was in the stall and secure, wrapped in a blanket, I closed the back doors.

"You drive," she said and gave a shudder.

I frowned at her. "You cold?"

"Cold and worried." She hugged her coat-wrapped arms around herself.

I shook my head to try and dismiss her worries. "He'll be fine."

"I hope so." And we ran down opposite sides of the trailer for the cab.

Inside, she crawled over and kissed me on the cheek. "My own driver." Then hugging her knees, sat with her back to the door.

"This thing ever warm up?" I said, meaning the engine heater.

"It will in a minute."

After a check of the half-iced side mirrors, satisfied I could see enough, I dropped the shift into forward. As we rolled down the long driveway, Benny and Rooster raised their heads up from grazing as if to see what was passing by.

"Those your roping horses?" she asked, twisting to look at them.

"Yes, they like to be outside."

"Look healthier, too."

"They got a good workout two days ago, getting up Gator's cattle."

"I bet. How's he?"

"Fine. Moans about paying child support all the time."

"They are his kids."

"Sure, but he needs to complain about something. His ex somehow found out he was going to Vegas with a lady friend this weekend and dumped the kids on him."

"He have a girlfriend?"

At the county road I hesitated, looked both ways and pulled out. "He had a female companion, anyway."

"Serious?"

"He won't admit it."

She put her lace-up boots on the dash and slumped down in the seat. "He'd be a good catch for some farm girl. You know—someone who drove a tractor, made crops, wasn't afraid of wild cows or bulldoggers." Then she laughed. "I bet there's a German girl down in the Texas hill country be just right for him."

"You playing cupid today?" At the state highway stop sign, I waved at Earl Gauge, a rancher neighbor on his way to check on some of his wheat pasture calves. He waved back as I pulled away.

"I just thought a farm girl would be right for him."

"Gator's a little soured on the marriage business."

"You, too?" she asked in a small voice.

"I made a big mistake—once."

"Hey, we both did," she said as she shifted up on her knees and reached past me for the seat belt. "I am going to buckle you up."

"Okay," I said at her fussing over it as I tried to see the highway past her.

"I don't want anything to happen to you." She quickly kissed me, then went back to sit in her own seat. I could feel her studying me.

"When I married Lucas, I thought our wedding was made in heaven. A horseman—well, he played polo. He liked my barrel horses. Anyway, he showed an interest in them before we got married. But that was all a put-on."

"He was an Argentinian?"

"International," she said with a sophisticated accent. "Yes, he came from there."

"So you had money, the glamorous life?"

"Come on. I fit in at those fancy balls about as well as Gator Bledsoe would."

"Your father sent you to the best finishing schools," I teased her, knowing the quality schools she attended. I felt Thunder shift around in the trailer, and his movements reminded me of our mission.

"That doesn't mean I liked it." She raked her blond hair back with a few brushstrokes and talked with a clip in her teeth until she wound it into a ponytail.

"You were drinking champagne and waltzing with playboys . . ." I said to make her continue.

When I glanced sideways, I met her peeved stare at me, then she shook her head in disapproval. "It was not a horse world. I was expected to dress up for those polo matches like the queen of England. Me, the jeans queen of the West."

I laughed aloud, imagining her trapped in high society. "You ever play?"

"Ha! Practice matches. Polo is a male sport," she said in a tight tone. "Wives do not play. They prance around on the grass in high heels and replace the divots."

We both chuckled as the miles rolled by. "So you weren't made up for it?"

"No. Then I found that black hearted SOB and the housekeeper in bed. She was a cute little Latin girl. He must have hired her just for that purpose. I left." She made a displeased grunt. "Brad, you don't think Thunder's seriously sick?" With a pained face, she stared at me.

"He'll be fine. They've got the best veterinarian setup in the country at OSU."

She drew up in a ball on the leather seat. "You know how hard I've worked with him. I don't think I could even face training another one to this point."

"You ever think he was the therapy you needed?"

"No."

"You've been so involved with him, you haven't worried about yourself."

"Perhaps."

"I think the staff down at Stillwater can cure him, but they can't cure you."

"Do I need to be cured?"

"That's a question you have to ask yourself, Zola."

I felt Thunder shift in back as I drove on. Nothing out of place, he wasn't fighting the trailer, his movements back there simply reminded me of our purpose. A horse's dry cough never sounded good. It was not the kind associated with everyday clearing a hay sticker from their throat, but a short hack.

"I've already asked myself."

"What was the answer?"

"I like being with you."

"But I go to rodeos for the duration. All my performances are in one place."

"Would I have to wear fancy dresses and replace divots?"

"No," I said and eased the rig onto Cherokee Strip Turnpike ramp. I regretted not having the Pike Pass from my truck in the window. "You have any change? We need to pay up here."

"Sure," she said and popped open the console. In seconds, she gave me enough quarters to pay the toll. I handed it to the gal in the booth and we were westward bound again.

"Can we leave it like it is for now?" she asked in a small voice.

"Hey, I appreciate your company." She left me an out. I wasn't all-fired certain I was ready for a big commitment. Still, the hyper blonde beside me meant more to me than perhaps I even admitted.

"Good. When we get big man back there all well, maybe I can think better."

"See if your cell phone works." I fished a handheld electronic directory out of my shirt pocket. "Look up the number for the vet services and call them. We should be there in forty-five minutes."

When she finished talking to them, she turned her phone off. "They said they would be ready for us."

I reached over and patted her on the leg. "He'll be fine."

"I hope so."

Under the bright lights, with assistants drawing blood and recording vital signs like an ER, the slender veterinarian in her white coveralls looked hard at the big gelding.

"Nice animal," Doctor Lee Ann Comfy said. "I think he has a respiratory infection. Doesn't sound like pneumonia or distemper. And he's had all his shots, so we can eliminate those. Whether it is bacterial or viral is hard to say, but being a barrel horse, he's been exposed to lots."

"You don't think it's serious?" Zola asked.

"Anything can become serious," Comfy said.

"Does he need medicine?"

Comfy nodded, folded her arms over her chest, and cupped her narrow chin in her fingers. "There's a new trial antibiotic out we have used on similar cases." She shook her head and made a sharp exhale as if she had a problem. "Oh, there's been no serious side effects using it. The only thing I have to ask you to sign is a release if I prescribe it for him."

"You say it will work, I'll sign." Zola looked at me and I approved.

"It's a little more complicated than that."

"Oh?"

"You have to also sign that he won't ever be used for human or animal food, since the medication is not cleared for usage in meat animals."

"No worry."

"It also requires that you send an affidavit of his disposal when he dies."

"I can do that."

"I'm sorry for all the precaution, but the only way that we get to use these new drugs is to assure the Food and Drug Administration that none of the residues will ever get into the food chain."

"I understand. What do they call it?" Zola asked.

"It has only a drug company's assigned designation. We call it 'Forty-five,' which is an abbreviation for all the numbers and letters in its name."

Zola reached out and caught Comfy's arm. "If he was yours, would you use it?"

"Oh, yes. We treated some horses that were a hundred times worse than he is and they completely recovered."

"Let's do it."

"We'll administer it," Comfy said. "But you need to leave him here for a few hours. We want to be certain that he doesn't develop an allergic reaction and that his vital signs are normal."

"Fine," Zola said and her shoulders sagged.

I wrapped her under my arm. "There's a famous hamburger joint in this town. Let's go have a burger and a shake. Thanks, Doc."

"Don't worry. He'll be fine. My, he's a wonderful horse."

"I think so, too," Zola said as I dragged her toward the exit door.

Chapter 8

The headlights of her pickup shone on the barn as I swung the pickup up to it. She bounded out, putting on her jacket as she hurried for the trailer tailgates. Great clouds of vapor escaped her mouth as she backed Thunder out. He whinnied at my horses and pranced around on his toes.

"I think he's better already," she said, leading him around in a circle at a jog.

"Acts that way," I said, going to turn on the lights in the barn. "I'm going to give those other two some grain. Check that waterer in his stall. Those heaters have been working good, but it's been real cold here recently."

From the feed room, I heard her say it was all right. Good—one less thing for me to worry about. Having poured the grain in the trough for Benny and Rooster, I went back to put the pail up in the tack room.

She finished fussing over his blanket and came outside the stall. The latch in place, she looked back in at him. "Sleep tight, big guy."

"He will."

She threw her arm around my waist and hugged me as we walked. "Kind of messed up our day together."

"Hey, I'm just glad that he's all right."

"Can I make it up to you?"

"You bet."

"Whew." She wiped the imaginary sweat from her forehead and flung it away. "I was worried you wouldn't let me."

"I'll even cook supper."

"Hey, that's great. Let me guess. Is it steak and potatoes or potatoes and steak?"

"You want something else?"

"No. . . . It wouldn't be good—whatever it was."

The answering service had several calls for me. A stock contractor in Utah wanted me to do a July rodeo for him. I looked up the dates in my handheld and found I was booked. When I called him, his answering machine came on and I told him thanks, but I was busy. Dale Rucker called and wanted to talk about some bulls. And a rodeo sponsor in Texas wanted me to cut him some TV ads; he'd be back in his office first of next week. So I put his name and number on my directory. The last voice message was from Gator. I called him up.

". . . and that trucker that took them cross cows to Tulsa, he called me when he got home. That society gal, who I figured never got her nails dirty—when he got there, she saddled a good horse and drove them sisters with a Border collie to the pasture where she wanted them. She told Ernie, this breeding for bucking bull business was hers." Then came Gator's deep laugh. "What you doing tonight? If you ain't doing anything special and you like the Disney channel, come over. I have the kids."

"That Gator?" she asked when I hung up.

"Yes, he's watching Mickey Mouse."

"Do him good."

"It's a lot cheaper then blackjack in Vegas."

"You calling someone else back?"

"After supper."

"Hey, I can operate that electric grill. You season the steaks. I can nuke taters, too."

"Sure."

"Who else called?"

"A man who wants to sell me some bulls, I guess."

"They buckers?"

"He hopes so."

She frowned at me from the kitchen sink, scrubbing the potato skins a lot harder than I do. "You mean he doesn't know?"

"He thinks that they're the greatest since Red Rocket. At least, I'd bet, he has them priced like that."

"Good bucking bulls bring high prices, don't they?"

"Good ones, yes. The rest are common and sell for a little more than hamburger."

"Why did he call you? Do you buy bulls?"

"I do sometimes. When they make money for me, I resell them."

"Oh, a side of you I didn't know about." She studied the dials on the cabinet microwave. Once satisfied, she placed both clean potatoes inside.

I dusted down the two sirloins with steak powder and pepper, then I went back to my recliner to call Rucker. From there, I had a perfect vantage point to admire the catlike swing of Zola's jeans as she fussed over the cooker, holding her hand over it to test the heat. Satisfied, she laid out the meat on the grill and nodded to me.

I approved and listened to the phone ring on the other end.

"Hey, hello."

"Rucker, Brad Turner here."

"Yeah, Brad, you keeping warm up there?"

"Heat pump still works and the North Hills Cooperative has juice. Should be fine until spring."

"I've got two super bulls down here."

That meant he knew where two bulls were that he could get his hands on to peddle. Guess you could call Rucker a bull jockey.

"One weighs thirteen hundred. Black, dubbed horns. Spins like a Wheezer. Man, he slings cowboys faster than you can say 'gone.' "

"How old?"

"Four." That meant he was seven or eight. Bull jockeys were like horse traders—they all lied a little.

"What's the second one?"

"Piebald longhorn. Man, he gets his butt high, drops down like a haint."

"They branded?"

"Yeah, black's got a ninety-two on his left hip. Longhorns got a Lazy-P brand on his right side."

"Who's been riding them?"

"No one. A guy down here just does junior rodeos, and they're too tough for them kids. He needs some dough to pay some feed bills."

"What did you think the longhorn would weigh?"

"Nine."

That meant he weighed seven-fifty, soaking wet. "I don't need a hatchet-assed bull."

"Hey, get a few pounds on him and he'll do the job. He's tough and young, I'm telling you."

"What does it take to get them to Woodbury, Oklahoma?"

"Your place?"

"Yes."

Pause. He was doing some fast calculating. "I can send them with a load going to Wichita, next couple of days."

"They don't get here by Tuesday, you feed them until I get back from Louisiana."

"I'll do that."

"What's his bottom dollar?"

"Three grand."

"Tell him two and I'll split the difference that they bring with him, if they can really buck."

"They'll buck."

"They better be super at that price."

"I don't ever lie to you. Hey, Brad, I don't know if he'll do it. Could you give twenty-five hundred for them?"

"If these aren't what I can sell, then what?"

"They're buckers, I tell you."

He had not answered me, though I knew if they didn't perform, I'd be stuck with them. "Lot's of difference between juniors and the pro boys."

"I know that. Have I ever steered you wrong?"

"No, but some were less than you thought they were."

"Them Brangus? He had them hopped up. I swear I'll never do business with that crook again."

"Let this guy think on the two grand."

"Twenty-five and no premium?" he asked.

"All right. But if you can't deliver before I leave here, you keep them."

"I'll let you know if he'll take that."

"Sure. Keep warm."

"You, too, buddy."

When I hung up, Zola came over and spilled in my lap. "Buy any?"

"Two. He said he had to call the guy back, but I figure he has them at his place already."

"Will they buck?"

"Yes, but how good, I'll have to see."

"Will they make money?"

"If they aren't super, there's enough small-stock contractors around that I won't lose any money on them. They'll need bulls in a few months for their rodeos this summer. But if they're super, I should make a good profit."

She squirmed in my lap and looked bewildered at me. "You just bought them sight unseen? No problem?"

"I know Rucker."

"But what if he—"

"Then he loses me for a customer. And I tell all the big contractors he can't be trusted."

"Blackball him, huh?"

"Rodeo is a small world. Word spreads like prairie fire."

"I better turn the steaks." She got up as the phone rang again.

It was Gator on the other end.

"How is the Disney Channel?" I asked, winking at Zola at the counter.

"You ever eat cheese pizza? I mean plain cheese pizza? Whew, they don't like nothing but plain cheese pizza." He made a deep inhale. "Their mother is going to make vegetarians out of them."

"Ah, they'd probably eat burgers."

"No. But they do like them fried-chicken chunks. Can you imagine, their old daddy makes his living in the beef business and they want no part of it."

"Could be worse. Mike want to take ballet lessons yet?"

"Aw, Brad, don't do that to me."

"Do what?"

"Hey, Lucy's really riding that pony. She wants to go to play days this spring."

"Sounds good. Your ex going to let her?"

"Hah! She can go to . . . that warm place." Gator caught himself before he cussed in front of his kids. "If Lucy wants to ride in those play days, I'll take her myself. What're you doing?"

"Rucker is sending me two bulls. Told him to have them here by Tuesday or to wait until I get back from Beauregard."

"Sounds all right?"

"You never know about bulls. My boy gets back from KC, I may let him practice on them."

"Hey, that's an idea."

"Tell him that your food's getting cold." Zola waved my plate at me.

"Got to run, supper's on."

"Hope it's better than plain cheese pizza."

"I wouldn't want to ruin your whole evening. Pass me the steak sauce, dear."

I heard Gator sigh before he hung up.

Thunder still had a small cough, but Zola left me for a rodeo in western Oklahoma on Saturday morning. Rucker called and said the bulls would be there that night, so rather than be her chauffeur, I stayed home to view my purchases. We parted all kissy-faced. Both of us were eaten up with regret about parting again.

"You think that he'll be fine to run, don't you?"

For the hundredth time I said, "Yes."

"I could pay the fine. Get a note from Doc Comfy—"

"Hey, go and run."

"Okay, I'll do that, but then I need to go back through Fort Worth and see Daddy."

"You're coming to Louisiana?"

"Yes, why?"

"I'll be by myself in the rig."

"No. I'll get a motel room. You can come there."

I leaned in the open window and kissed her again.

"Let the good times roll," she said and raised the electric window as she pulled away.

The bulls arrived near eleven at night. I had fallen asleep in the recliner when I heard the air horns. There in the yard was a sleeper-cab Freightliner, lights flashing like a Christmas tree and a pot trailer hooked on behind.

"You're Brad Turner?" the driver asked, climbing down off the clucking monster.

"Yeah. We need those bulls off over at the loading chute."

"Fine, but they ain't good-dispositioned."

"Do they want to fight?" I frowned at the man in the coveralls and ball cap. "Not good-dispositioned" sent a wave of concern through me. My old buddy Rucker might have sold me some real flakes.

"That longhorn looks and acts like a messikin fighting bull. Black one, he ain't too nice, either."

"Where are they?"

"On top with a bunch of *corrienta* steers. We need to cut them off."

"You're saying that we need to unload the deck and then reload the roping stock?"

"Yes, I ain't going in that deck with them two in there. Only way that we could load them was with them little steers."

"This calls for lights," I said, blowing big puffs of steam in the cold night air.

"It calls for a lot with good fences."

"I've got that. My pens have held buffalo and that's the real test."

"Yes, sir, but these two're crazy."

"Let me turn the lights on, then I can spot you at the chute."

He agreed, told me his name was Joey, and we shook on it.

With a roar of the engine, he backed the trailer as I waved him into place. We cranked up the chute and he dropped the floor and opened the door. The dazed-looking, short-legged steers came off in orderly fashion until the two bulls began hooking their way out of the top. The longhorn stopped in the trailer's doorway, looked over everything and then sailed over a couple of those steers into the lot. He tore around the pen like a mad dog, shaking his hat rack at the welded pipe like he intended to put the fear of God in it. Number ninety-two soon joined him, tossing steers around like hay chucks and bellowing in defiance at the night, the pot, Joey the driver, and me.

What in the devil had Dale Rucker sent me? If I had been a junior rodeo cowboy's parent, I'd pull my kid out of bull riding before he would get near one of those two crazy creatures. They looked like a wreck about to happen at any moment.

"They're sure upset, ain't they?" Joey asked as I studied my twenty-five-hundred dollar investment. Man, in the glare of the pen lights, they looked like eight thousand dollars' worth of broken bones and stitches.

"How we separating them?" he asked.

"If we can get them all in the sorting alley, we can peel those two off."

"I ain't chasing them in no alley."

"We can get them there," I assured him. "Those little steers don't like them any better than we do." I took him over to the pen and pointed it out. "You open that gate and let them into the alleyway. You can get on the fence if they charge you. I'll try to get them headed that way."

"Sure."

"I'll get my Hot Shot and be right back," I told him.

In the tack room, I found a six-foot-long Hot Shot. That might give me the distance I needed. Loaded with fresh batteries, the whip-ended yellow cattle prod looked deadly in my hand. Wary of the two bulls who stood with their butts to the barn, craning their heads around to look for something to ram, I started over the pipe fencing with my wand. Hardly a tooth fairy's wand, the two contacts could make blue fire jump between them.

"Open the gate," I said to Joey and he ripped it back. The *corrientas* charged down the alleyway like range sheep. The two bulls, Blacky and Dummy, freshly christened in the twenty-degree frosty Oklahoma night, held their vigil. In other words, they didn't go out after the steers as I expected them to. We needed the two in the next pen so we could reload those steers. Anywhere else in this labyrinth of number-one sorting corrals was fine, except this one.

"Watch yourself," Joey called out from behind the two and a half inch stem gate.

With my feet on the ground and one hand on the fence, I waved the magic wand threateningly at the two bug-eyed bulls. "Hee-yah!" Blue sparks on the end punctuated my cry. Those two dumb bulls simply rocked back and forth like track stars in their starting blocks. They stood in place like head-tossing statues. Dummy had already proved his athletic agility when he came off that truck. He could run like a gazelle and use those deadly antennas. Blacky's murderous ways had not escaped my notice, either.

"Wave the gate at them," I shouted to Joey.

"I will. Hey, have you considered buying them *corrientas*? I'll just leave them here."

"No, I don't want the roping cattle." Ready to scramble up the fence, I slowly moved along its length. My eyes were fixed on the sullen bulls for any flicker of movement. The main thought on my mind was on how to get up fast enough so I would not be smashed should they charge.

"Hee-yah! Get out of here!"

Dummy threw snot at me. Then he slung his three-foot horns around with deep intent, as if to say, I'm going to hang you up and plaster the ground with you. The sizzling prod only made them more resistant to moving. What in the Sam Hill was I going to do? The two bulls and I were at an impasse. Call it a Mexican standoff, but the bulls were winning.

"Bring the steers back," I shouted to Joey. "Maybe they'll go out with them this time."

Joey was standing on the gate and leaning over the top, looking pensively at the pair. "Naw, they won't go. They've got something figured out."

"I've never had two stupid bulls outfox me yet. You bring those steers back in here."

"What are you going to do?"

"Get on the barn roof and reach down and tickle them with this Hot Shot."

"That might work. I'll send the steers back."

From inside the barn, I carried out a stepladder. The roof's edge was only eight feet high. I leaned the ladder against the fence. In moments, I stood on the sheet iron with my wand. The frost had fallen and in two steps, I almost went flying off, but managed to find some traction at the last minute. Ten shaky steps later, I stood over the bulls. The steers charged into the pen and circled around, looking for an escape hole.

"Ready?" Joey shouted at the gate.

"Yeah—" I started to say. My boot leather hit a patch of ice and the right one flew in the air over my head. My butt hit the sheet iron and I went sailing like I was on a schoolhouse slide. With a wallering scream, I flew off that roof and right onto the hard frozen ground. Those two dumb bulls must have thought the biggest all-time Guiness Book of Records bald eagle was coming for them because they broke for the pen after the steers.

Joey closed the gate and ran over. "You hurt?"

"Just my pride," I said and managed to get first on my knees, and then at last on my feet. That landing sure made my vertebraes a lot closer.

"What we going to do now?" he asked.

"I can reach them from any side of the fence with this Hot Shot in the rest of these pens. We'll sort out them Mexican steers."

"Good," Joey said. Ten minutes later, the *corrientas'* hooves were clattering back up into the top deck. As for Blacky and Dummy, they were lowing to themselves in the back pen. My compassion for those two had hit a low ebb. My hands on my sciatic nerve, I walked Joey to the cab. I signed for the pair and offered to make him coffee. He had had enough of the place and told me he needed to head for Wichita.

Somehow I managed to wave good-bye and kept from crying all the way to the house. Joey revved up the diesel with a ground-shaking roar and headed the big rig down the drive. I went inside the warm house and decided I needed four aspirins—two would never cut it.

I awoke to the phone ringing. Daylight streamed from outside. How long had I slept? Then the knifing pain in my lower back jabbed me.

"Hello."

"Brad, you sound asleep?"

"Gator?" I rolled over on my back looking for a comfortable place to lie. "I wasn't asleep, I was lying here awake waiting for you to call me."

"Yeah. Them bulls arrive?"

"How would you like to buy two of the best buckers in West Texas or East Texas, south or mid, junior rodeo dandies?"

"Oh, something wrong with them?"

"Don't mince words. They are meaner than billy goats and twice as fast."

"You don't know if they'll buck, then?"

"Buck, I doubt, but they'll be wonderful at butting. Need a money-the-hard-way bull or a poker bull? I've got them."

"You calling Rucker about them?"

"No, I'm personally going to go down there and stomp his backside."

"Let me go for you."

"No, I want to do it myself. When you get time, you bring Dawg over. I want them separated and in different pens."

"No problem. You going to be around there?"

"Yes. I'm going to be in bed."

"What's wrong?"

"I fell off the barn roof."

"How did that happen?"

"I'll tell you when you get over here. Bring some whiskey, I'm going to run out."

"You—whiskey? I'll be right over when I get the kids ready."

"Soon enough."

I used the bathroom, drank a half of a glass of bourbon straight, found the heating pad and went back to bed—gingerly. The soreness had set in and on Sunday morning there wasn't a doctor or a chiropractor around, save for the emergency room—and I had my own aspirins. That was what they would hand me anyway. If I wasn't dead or better Monday, I could come back.

I awoke from my foggy sleep. Gator stood over the bed, beside him four bright blue eyes, wide open, inspecting a man asleep in the middle of the morning.

"Hi, kids," I managed in a husky voice that shocked me.

"Daddy said you were hurt, Uncle Brad."

"I'll live, honey." I sat up and tried to clear the cobwebs.

"Daddy gets like that when he drinks a lot," Mike said matter-of-factly.

"Kids, hush," Gator said gently. "Uncle Brad fell and hurt himself. How did that happen?"

They laughed at my story, and even Gator joined in when I told him the part about the big eagle scaring them.

"You need someone to drive you in to the doctor's tomorrow, I'll volunteer. The kids will be in school."

"If I can't get myself there, I'll call you."

"What are you going to do now?"

"Get out of bed and get dressed. I want to see those two bulls again."

"All right. Come on, kids, we have to let Uncle Brad get dressed."

Once clothed, I came out of the bedroom.

"You don't have Disney on your TV?" Lucy asked.

"He don't have any kids," Gator explained.

"Lots of grownups watch it and laugh. You do."

"Oh, yes, darling, I sure do watch it. Brad, you all right?" He frowned, concerned.

"I'll make it to the pens. You may have to wheelbarrow me back, but I can walk that far."

"Stay here. I can sort and feed them.

The icy chills of pain ran up my face every step to the corrals. Despite the sharp wind, I was sweating inside my goose-down jacket when I took hold of the pipe fencing. Then I saw the pair. I wanted to grind my molars together at the sight of them.

"Wish you would have called me. I'd brought Dawg and we'd had this done."

"It was midnight. They had loaded those two with a swarm of *corrientas* in the top deck because they were so crazy."

Gator shook his head looking through the pipes at the two. "No one could rodeo with stock like that."

"I'm calling the man who sold them to Rucker today."

"You want them separated and in them back pens with the waterers?"

"Yes, until I figure what to do with them."

"Dawg!" he shouted and the red blur came bailing out of Gator's truck and charged over to prance around the kids.

Lucy waved a finger at him and he immediately sat down. "He minds me, Uncle Brad."

"He sure does," I said, impressed.

"Not bad for a girl," Mike said and shook his head in disgust. He turned back to watch his father.

When Gator started down the pens, he called the heeler to him. I watched Gator go down the alleyway and set the first pen. He came back, unchained the gate and hissed Dawg on them.

Dummy went berserk, and began running around the pen, hooking his horns at the fence. Blacky made a break for the gate with Dawg in full pursuit. Gator slammed it shut and they were separated. In less time than I took to get the ladder, Blacky was in his own pen. Then Gator came back and unchained the gate. Dummy had gone to a neutral corner and would not come out. Head down and threatening with his antlers despite Dawg's passes at his heels, he would not leave.

I hobbled down to the corner near the loading chutes and found my yellow prod on the ground. Then, with pain-filled steps, I carried it back.

"I'll get it." I waved Gator away.

When I stuck that wand through the fence, I pressed down hard on the button for full voltage. The blue electricity flew. Dummy let out a cry like he'd been murdered and left that pen bucking every bit as good as Rucker said he could. I mean his butt went over his head. He danced on his front feet and went through the gate in high flight.

Gator penned him. "Whew, you see him buck?" he asked, coming back. "You still calling Rucker?"

"No, I'm waiting for my bull-riding expert to get back from Kansas City."

"Good idea. Wonder what happened to him?" Gator said, climbing over to join me and the kids.

I had to close my eyes, my back hurt so bad.

"You kids go with Uncle Brad to the house. I'll toss them bulls some hay and be right there."

"Thanks," I managed. Whew, I needed to be well enough to drive to Louisiana by Wednesday.

Zola called when I got in the house. She was on the road, with first-place money in her pocket, telling me that Thunder was over his coughing. She sounded upbeat.

"Of course, I'll be at my father's place by afternoon," she said, as if that would be like taking medicine.

"He'll be glad to see you. Gator and the kids are here."

"Tell them hi. I better boot scoot if I'm ever going to get there."

"Love you."

"You too."

I never mentioned my back or my stupidity. Going home, she had enough to worry about. Her father might support her barrel-racing habit, but it sounded to me like he lectured her regularly about doing something else constructive with her life.

When Shoat came back Monday morning, he drove me into Doc Watson's office, the old family doctor in Woodbury, who ruefully shook his head at me over my wrecks since I was fourteen. He took some X-rays, decided I would live, gave me a prescription for muscle relaxants and pain pills that I couldn't mix with driving. He also told me to wear the brace hanging in my closet.

And I had three performance to work in Beauregard that week.

Chapter 9

Zola called from Fort Worth. "Hey, Thunder's doing fine."

"Wonderful. You at home?"

"Oh, yes. Doing the little-daughter things. I went to a gathering last night with him in Dallas." Some social or business event, I surmised.

"Sounds exciting."

"Oh, it was. What are you doing?"

"Getting ready for Louisiana."

"Shoat come back?"

"Yes, he's feeding stock for me right now. He says he's lots better."

"Good. I'll see you down there."

"Can't wait."

"I'd go today," she said a low voice. "If you were there."

"Me, too."

The phone clicked and Shoat came in the front door.

"Them bulls are settling down. I think they they'll be fine," he said, stripping off his coveralls.

"Boy, they were wilder than billy goats when they came off that pot."

"We get back from Louisiana, I want to ride 'em."

"You be well enough by then?"

"Oh, yes."

"We can take them over to Ule's indoor arena and try them out. There's usually some boys over there that can fight one, just in case."

Maybe my purchase would work out after all. Rucker had never called me. He knew something was bad wrong with those two or he'd been bugging me about the "good deal" he made me on them. He'd still get his though, if that pair didn't do better than they did upon arrival. I could still see that hatchet-butted longhorn Dummy circling the pen at ninety miles an hour. Showing off his horns like it was Sunday in Madrid.

"Hey, I can drive the rig for you," Shoat offered, sitting down to breakfast.

"You'll probably have to."

The red sun shone across the frosty hills and I half closed the blinds. The cold sure hung on. Usually in this country, it was warm a few days then cold a few. But this winter turned cold and went colder. Some moisture wouldn't hurt, either—we'd need it for the spring grass and the tanks. This far north, it could come as snow or rain or ice. The latter, I could do without.

The TV network morning show was interviewing a movie star. My back still hurt and the brace made me feel like a turtle in a shell.

"That guy was paid ten million bucks to make a movie and thinks he did them a favor?" Shoat said, setting down his fork.

"Movie stars make a lot more money than cowboys do. Hey, you sure can drive that rig for me?"

"I'll do it," he said sipping coffee and watching the tube.

"What would you do with ten million dollars anyway?"

"Go on rodeoing until it's all gone."

We both laughed. He carefully never mentioned anything about his trip to KC. I didn't pursue it, though he acted like he felt better about things in general. But that was his business and I'd keep my nose out of it.

We spent the rest of the day getting things ready. I picked up my laundry at the cleaners. Madra, the chubby girl who worked there, had to ask me about the guy with the cute butt.

"Shoat Krammer, this is Madra," I said, writing a check for the bill.

"Pleased to met you, ma'am."

She blushed and sucked in her lower lip. "Yeah, me, too."

"See ya," I said and waved to her. Shoat carried the starched Wranglers and shirts under the flimsy plastic.

Once in the truck and settled in the passenger side, I looked back at the sign in the window. Extra starch a specialty. Maybe Madra would do for Gator. A farm gal, she sure wouldn't mind some cow manure on his boots. Have to think on that. He'd kill me for even mentioning her.

"You feeling better?" Shoat asked, looking both ways before backing out on Main.

"A little."

"You look and act better."

"So do you. KC must have been good for you."

He shook his head and made a pained face. "You ever met a woman you couldn't forget?"

"Several. My ex-wife, for one."

"You can't forget her?" He blinked at me.

"Now I can, but for a long time I couldn't, and I tried and tried to get back with her."

"You were saying before that we need feed." He glanced over at me for directions.

"Turn in at the Co-op." The familiar oval sign was on the right. The store and warehouse were easy to see across the potholed parking lot.

"This woman—I mean, she eats my guts out."

"Yeah, mine did that, too."

"Guess I'm still a kid, huh? If I was grown-up like you, I wouldn't feel that way."

"I wouldn't say that. Zola gets to me. I'd like for her to be here."

"You and her?" He backed up to the waist-high dock and parked. Then he turned. "You and her serious?"

"I am."

"Yeah, but you've got a ranch and lots to offer her."

"She hasn't bit on it yet."

"If I had more, I would do something myself."

"Maybe time will work it out."

"I hope so. I ain't never been so confused in my life. I mean, about what to do."

"Let me know if I can help." As I pulled on the door latch, the pain shot up my back. "Have you ever announced on horseback?"

"No, sir, and I ain't going to try, either. I can get the feed."

For a long moment I sat there and let the pain recede, then I slipped out of the pickup.

"You're hurting?" Shoat said when he saw me, looking at me critically. "What if you can't announce on horseback?"

"I'll do it from upstairs."

"Yeah, I hadn't thought about that. Most announcers do it from there, anyway. Bet you won't even remember this rodeo, but I sure do," he said. "When you once opened a rodeo on a bucking horse, and he really bucked. You managed to land on your feet and the crowd went wild."

"Fort Smith, Arkansas."

"Yeah! Jasper took a bull down there for them to try. I went with him."

"He brought a one-horned bull right?"

"How did you remember that? We always said that he left the other one stuck in a bull rider. Jasper called him Boulder Mountain."

"Pretty decent bull. But no, I never ever tried saddle broncing to open a rodeo again."

"Out back the cowboys were all laughing, saying they had switched horses on you."

"I know. He was supposed to barely buck." Funny, I didn't recall Shoat from that day, but he was probably just a kid standing around back then.

When we entered the store, the smell of fly dope and feed filled my nose. Harvey Grayson looked up and smiled. "Half a ton of special horse mix?"

"That and some bull feed," I said, then introduced Shoat.

"This your new man?" Grayson asked, reaching under the counter and handing each of us a red ball cap.

"No, Shoat rides bulls. He's just visiting."

"Nice to meet you."

Gator was set up to feed the stock while we were gone, so he'd have plenty on hand. After a trip by the bank to make a couple of payments, we ended up at the diner for lunch. It was beginning to fill up with locals so we found a side table. Milly, a pert gal in her late forties with shades of gray, brought us menus, then whipped out her pad and pen.

"Tired of your own dang cooking, huh?"

"All the time. Milly, this is Shoat. He's a bull rider."

"I ever see you on ESPN?" Her eyes shone like diamonds as she inspected his face closely.

"No, ma'am, but it's nice to meet you."

"They need Brad to announce them sports programs. You know what I mean?"

"He's a great announcer," Shoat said.

"Best one in the land. Now that I've swelled your head up two hat sizes, I hope you'll have the appetite to match. I've got beef roast on the special."

"Special and an ice tea."

"Same here, ma'am," Shoat said. "Kinda like home, everyone knows everyone," he said putting the napkin in his lap.

"And everyone's business."

"Yeah, that, too."

From the look in her eye, I knew when Liz Clayton pushed in the door that she was going to come by and speak.

"Oh, you *do* come home in the winter," she said. Tall, wearing a red-and-black business suit, she looked overdressed for Woodbury. Her shoulder-length brown hair looked a shade lighter than usual.

"I don't get to do many Florida rodeos."

"We're having a band at the country club this Saturday night. Out of Tulsa. A rather good one."

"Sorry." I smiled at her. "Shoat and I'll be eating crawdads.

I saw her lip curl. Then she smiled. "Oh, well, busy people have little time to flitter with homebodies."

"Hey, keep the invitation open."

"Oh, I will. Don't eat too many of them crayfish."

"Who's she?" Shoat asked.

"Used to be the state senator's wife. Liz Clayton. She's Woodbury's answer to a society matron. On the hospital board, all that."

Shoat half smiled, then in a low whisper said, "I think she wants you on her board."

After being certain she was busy talking to someone else with her back to us, I shook my head.

"The only way that this cowboy got on her list is because I do things outside of the city limits, like announce some pro rodeos. She's too uppity for my lifestyle. Besides, the smell of horses might permeate her tailored woolen suit."

"She could sure meet big people. I mean, she would know what to say and things like that."

"I don't need a translator."

"No, I know you don't."

"If you're thinking about her for you, forget it."

"Naw, you don't understand. A guy like me from the sticks? Say I make good some day—"

"You will, Shoat. Some day you will, if you apply yourself. But the worst thing you can do is try to be what you aren't. You ever see that old show *Beverly Hillbillies?*"

"Yeah, I've seen them reruns."

"That's what I mean by being out of place."

"Here's lunch, cowboys," Milly said, suddenly appearing and delivering the plates filled with sliced beef, mashed potatoes, gravy, green beans, and salad. "I see that Miss Astor came by to speak to you." She plopped down fresh yeast rolls and a butter dish.

"Our day, huh, Milly?"

She whipped out a ticket from her apron pocket, checked to be certain it was ours, then slid it on the table. "Ain't everyone that she'll speak to."

Shoat and I chuckled to each other.

"You want pie, I'll be back," Milly said

"Just like home," Shoat said, busy cutting his beef. "Where's your girlfriend?" he asked.

"Zola's in Fort Worth having to dress up and meet all her father's friends and associates."

He threw his head up and looked hard at me. "Glad she's there and not me."

"Hey, quit worrying about those kind of things. Those folks pull their pants on one leg at a time."

"Yeah, but they know what leg to put in first."

His words made me so tickled I had to stop eating to laugh. He shook his head, acting intent on his food, but I saw the mischievous grin.

"You rodeo clowned too long," I said.

"Maybe. Hey, I want to do my share. We get those groceries for the trip, let me buy them. I've been mooching off you."

"You've been a lifesaver. I'd have had a hard time getting around without you."

"I been a thinking. After that car-rental deal the other day—after I found out I couldn't rent a car without a credit card?"

"Yes?"

"I better get me one."

"I'm sure you can. They send me applications every day."

"Yeah, but you're famous."

That about choked me. I finally managed to swallow and speak. "Away from here, I'm just another guy wearing a Resistol."

"Well, I don't have much of the collar-stuff them bankers like."

"Collateral?"

"Yeah, that's it. Down home, that banker Dan Sipes said, 'Krammer what've you got for—' that word you just said. I asked if it was like rickets." He sat down his fork and wiped his mouth on the napkin. "Made him laugh, by golly."

"Were you after a loan?"

"Oh, yes. I wanted to buy a pickup to drive to rodeos."

"You get the loan?"

"Naw. See, Old Man Bartlett had that First National Bank. He sold it to this big city bank. They got a new sign. This Sipes guy wanted to loan me money to build a big chicken house. But he didn't want to loan me no money on a pickup."

"So you didn't buy it?"

"Oh, yeah. Carl Jones financed it himself."

"Where's the pickup at?"

"Mexico, I guess. Someone stole it down in Texas on the border."

"What did the police say?"

"Said they did it all the time down there. Them Mexican car stealers, they liked them four-wheel drive rigs."

"How new was it?"

"Oh, it wasn't new. Ten years old, but Carl had put a new engine in it and it ran real good. Needed a paint job was all, and the right door was dented bad. Never bothered the Mexicans none, they must have liked it."

"Was it paid for?"

"Almost. Sis sends him the payments each month for me."

"Have any insurance?"

"Yeah, but it wasn't no good within a hundred miles of the border."

"What?"

"That's what I said on the phone. Carly Tattum said he wouldn't have sold me that policy if he'd known I was going way down there. He thought I'd be staying up there in Murphy County and Arkansas and tried to save me some money."

"You need a guardian."

"Well, I'm learning."

"Dang sure the hard way."

"Yeah, but I'll know better the next time."

What kind of guidance had he had in his life? He was a self-made bull rider and he learned a lesson. Perhaps with enough beating around in this old world, he would survive. But if that beating he took in Jackson was over the gal in the sports car marked HONEY-1—he still had a lot more to learn.

Chapter 10

Before the sun even thought about coming up, Shoat herded the big rig south toward Louisiana. In the predawn, the headlight beams shone dully on the county road and the fencerows. We settled in for a long drive.

"When we get back, I want to get on those two bulls," he said. I considered taking a sip of the coffee from my thermal mug and adjusted for the road bumps for the sip. He pulled out on the smooth blacktop and I finished the drink.

"Fine. They've settled down a lot. I'd like to see them buck."

"That old boy never called you?" Shoat sounded a little amused.

"Rucker knew from talking to that truck driver how upset I was. He's hoping I'd cool down."

"Wish I'd been there."

"What—to see me do the Russian ballet on the tin roof?"

"Ah, I feel real bad about your back. I'd just liked to have been in the excitement."

"Buddy, that Dummy bull can run like a greyhound."

"He looks like an athlete."

"He is one. He bucked going out that gate that night like a supercharger."

"I'll be healed enough to try him next week."

"You sure?"

"Positive."

Thursday night, Golden Boy looked to be in fine shape standing on fresh shavings in his panel stall. Upstairs, seated on a high stool with the timekeepers and the rodeo secretary in the box over the chutes, I could survey the good-sized crowd taking their seats. It would be different to announce from there after three years of coming blazing into the arena. It bothered me a little, my loss of a close rapport with the crowd—but there was no getting on Boy and playing Roy Rogers with my sore back.

A few minutes earlier, before I went upstairs, Skip Evers spotted me walking up the aisleway under the huge shed where the rodeo livestock was housed. He frowned hard.

"Son, you look like you've been in a wreck."

I nodded.

"What happened?"

I gave him the highlights of my accident. He nodded and agreed that I belonged upstairs. No one but me acted upset over my appearance in the box. It would be different from there, though, and even the prospect of a major change in work habits can make your stomach churn. Mine had more butterflies than a meadow full of wildflowers in the summer time. Announcing is a natural thing to me. I step up, take the mic, and my mouth goes to work—hopefully, its fully connected to my brain. Crowds that would make Shoat shrink to a midge, well, they warm my heart. Those folks came to rodeo; my job is to inform and entertain them. It's an opportunity for me to convince them that when they go out the exit gate after the last bull, they feel like they've been through the greatest sports event they ever experienced, and never begrudge the price they paid for that seat.

"Good evening, ladies and gentlemen, cowboys and cowgirls big and small, welcome to the South's biggest festival—we call it the Crawdad Dance! My name's Brad Turner and coming in on their quarterhorses are the super pickup team. Let's welcome them." Things went smooth through the intros. By the time they cracked out the first bareback rider, the fans were into it, and I felt better.

A chute fighting horse brought Skip into action.

"Hey, Bradberry! Why ain't you out here with me? That Oklahoma bank repossess your pretty yellow pony?"

"No."

"If they did, I want to buy it."

"No, I had an accident."

"I heard about your accident."

"You did?" The rider had gotten off and was standing on the platform, pulling on his glove. We had time.

"Yeah, you folks all know what chicken poppy is?" Skip asked and used his hands to shade his eyes from the bright lights. "I figured you did. Well, Bradberry was over at his neighbor's house, going to steal him a chicken. His neighbors up there in Oklahoma got big chicken houses. Thousands of chickens in every one of them big long coops. They ain't going to miss one chicken." Skip put his hands on his hips. "Seems that when our friend and announcer Bradberry snuck in, those clucks took an instant disliking to him. Way I hear it, them hens pecked at Brad's behind so hard, he can't ride for a month of Sundays." The crowd guffawed.

"Skip," I replied, "you deserve to be tarred and feathered."

The cowboy was ready, the gatemen on the end of their ropes. "Ladies and gentlemen the cowboy from North Dakota, Mike Tease on Baldy," I announced.

The cowboy made a ride, but seventy would be a high score for his effort. The scores came up and Tease had seventy-one. Skip tracked the rider coming back up the arena.

"Son, you better check your britches. We ain't got no chickens in here but you got some poppy on your backside." The cowboy never turned, just brushed his seat off, which made the crowd laugh.

The crowd was into Skip's "poppy." It went on until down in the barrel setup, continuing the wild chicken story about how I then slipped in the coop and hurt my back trying to steal a chicken and thus I couldn't ride my horse. He received ten miles of laughs on that one. I knew when I said good night to the fans that story would be the topic of conversation the rest of the weekend.

"Don't slip going down those stairs," Dale, the rodeo secretary, said to me.

"Thanks. Good night."

"Was the sound okay?" Swing asked, taking off his headphones.

"Sure, fine."

"Ha," he said. "You need to be up here every performance. You're sure a damn sight easier to please up here than down there."

"I'll listen better tomorrow night."

At the foot of the stairs, up swaggered Skip. "Well, if it ain't old cripple poppy boy."

"You going to the dance?" I asked.

He gave a look at the tractor busy harrowing the coliseum floor. "Bradberry, I don't think so. You going?"

"It depends. I sure can't dance."

"Yeah, but that little blond-headed lady sure can." Skip nodded behind me.

"Hi, Skip," Zola said joining us.

"My, my, honey," Skip said, "why don't you go out with me? He's all crippled up from stealing chickens and won't be no good for nothing."

"I loved that story," she said and beamed at him. "But he never told me about it."

"Aw, that chicken he took was too tough to eat. I wouldn't have mentioned it, either." He wiped his forehead on his sleeve then frowned at the makeup that came off on his white and red shirt. "Look here, I'm coming apart. See you two."

"Yes, good night, Skip." Zola then turned to face me. "What did you do to yourself?"

All the way back to Boy's stall, she chewed on me, mostly for not telling her about my injury on the phone. I saw Chester walking up the alleyway on horseback.

"Hi, Zola," Chester said and dismounted. "Shoat said he fed Boy and he is going to the dance with the guys. He said he'll see you later."

"Thanks, Chester."

"Once I get these last bulls sorted out, I'll be there, too. Save a dance for me, ma'am." He tipped his hat and rode on, with her promising him that she would.

"You all right to go down there?" she asked, concerned.

"I'll make it."

"You taking pain pills?"

"Did I sound like it during the show?"

"No, I was only asking."

"I'm taking one soon, but I sure didn't want to sound all loopy up in the booth."

"You didn't, you sounded great. I like you better out in the arena, but I understand looking at you that you needed to be upstairs."

"Maybe Saturday night . . ." A guy could wish he would be well enough by then.

"Don't rush it."

Beauregard's civic center was a great sprawling circular building, wrapped in colorful crepe-paper strips, banners, and sponsor signs. Fiddle and accordion music filled the air; straight-armed dancers circled the slick floor as we came inside.

You could smell the crawdads boiling and see the beer kegs carted around on dollies. Let the good times roll.

"Hey, Brad," Gusto Bernadine shouted greeting to the two of us. The white-shirted tall man in his once-a-year to wear a cowboy hat was a committee man.

"Ah, I never met the lady."

"Zola, meet Gusto."

"Such a pleasure, madam. You two had any food yet? Some red wine? We got some good whiskey."

"I'll have a soft drink," I said, looking around.

"I love red wine," she told him, and I could tell Gusto was already putty in her hands. He ran off to get us some drinks.

We were soon seated with the committee men and their wives at a long table where we shook hands and made intros. In no time they had Zola dancing. Since I couldn't shuffle, I was pleased that she was having a good time. To be friendly, I ate some of the mud puppies they served, piled on big trays on the table.

Monica, Gusto's motherly wife, went and found me some of the largest iced shrimp they had in the Gulf.

"You don't drink wine?" she asked with a frown, holding up a gallon of the grape to refill her plastic glass.

"No, ma'am. Coke's fine."

"My, even Jesus drank wine."

"I know, but I don't have his willpower."

She laughed and clapped me on the shoulder. "I'm going to tell that to my aunt, that's a good one." After she set the jug down, she waved at a young person to bring me another pop.

"I can go get it," I protested.

"You're my guest. Heavens, you see all those sisters a-going by and looking at us, seeing me sitting with you." Her dark eyes danced with mischief. "Their tongues will wag tomorrow and I will be the point of it all, no?"

"I guess so."

"Good. It isn't bad for them to tell gossip about a fat old lady and a handsome man. They'd all be here if they had any nerve or half a chance." Then she threw her head back and laughed aloud like I'd tickled her.

"You ever do this with Skip?" I asked.

"Oh, yeah. One night two years ago."

I could imagine how exciting that could have been. Skip was wild when things got started. The pills had begun to ease my back some, and the shrimp filled me up. A barrel racer, Louise Taylor, stopped by and asked over all the noise and music if I thought that the vet school at OSU could help her crippled horse.

"Zola said they had a great setup," she shouted at me.

With a nod, I stood up with some discomfort, found

Dr. Comfy's card in my wallet, and told Lou to call her.

"I will, thanks!"

"You and that girl serious?" Monica asked with an elbow in my side when I sat down.

"No, that's Lou—"

"No, I mean the blonde that's wearing out dancing with all those old men on the dance floor."

"They'll be wore out, she won't."

"That's what I am worried about. After this is over I still have to go home with one of them old farts." Then she laughed aloud and dumped more fresh shrimp on the paper plate before me.

"Zola and I are good friends who live in different worlds. She wants to win the world title in barrel racing, and that means driving hard and going lots of places. I stay at one place and announce."

"Yes, but she better get smart and stay in one place."

"That's her decision."

"I tell you what, once she gets older, she'll wish she had done that."

"Yes, but she's not that age yet."

"It comes faster than we want it to."

"It does, it sure does."

Zola came by, stole some shrimp, drank a half a glass of wine, and was dragged away by another native to dance. Without an intermission, they shoved another band in to play.

Finally out of wind, Zola returned and collapsed on a folding chair behind me. "I'm done in, Brad."

"There are two more nights of this. You should save yourself."

"Oh." She put her hand to her forehead. "Can you die from having a good time?"

"Not a chance, honey," Monica injected with mer mouth full.

Hours later, when we went to Zola's pickup, I asked if she had seen Shoat. She looked around the parking lot as we crossed to her pickup. "No, come to think of it, I didn't."

Neither had I, but the place bustled and I could have simply missed him. Strange, though, that I didn't see him once.

"That deal is wild. I'd never been before. Always heard about it, but usually had another rodeo to go to after the performance."

"Cajuns have a great time. This committee is no exception."

"That Monica looked like the queen bee."

"That's the way she wanted it to look," I assured her.

In the coolness of the night, I gave one last search across the cars. No sign of Shoat out there. I eased in the passenger side and she frowned at me when she climbed in the truck.

"I have a king-size bed at the Holiday, you know."

"Be a shame to waste it," I said and grinned.

She shook her head as if I was hopeless.

"Tomorrow," I began, "I'm going to a chiropractor. Monica gave me his card. She says he's wonderful."

"If you can even get there," she said as she leaned over and kissed me.

I would. But still the question nagged me: Where was Shoat?

Chapter 11

When I got to the coliseum the next morning to check on Boy, Shoat had already cleaned his stall, fed, and watered him. I found him busy sorting stock with Chester and Glen.

"Everyone have a good time last night?" I asked, watching Shoat work the cut gate.

"Too good," Chester called out, bringing another bucking horse down the alley ahead of his sorrel. "He goes out tonight," he said, reading off a list as he came with him. "Shoat send that big gray to Glen. Put him in the holding pen. He's a reride horse."

"I see Boy's cared for," I said to him.

"You didn't need to come back so early. I'll take care of him for you," Shoat said.

"Thanks. I needed to go see a doc, anyway."

"Back worse?"

"No, but according to a lady friend, he's the best in the swamps at unkinking you."

"Hope it helps," Shoat said, then looked up in time to face a head-shaking horse. "Where does this one go?" he asked about the walleyed bronc coming at him.

"Goes outside."

"Got it. See you, Brad."

"Supper at five?"

"I can be there."

"Steaks at the rig."

"Wouldn't miss it." He grinned.

Zola took me by the RV. I checked the refrig and saw that we had plenty of fresh-cut steaks and potatoes in the bin. She headed me for the chiropractor's office.

The doctor worked me over and I felt much better. He wanted me to come back the next week for more, but I told him I needed to head home Monday morning, thanked him, and learned from the receptionist that Monica had already paid my bill.

"Nice of her," Zola said as we went out of the office to her pickup.

"She ain't getting much but a shrimp-eater for her money."

Zola shook her head in disapproval. "Maybe all she wants is the attention."

"Might be." I climbed in the pickup with more ease than I ever had in several days. I looked hard at the sign on the door. DR. LEO CHARBONNEAU. Well, old Char sure knew his business. Maybe he ought to come to Woodbury and work on the old busted-up ranchers and cowboys. They ever found out how good he was, they'd be lined up clear down to the Co-op waiting for a turn.

"Listen, cowboy, don't rush this business," she warned and I heeded her advice.

My back felt even better by Saturday, but I still worked the last performance from the crow's nest. No bad wrecks, and our injured list of contestants was very low. Plenty of top hands were up at each performance, so the hometown folks were pleased. Beauregard went well for me despite my being upstairs. The committee men said their seat sales were up over the year before.

My contract to announce for them ran for two more years, so I had nothing to worry about. Johnny Farmer's stock contract was also still on, so it was hand-shaking time Saturday night at curtain time with the committee men congratulating each other for another great year.

"Now let's go dance," Gusto announced and Zola took his arm.

"Put that in your contract. You got to bring your pretty lady back next year," Phillip Derousseau, another committee man, said, taking my arm.

"He couldn't keep me home at the chicken farm," she said over her shoulder.

"No free hens for you, huh?" Phillip asked.

"Right," she said and we all laughed, including Skip who was tailing along with us.

I slow danced with Monica, and two other director's wives. My real craving for crawdads, shrimp, and anything else dipped in tabasco sauce had slackened by the third night.

On my way to the men's room, Shoat appeared out of nowhere and caught my arm.

"Brad, I want you to meet Mona."

I removed my hat and smiled at the dark-eyed girl in the tight blouse and jeans. Black hair and those sleepy eyes, plus she had a figure that wouldn't quit. Either she wore a very expensive bra or she had a set that stood up and pointed at the moon. Whew.

"Shoat's told me how much you've helped him and all. I'm so glad to meet you at last," she said.

"Yes, ma'am. He's a great cowboy."

"Oh, yes," she said, holding his arm in both hands possessively.

I wanted to shiver at the thought of my own mistakes. She was obviously older than he was. But she sure was a firecracker, and she even got to me. Was this HONEY-1? I smiled, told them to have fun, and went on to the rest room.

"That's her, the one he introduced you to," Chester said, washing his hands beside me in the men's room.

"The one who drove the fancy car?"

"Yeah, I seen that Ghia of hers show up Thursday night after the rodeo. He got in it and drove off."

"Hmm. No sign of trouble?"

"No sign of them other two," Chester said and dried his hands on the too-small brown paper towels.

I tried to think. Friday night, Shoat had shared steaks with Zola and me at the trailer. He never mentioned Mona or anyone else then. Obviously, he went out with her after the show. Wasn't any of my business, but he'd sure spoiled me, driving, doing all my chores while I had been so sore. I'd miss him when he left, that was for sure.

Back at the table, Zola pointed them out to me. "Her name is Mona. He introduced her to me. This is the same one?"

"Yes. Chester says she drives a Karmann-Ghia."

"Boy, she does look like a movie star." Her eyes went to the ceiling in an oh-my expression.

"And that boy worries all the time about being adequate in public."

"He does?" she whispered. "Well, her bust line would give me an inferiority complex if I had to look at them for very long."

Zola looked at the crepe-paper decoration overhead and then gave me an exasperated exhale. "This is a slow song. We better dance. You might get ideas."

We left to go back to the rig about midnight. She

came in and we had a soda. It was parting time again and neither of us wanted it to end. Her plans over the next few weeks were to take a sweep through the southwest and then make some shows in California.

"You going to do anything exciting?"

"Probably help Gator some. Buck my bulls out a few times."

"Those dang bulls are going to be the death of you yet. Don't do anything silly again." She sat across from me at the kitchen table, he knees drawn up under her chin. At times, it hurt just to watch her body contortions.

"We'll meet again in Fort Worth?"

"Yes, ma'am."

"I'll run there and stay there for that week."

"At home?" I asked.

"No. I'll stay at a motel."

"You can go home."

"You want me to?" Her frown an indication I'd said the wrong thing.

"No."

"I don't even want to leave you tonight." She shook her head ruefully.

"Me, neither."

"You need to get up early and go home. I'm going to run by Dad's place going west and pick up some things." Her blue eyes searched the ceiling of the coach.

I reached out for her hands and squeezed them. "It was a nice time. Very nice."

"Oh, Brad, I'm not going to get teary-eyed. But you be careful and call me. You have my cell phone number. Tell me how your back is."

"Yes, Mother."

She bolted up and reached across the table and kissed me. Then she wiped a tear from her eye, shook her head, and started for the door. A little less agile, I got up and followed her outside.

"You be careful, too," I said, then hugged and kissed her. She nodded and then climbed in her pickup and drove off. That left me looking at her taillights and wondering what we should do next. In three days together, the status of our relationship had hovered over both of us, more so than ever before.

I went back inside the rig, locked the door, undressed, took off the brace, and hit the mattress.

Shoat missed the coffee I made early the next morning. No sign of the boy—he obviously hadn't come in to sleep. I needed to find my trailer, hook on, and load Boy. Soon enough, someone pulled up and then rapped on the door.

"You up, Brad?" It was Shoat.

"I'll dolly down the trailer first," he said as he went behind the pickup and began cranking down the jack wheel.

That completed, he came inside out of the chilly air and tried the coffee I'd poured for him. "Boy's ready over at the coliseum. Got his blanket on."

"You want some cereal?" I asked.

"Naw, I ate late last night. Hey, I'll run Chester's pickup back to him and then we can hook this rig to the trailer."

"I'll do that."

"No, you stay in the rig and eat your tiger berries. I'll take care of this."

"Yes, sir."

I wondered over the next spoonful of milk and cereal what I would learn on the way home about Mona, if anything at all. Odds were, he would not say a thing about her. Case closed.

Sun-up found us Oklahoma-bound, peddling the interstate, the horse trailer and Boy on behind.

"You awake enough to drive?" I asked.

"I don't take much sleep."

"That's well and good. But you get tired, we switch drivers."

"Yes, sir."

"You're supposed to say, 'Aye, aye, Captain.' "

"You ever in the Navy?"

"No."

"Just wondered. By the way, I watched them bulls close this weekend."

"Never figured you had time."

"Hey, you know that Cody bull, the white one Johnny calls Bill Cody?"

"The one that bucked down Lonnie?"

"Right. He always bucks light coming out?"

"Most times, except for that time with Lonnie."

"I think that if a man rode him loose, the first jump then got ready for a wild second ride, he'd fool that old bull."

"Might work."

"That boy that got on Monkey should have ridden him. But it seemed like he wanted off as soon as the gate came open."

I agreed. More cowboys were bucked off mentally than physically.

Shoat had fallen into the how-to syndrome that affects most full-time rodeo cowboys. How should he ride the bad ones? What made those buckers so tough, and how could you give yourself a winning edge? I figured the next fifteen hours of driving would be full of questions like, Does the bull always go out like that? Or, Could a man get enough steel in his craw to ride that tornado? It was that way in my days; now things were even more advanced—guys like Shoat could get detailed computer sheets on every bucking animal.

"I'm kinda anxious to get back on some," he said, when we pulled over at a truck stop in Shreveport about midmorning.

"You thinking about my bulls?" I asked, slipping on a jacket and coming off the rig.

"Yeah, they're supposed to be tough stuff."

"Well, I paid for that."

"We get home, I'll be ready to try them."

"Good."

All the way from Beauregard he'd never mentioned Honey One. I wondered what happened to her as I went back and checked on Boy. We unloaded him and walked some of the kinks out of the palomino. My back felt better. Not totally great, but not killing me.

"That's a heckuva horse, mister," a trucker said on his way to his rig.

"Not bad, thanks."

"He's a beauty," the man said, obviously awed by the golden horse.

"Where did you get him, anyway?" Shoat asked me as he led Boy back inside the trailer.

"Southern Arizona. A gal had him down there and I got a call about him from a guy I knew who lived by her. He said she's got the ideal horse for me to announce on. My next question to him was 'What does he cost?' Man, I figured we were talking thousands if he had the color and disposition that the guy described on the phone and all.

"So he says, 'You're going to have to ask her yourself what she wants for him.' So I got the number and phoned her. She came to the phone and sounded all excited. When could I come look at him, and see if he fit me?

"Then I had to decide: fly or drive. I didn't have any idea what she wanted for him and she wasn't saying. Like, if you have to ask, then you can't afford him, right?"

Shoat nodded as we pushed inside the truck stop, grabbed us some coffee and began waiting in line.

"What did you do?" Shoat asked.

"On a whim, I drove my pickup and trailer down there."

"And?" He paid for both of our coffees and snacks at the checkout.

"She was on the front porch when I drove up. She was in a wheelchair. Sun shining, warm day, it was springtime down there. She explained that she would never be able to ride him again. Car wreck. So we went to the corral. I stepped in the lot and he took to me while she watched.

"I fell in love with him. Stout, great disposition. I got on his back and rode him with my knees, no bridle and she nodded in approval. When I slide off and went to the fence, I asked for her price She looked up at me and said, 'What can you afford?' Told her not anything like that he would bring at a sale."

Shoat and I pushed our way out of the glass doors into the sunshine and headed for the RV.

"What happened next?" Shoat asked, taking a chew off a beef jerky stick.

"She said, 'I'll rent him to you for a hundred dollars a year.' "

"My gosh, Brad, you rent him for that?"

"No, six months later, she came to a rodeo I did in New Mexico and gave me the papers, transferred to my name and all."

"She must have been an angel."

"She was, Shoat. She really was." I felt a knot growing in my throat.

"You go by and see her?"

I shook my head. "She couldn't stand the confinement of the wheelchair. Two weeks after she gave him to me, she committed suicide. I think she had already planned it when she signed him over to me."

He gave me a grave look.

All I could do was nod and blow my nose hard.

Chapter 12

It was all set for us to buck the two bulls Saturday night at an open rodeo. A skiff of dry snow swirled in from Kansas and I was ready to declare this the toughest winter on record for cold in northern Oklahoma. Whew, it was nearly March and the arctic weather still hung on. Bundled up like stuffed scarecrows in coveralls and ballcaps with scarfs, Shoat and I convinced the two bulls with much shouting and arm waving to get in the Gooseneck trailer.

On a gray afternoon, we headed for the Lazy-U arena and the small weekly rodeo, picking up Gator and his two horses along the way. I didn't feel up to team roping, even though my back pain was down to a couple of aspirins a day. That was close to normal, but still, I didn't need to aggravate it.

Gator came out of his white-framed farmhouse, puffing vapor clouds in his usual blown-up fashion. I could see he was in a heat before he ever left the porch. His ex must have jabbed him.

"You look like Dawg bit you, and then you burnt the toast," I said as he stormed up.

"Worse than that. An old boy called from Nebraska and turned down a potload of calves. I need to stay home and sell them."

"We can take your dogging horses up there for the kids to use."

"No, I ain't in the mood to talk to nobody about those calves. I ought to drive up there and punch out his lights."

"He ordered them?"

"Yeah, he did. Called me for them. I was down at the Joplin Yards and those calves were farm fresh."

"What was the matter?"

"Said they were fifty pounds too heavy."

"Were they?" I asked as the three of us strode down the hallway of the old barn to get his horses.

"Brad, they ran 501. He wanted four-fifty to fives. That ain't fifty over. He wanted lighter cattle, he should have said so."

"Done business with him before?"

"Couple of times. But he never kicked on me before."

"Might be his credit has gone bad," I suggested while Shoat led out Gator's bay heeling horse, Chaw. Gator caught the sorrel dogging horse he called Strike King and we led them both down to the tack room. He unlocked the padlock on the door as if still deep in thought.

"You know, Brad, that might be it. Shoat, don't never get in the cattle-buying business; it'll make an old man out of you."

"A potload of cattle?" Shoat frowned at him. "Why, if I had to pay for them—it would bankrupt me."

"Ah, they're good cattle. I've got them off at a friend's place who'll take care of them. I'll be fine. Just got to get calmed down." He drug out his dogging saddle and pad. In his haste to throw it on Strike King's back, he boogered on the lead. For a minute, I worried for the horse's safety, but Gator settled down some and coaxed the high-strung horse to accept the saddle.

He looked at me and shook his head. "I knowed what you were going to say before that horse found the end of the rope. 'Go easy, Gator.' "

"I've been calming you down since we were kids in the sandbox."

"That's a fact. Shoat, years ago, we were down at the fair at Tulsa and this old boy from Ada made a mouthy comment to me about how badly I had judged some hogs. Brad grabbed my arm and shoved me down on a bale of hay. Saved that old boy's life."

"I don't recall that," I said, trying to remember the incident. I could recall him bailing into the whole Barnsdale FFA down at OSU once during a high-school judging meet. We all got called on the carpet over that when we got back home.

"I dang sure do."

"You've got a better memory than me," I said and we loaded the horses in the back of the trailer. "Are you going with us?" I asked.

"Sure, what's ten-twenty thousand? I might win fifty dogging over there tonight."

"Or lose it," I added and they both laughed.

Shoat got in the bench seat and we were off for the arena via Harry's Chicken Shack. It was a ritual. If we didn't stop and eat some of Evonne's greasy chicken, we would be cursed with bad luck and not win a thing. Evonne had bought the place from Harry and never changed the name; she didn't improve the chicken, either.

The three off us piled into the place and, lucky for us on a Saturday night, we could get to the counter easily and place our order. Evonne, a good-sized gal in a blue waitress uniform that hugged her ample figure, smiled big at us.

"Well, you pros are going to work over the kids tonight, I bet."

"Probably lose our shirts," Gator said, looking at the menu on the wall as if he had not read it ten thousand times.

"Be cold driving home—without your shirts."

"That's why we're eating now. I seen that sign, 'No shirt, no food,' by the door."

"Gator Bledsoe, what do you want?" She smiled at a family with children who came in and stood behind us.

"Crispy dark meat, fries, slaw, and extra biscuits."

"You want a side order of biscuits?"

"I want enough to eat with my meal."

"Iced tea?"

"Yeah, got to have that, too."

"Comes to four-eighty."

"I've got to feed Shoat and Brad here; they're hauling me."

"What do they want?"

"Better ask them. Shoat Krammer there is single, too, by the way."

She looked at the ceiling for help and shook her head. "I'm through with men."

"Shoat and I want the chicken breasts, fries, and slaw. He's drinking soda, I want tea."

"Good to talk to a man knows what he wants," she said and rang the total up, taking the money Gator dug out of the front pocket of his Wranglers.

"It'll be ready shortly," she said and then took the family's order.

We sat at a picnic table and went to undressing—the heat in the cafe was hot on coveralls. Gator spoke to an older man and his wife at a side table.

Some young cowboys came in and ordered. I recognized them as hanger-ons. One, the Beadle boy, came over and asked about the bulls in the trailer.

"They're suppose to really buck," I said. "But you know about that."

"You got someone to ride them?"

"Shoat's going to tonight."

"Oh, yeah, I just wondered. Thanks."

"I get some lighter ones I'll sure let you try them," I said, and the boy politely nodded.

"Couldn't ride a gnat," Gator said and shook his head in disapproval when the youth walked off.

"He wants to."

"No, he don't. He wants to be a bull rider by hanging out with them." Gator scowled, looking ahead. "No guts, no glory."

"Here we go," Evonne said serving our meals on wax paper in plastic baskets. She set the drinks down and looked us over. "Anything else?"

"No," Gator said. "You got it right this time." Then he ducked as she threatened to hit him on the head with the tray.

"Thanks," I said to make up for Gator.

"She likes the attention," Gator said to Shoat with a wink and reached for the ketchup. He always drowned things in the stuff.

My mind was more on the bulls and how they would work out. In my vision I could see myself landing on my butt atop that hard ground and both them bulls giving a snort and quitting the pen. Oh, well, you can whip yourself with dumb moves you've made until you're depressed. I had Zola in my thoughts, too. She was running in Arizona tonight and then off to California in the morning. And looking at Shoat wiping his mouth on a napkin, I realized there had been nothing else said on Mona since Beauregard.

When we had unloaded Gator's horses and backed the trailer up to the lot gate, Ule came out. We'd talked on the phone about bucking them so he expected the bulls.

"Put them in pen ten."

"I'll go set the gates," Gator said.

Shoat took the Hot Shot and never said a word. Up in the trailer he went, saying, "You sure don't need to get knocked down again."

"Thanks," I said, going to open the center cut gate. "Don't rile them up."

"I won't. I've been chewed out too many times by Jasper Northcutt for even thinking about it."

The bulls came off easy and craned their heads around like two studs looking for a cow. They smelled the air; Blacky lowed to warn any adversaries that he was there. Dummy trotted down the dim-lighted alleyway, and his cohort soon followed.

"You got them out of Texas?" Ule asked.

"You know they're supposed to be pro bulls?"

"I used to think that horse traders could outlie anyone on the earth. The guys with bulls are worse."

"Shoat Krammer there is going to try them when you've got time."

"Hey, we'll do one early, one late, and give him some rest."

"Appreciate it."

"No problem. If some of you guys hadn't helped me get this thing going, the bank would have owned this place years ago."

Despite the cold, a number of folks bought tickets and were filling up the stands on each side. Kids were having fun while their parents visited. It was something to do on a Saturday night besides watch the tube. Here they got live action, sometimes more than they wanted.

Familiar faces were gathered around the heater behind the chutes. I spoke with several and shook their hands. I stripped off my cotton gloves and unzipped the coveralls. The humidity was causing a foggy haze to form inside the building. Several young contestants were there along with some guys who simply rodeoed close to home.

Sam Howard, the announcer, came down from above the bucking chutes. He made a big deal of shaking my hand. He enjoyed announcing but never got more than twenty miles from his car-lot business. From time to time he'd call me and ask for a critique. I always said he was great. In truth, I wanted him to tape a few performances to let him listen to how redundant he was. He worked hard for Ule, though. The cowboys that hung out with Sam liked him, he gave scores and times loud enough and bragged on them.

"You ever lose your voice," Sam said, "you feel free to call on me."

"I ever do, you'll be the man." I smiled and he nodded. Then he went over and talked to one of the judges, a big Indian from Watts. John Stills stood six-six in his bare feet. He had the respect of the cowboys and they never argued with him or Dub Price, the area rancher on the other side.

With the barebacks penned at our backs, George Hanks and I visited about the weather. A ruddy-faced man in his fifties, he always looked windburned. He ran mother cows, and at one time was the biggest hay dealer in the area, though he'd cut back in recent years.

"You must not have a rodeo this weekend," he said.

"Got a few weekends off this spring."

"I would imagine you get road-foundered."

"Not bad," I said. Seeing Bobby Knight, the bull-fighter, come by, I collared him. "I've got two bulls here to try. I'd say that the longhorn Dummy is the toughest. He's a fast cat."

"You got riders?"

"Yes, Shoat Krammer's going out on them."

"Never heard of him."

"You will. I just wanted to warn you."

"Hey, thanks."

"No problem. They're supposed to buck."

Knight grinned big. "Ain't they all?"

"If they don't, that longhorn will make a poker bull."

"I'll watch him."

"You make any money on those bulls?" George asked.

"Win some, lose some. These I'm worried about. I may have some duds."

Sam's national anthem tape hissed, his PA system sounded like a cracker box, but the four bareback broncs went without a hitch. Mostly jump and kick horses, with Gator helping Ule pick up the riders. One boy leaped for Gator's back and I thought for a moment they would both hit the dirt, but they didn't. Hard to unseat that burly cowboy.

Couple of good hands were there to calf rope; a former top roper tied a calf in nine flat. I knew him from competition; despite some gray hair, he came mounted and still could wrap and tie in a hurry. Ule's crew of boys were sorting stock and had Blacky in the chute next to the last one. If he acted up and we needed to move him up to try and settle him again, we had the space.

"We can buck him after the calf roping," Ule came by and told us. I nodded.

Without any references on which way and how the two bulls bucked, it left a lot of questions unanswered. Another reason to kick Rucker in the seat of the pants. The four chutes were all right-hand turnout. Some bulls will buck better on a left turnout than a right. Shoat had his rope rosined and climbed up on the back platform with me. He threaded it around the bull's belly. The bell underneath was ringing as he sought the place where he wanted to secure his hand on the animal's back. Bobby gave him the tail end of the rope. Gator showed up to pull it tight for him. I stood on the back of the chutes with the flank man, Graves, who adjusted the rope on the bull's flank.

"Tight?" he asked me.

"Danged if I know. Try him medium. Then I'll know more." I stood over Shoat, ready to pull him out of harm's way if Blacky tried anything like jumping around in the chute. The bull acted fired up and that made me feel better. I could tell by the way he stood through all this that he was a veteran of the game and not chute-crazy. He kept trying to see out the gate and Shoat forced his head back with his foot.

"Who's riding?" Sam asked from above us.

"Julio Juarez," I said, making up a name. The chute crowd laughed at my choice.

After the last calf roper missed and took a no time, Ule came over to help pull the gate. Bobby Knight, the bullfighter, ran out in the arena, backpeddling and dancing in his tennies with all his attention on the gate.

"Here from El Paso, Texas is Julio Juarez on the great bull, Black Magic. Just a quick snapshot of all the bull riding we'll have later tonight, folks."

Shoat slid up on his hand and nodded. When the gate flew back, Blacky hesitated for one-hundredth of a second, then he simply soared out in the air. He threw his head left before his front feet hit the ground and slung his hind end around like a whip. His speed impressed me as I counted a thousand and one, a thousand and two. At six, Blacky reversed direction. Then Shoat jerked his rope with his free hand, gave a kick and landed on his feet. The buzzer came slow. He loosened his hat and nodded to Sam's praise of his ride as he swept up his bell and rope. Without hardly a bobble, Blacky left the arena.

Shoat climbed over the gate, grinning at me. "He's a keeper, ain't he?"

"Sorry, folks," Sam said over the PA. "No score for the cowboy. Didn't stay on till the buzzer."

I nodded to Shoat, feeling a hundred percent better over half the deal. "I can get my money back on him. You don't have to try that longhorn tonight. You sore?"

"No way." Shoat shook his head like I was crazy. "I'm just getting warmed up. There's lots of contractors could use him."

"I think so. Ule wants to do the longhorn Dummy last. Bring down the curtain with him."

"Fine," Shoat agreed, as unruffled by the ride as someone who had just done five pushups.

The crowd hadn't noticed; they thought Julio had misjudged the time by pulling the tail of his rope before the whistle. But I knew and so did several others—Shoat wanted that bull to think he had thrown him. Not ride him into the ground. The boy had been around enough to know the hows and whys of this game. I felt good about the first one, but the snaky longhorn still had me concerned.

Gator dogged his steer in six flat. Three of the high-school boys used Strike King. They came up respectable under nine seconds on their steers. Of course, Gator hazed for them, riding on the far side and shouting his instructions at them about what they needed to do. Breaking hard out of the box beside the steer, he shouted at the last boy, "Get down!" He did, lost his handhold, and ended facedown in the dirt.

"If your mama complains about your dirty clothes, son, blame it on Gator Bledsoe," Sam said and the crowd laughed.

Ule's bulls were mostly young, but tough enough for the amateurs. A guy in his thirties by the name of Signs rode a slow spinner. Gator told me that Signs never left Oklahoma to rodeo.

I frowned at him.

"Lives with his mother, ain't never been married either. They've got a ranch and some cows. He grows some wheat and beans."

"Why ain't he ever rodeoed out of state?"

"His mother got him to promise her that years ago."

When Signs came out of the arena, he nodded, smiled, and put out his hand. I shook it and complimented him on his score.

"Aw, I'm glad I didn't have to ride your black bull. That one was easy."

Old Blacky had begun to build a place in my heart. My mind was going back and forth about Rucker, and whether I needed to turn Gator loose on him or not. They loaded Dummy in the last hole. He was slinging snot and rattling horns on the bars. Several of the younger hands looked at him in awe. Shoat had his bull rope on him and tied off to speed things up.

The slow pace of the rodeo reminded me of my days in Arizona at the weekend rodeo. Inexperienced riders, uncertain if they wanted to ride the bell-ringing creature waiting to explode beneath them could take forever to get ready. The bull would wiggle a little, and they would jump off him and need to repull their bull rope. They seldom rode eight seconds because by the time they'd nod, they were scared to death.

Shoat was finally in the second chute ready to ride. Ule's last green bull bucked off a kid and then he refused to come out of the arena. The two ranch hands on horseback were making passes in at him, but his head-tossing and loud bellowing made their horses gunshy. At last, in his baggy pants and scarves waving, Knight appeared armed with a yellow, six-foot-long Hot Shot.

A light came on in that bull's pea-sized brain as Knight grew closer waving his wand—that thing he knew would zap him. He made a lurch at Knight, missed the clown, and ran with his tail over his back for the gate.

Finally, it was Shoat's turn. Graves set the flank tight on the Dummy and I nodded in approval. Standing in the chute gate, Gator pulled the bull rope and Sam told everyone to stay in their seats for one last great ride. Dummy was fighting the chute, blowing fire at the gatemen, and I stood ready to pull Shoat off at a second's notice. This critter acted like he was electrified.

"Good luck," I hissed at Shoat and Shoat nodded.

The gate flew open, and the long horn threw himself to the right. Hopping like a bunny rabbit, he headed for the calf chutes on the north end. Knight was running hard after him screaming for the bull's attention. Halfway down, Shoat jerked his tail and spun off, then headed for the fence. Dummy was at the far end before he turned back and spotted Knight.

"Get out of there!" Gator shouted in warning to Knight.

The rest of the action looked like it happened in slow motion. Dummy, despite the restraint of the flank rope, raced for Knight with his head lowered. Before the clown could dodge aside, Dummy tossed the bullfighter in the air. The crowd screamed. Off the fence and swinging his hat over his head, Shoat charged the longhorn to save the fallen clown.

Distracted from his quarry sprawled on the ground, Dummy headed for Shoat like a cheetah. He missed him the first time. Shoat was smart enough and never turned his back on the bull unless it was to twist away. Both men in the arena on horseback were fighting their horses to get close enough to toss a rope on the enraged bull. It was Shoat's show and he skillfully dodged the bull's lightninglike lunges, barely missing the tips of the horns. Bouncing on his feet, he soon had Dummy halfway down the pen.

Knight was up and raced for the return gate, yelling and shouting for the bull. Tired of not being able to gore the elusive Shoat, the longhorn headed for Knight, who led him out. The audience gave both bullfighters a thunderous hand.

"I might have missed the flank rope," Graves said, apologizing as if that was the reason he didn't buck. "Maybe it should have been tighter."

"No, you did fine. He's a dud. Flanked him any tighter, he'd have fallen down running away."

Gator joined me. "Get a fertility test on that longhorn. I know a guy needs one to breed a set of heifers."

"What about sending him to the hamburger factory?"

With a frown of disbelief, Gator looked at me. "You going to give up on him that easy?"

"No, I'll call Texas and find out what I did wrong."

"Good idea."

"We going by the Shady Point dance?" Gator asked.

"I guess."

"Let's load up them oxen and horses. I've got to practice team roping more. Did you see me miss those heels tonight?"

"Sure did. Glad I wasn't roping with you tonight."

"Whew, that Dummy is a cat," Shoat said, finally coming around behind the chutes.

"Think he can buck?" Gator asked.

"If he wants to," Shoat said. "He's got mad on his mind right now. Jasper had a bull like that he turned out with some cows and when we got him back, he bucked like fire."

"There you go," Gator said.

"We'll fertility test him Monday. Doc Foster can do that."

"I'll call Johnny Ross and tell him he can use him free. He'll feed him good before he turns him out with the heifers."

"Good enough."

"Let's get loaded, guys," Gator said impatiently.

"Where are we going?" Shoat asked.

"Boot scooting. Gator's anxious to get there," I said.

"Sure," Shoat said and tossed his spurs in his war bag. "I'm ready."

Maybe turning Dummy with a set of females would help. Who knew? Rucker sure owed me one. Dang, the folks in this world you had to deal with were sometimes more than a fellow could handle.

Shoat took my keys and went for the rig. I led Gator's roping horse, he grabbed Strike King's reins, and we went outside of the building into the cold air and glaring light. Along the way, we thanked Ule and all his helpers as they hustled around to get their chores completed.

The two bulls were settled some when we loaded them, and I double chained the cut gate shut. Looking through the sides at them, I could see Dummy acting snorty. Then we put in Gator's horses. With him still complaining the whole time about his poor roping, we climbed in the club cab and headed for Shady Point. It wasn't really his misses that had him so upset—but rather that potload of cattle in Nebraska the guy turned down. I knew Gator Bledsoe too well.

Chapter 13

Sunday morning, a weak sun tried to shine into the cold portion of the world where I lived. Shoat was busy looking over rodeo schedules on the kitchen table. I'd gone to the mailbox out at the road and brought back the Tulsa Sunday paper.

"I may get cleaned up and go to church," I announced. Services wouldn't hurt me, but I didn't know anything about Shoat's faith or preference.

"I'll go, too."

The Presbyterian Church roof didn't cave in over our appearance. We came outside after services, and it hadn't warmed up much. After turning down two offers of dinner from some sweet gray-haired ladies I had known all my life, we went back to my place and ate a frozen pizza.

"Your folks not alive?" Shoat was asking me.

"No, I was raised by my grandfather. I lost them both in a car wreck when I was ten."

"I wondered."

"Oh, I've got some kinfolk around the state, but no one I'm real close to. That lady I called Aunt Ellen at church was really my mother's cousin."

"So all you had was your grandfather?"

"Grand old man. I lost him ten years ago."

"This the old family place here?"

"No." Something in my tone must have hardened.

"Hey, I don't mean to be nosy," Shoat said.

"No problem. The old family place is north and west of here. It was four sections. My great-grandfather came out here from Indiana and put it together in the 1880s. I bought this one about four years ago."

I stared out the window, not wanting to think about those familiar grassy hills. The big oaks and pecans along Clear Creek. The huge barns filled with prairie grass and alfalfa bales, smelling so pungent and sweet. The windmills I'd greased, and all the trophy deer that hid out in the breaks. The big white-faced cattle that Turners had bred for over a hundred years.

Of course, straight breeds were out these days. We should have crossbred years before I managed to talk Gramps into doing it. No matter—the breed, like the land, were a family tradition and there was no good reason that ranch shouldn't still be owned by a Turner.

Too much drinking, not enough sense to see that my reckless ventures in oil drilling ate up my resources. When oil prices plummeted, so did my fortune; the worst thing was the auction of the assets and the sale of the ranch. Pen after pen of cattle carrying the T-Bar-T brand were sold the first day. I listened to all of them saying how they would've brought more had they been black baldies. Day two was the hardest—the farm machinery and the antiques from the house.

I was left with a three-year-old pickup, a horse trailer, two horses, saddles, and the clothes on my back. I felt lucky I had that much. I was even with the banks and the rest of my creditors, but I'll never forget the screaming red-tailed hawk that ruined my last ride across those empty hills. In the ten short years since I had graduated from OSU I'd managed to mess up a marriage, screw up an oil deal, failed in my attempts to make the finals in bull riding, and lost the family land.

That was the day I quit drinking. Cold turkey. I decided to do it as I rode an aging Skipper-bred horse across the grassy hills that had been Turner land for over a hundred and twenty years. The tears burned like acid on my checks, running down in rivers. A man can sink so low that there isn't room for him on this earth.

Gator found me up at a pond we used to swim in when we were teenagers. He never said a word. Rode up, hitched his horse; I heard his spurs jingle as he came through the grass. He dropped down close by, never looked at me.

"This ain't the worst day in your life," he said, still looking off toward the north.

"That ain't hard for you to say."

"The worst day in your life will be when you can't remember your own name."

"What're you saying?"

"You know my daddy's up at the nursing home with his Alzheimers. You and me, we've still got our minds. We ain't so busted up that we can't dig ditches if we need to eat. You tell me where you're going to start over, and I'll come help you."

"Well, I'm not going to go on another drunk."

"I understand."

"What the hell are you doing up here, anyway?"

"You remember when Debbie served me them divorce papers and took the kids?"

I stood up and skipped a flat rock three times across the water. "Yeah."

"Who came and got me out of that bar and sobered me up?"

"That wasn't nothing."

Gator stood and made four skips with his rock. "The hell it wasn't. I'd have killed someone that night if you hadn't done that, and I'd still been in prison."

My next rock made three. I wanted it to make six. We really became hot and heavy at the rock skipping. His four went unbeaten.

"I promise I won't do anything stupid," I finally said. "Let me ride some more over this place by myself."

"You've got to be at my place by seven tonight. I'll have steaks on."

We shook hands, hugged, and clapped each other on the back. I could recall two pale-skinned boys skinny-dipping in that water on a day like this one, when the blue sky reached across the whole horizon and this was all Turner land.

"I'll be there," I promised him.

We sure weren't boys anymore.

"I think I'll call in and enter this rodeo in Texas." Shoat's words brought me back to the present.

"Sure," I said, then considered the last piece of pizza left on the round cardboard server. I put it on a plate and then into the microwave.

The phone rang.

"Hi," Zola said, sounding bouncy on the other end. "Warm out there?"

"Yes, real nice. Cold back there?"

"Yes, it's wintertime. You winning?"

"Winning, yes, but it isn't as much fun as I like."

"Why not?" I asked absently as the microwave buzzer went off.

"You aren't here."

"Oh, well, Shoat and I have had some grand dining here, we've had store-bought pizza for dinner. In fact, I'm reheating my last piece."

"You guys sound like gourmet chefs."

"Where is that rodeo you're going to?" I asked Shoat.

"Oh, a little place in east Texas. Green Town."

"Why don't you get up to Green Town, Texas next weekend?" I asked Zola.

"You're going to be there?"

"Shoat and I are going there." He nodded his head hard.

"You aren't announcing?"

"No, I'm off these two weeks."

"See you in Green Town."

"Love you."

"Love you, too." I hung up and wondered if I'd ever said that on the phone to her before. Why couldn't I find for myself that German farmgirl I wanted for Gator? One that cooked, canned, made garden and hung her wash on the line so the sheets would be stiff. Because I didn't love some chuffy farm girl, mine was a thin, hyper, wiggle-worm that couldn't sit still ten minutes. I looked to the ceiling for help.

"You don't have to go down there," Shoat said.

"I told her I would."

"I'm such a burden to you—"

"When you get to be a burden, I'll tell you about it."

"You better. I'm sure enjoying being with you and Gator."

"No problem. Tomorrow, we'll take the Dummy to town and have him fertility-checked."

"I've never seen that done."

"When you see it, you won't ever want them to do it to you. But if that bull's got a high enough count, it may spare him the butcher shop for a while."

"Jasper told me that lots of bucking bulls become infertile."

"So do lots of pasture bulls. Best way to lose a calf crop is not to test your bulls."

"Funny thing, I figured a bull was a bull and you could turn him out and he did his thing."

"Nope. Much more complicated than that. Years ago, my grandfather would wonder why some good cows missed having calves. He bought a high-priced bull up in Kansas at a sale. We were pretty sure we never had a calf out of him, because he had some deep pigment around his eyes and no calves showed it. So Doc Foster checked him. Sure enough, he couldn't settle anything."

"What happened?"

"The breeder claimed he was sound when we bought him so Gramps went round and round with them. They finally replaced him with a younger bull that was all right."

"That's interesting."

With flying colors, Dummy passed the test. On the drive back to the ranch Shoat sat uneasy on the passenger side still recalling, I figured, how Doc Foster inserted the electric probe inside Dummy and turned on the charge to collect his semen. Such treatment was enough to make any male squirm.

Green Town, Texas is in the piney woods. Shoat

drew up Saturday night, Zola on Friday, so we left on Thursday with Gator in charge of the stock at home. We hit some rain in southeast Oklahoma and the big wipers on the rig swept sheets of water back and forth. Across the Red River, it let up and we drove around Dallas, then south into the pines.

At the rodeo grounds, we parked in the back parking lot. There were no hookups, but the rig had a generator if we needed power. Shorty Hankins had the stock for the show and most of it was in the older pens. We found him in the rodeo office.

The LBJ hat cocked on the side of his bald head, he bolted up from his chair.

"What brings you down here?" We shook hands.

"Shoat's in the bull riding. I'm taking a holiday."

They shook hands at my introduction.

"You're running around with tough company," Shorty warned him.

"I appreciate it, too," Shoat said.

"If I'd known you would have been here, I'd have hired you to announce."

I shook my head to dismiss any of his concern. "Didn't know I was even coming until last Sunday," I explained.

"Got some top hands entered here," Shorty bragged.

"If the rain stays away, you should have a great weekend."

"This town has a good little committee. They try hard."

Shoat was looking over the stock and pointed out one of them out. "That bull 768?" he asked.

"Yep, came from Harvey Thornton. He's been hauled. Usually spins to the right."

"Good to know. I'm anxious to get on him."

"You won Jackson, didn't you?"

Shoat nodded.

We went back to the rig. I started the generator and we grilled some burgers. Then we watched fuzzy TV and relaxed. About ten o'clock, a horn honked, startling me.

I put on my slippers and opened the front door. There sat her rig, no trailer. She let down the window and waved to me. "Come on."

"I'll get my boots," I protested.

She leaned over shaking her head. "Come on."

"Where's Thunder?" I asked.

"Got him at a friend's place east of here."

I jumped in the cab, feeling half-dressed, no hat, no boots, still wondering what she had in mind. When I closed the door, she tackled me and smothered me with kisses.

"I sure missed you."

"Missed you, too."

"Where're we going?" I asked as she slid back under the wheel.

"They must have a place to park around here. I saw a sign at the edge of town—said some lake was up ahead."

"I need my fishing pole?"

"No, silly."

She drove down a rutted road and we were soon parked on the bank of a lovely lake, lighted by the quarter moon. Far enough south, the frogs and cheepers were already out, and she led me by the hand around in back and into her camper. Inside, I was forced to duck my head. The interior held those musky female scents mixed with perfumy sweetness.

There was a queen bed made up in the back. The bedsheets were so fresh they crinkled while we made love on them.

Later, like two drunks, we walked around the shore, holding each other up. The night air was cooling, but we never cared. We had each other.

"It's getting worse than I thought it would be," she said.

"Much worse," I agreed.

"What will we do?" she asked.

To solve the problem I stopped and kissed her. Did I want to make that big of a commitment? I'd failed the last time and when I married Stormy, I thought I couldn't live without her, too.

Why was I so reserved when I should be pressing to make this permanent? I had no good answer. I wanted her in my arms always, but was that just a sexual thing? No, there was more. Her company illuminated me. It was more than that, I said to myself. *Damn, Brad Turner, you better decide something fast.*

Chapter 14

Saturday night I pulled his bull rope Shoat nodded he was satisfied, but I wondered if he really was there, really had all his power of concentration on the job at hand. Something had distracted him lately. I had been around him enough. Whatever it was, riding this bull was not his main focus.

"Cowboy up!" I shouted from behind the gate man, hoping to jar him into a riding mode. Forced to get back, I saw him nod. The bull came out smooth enough, dipped his right shoulder and began to spin. Shoat's right boot slipped and flew back. He did a bellydown ride on the bull's back, stopping my heart. He didn't need to go in the well—that was where riders got stepped on, even killed. For a split second, it looked like he was going down; then the bull flung him away.

He landed before the chutes on his knees. In a bound, he was up and on the gate. It didn't matter the bull fighter had the bull distracted. Shoat recovered his hat and bull rope, then joined me out back.

"He outdid me."

"Or you outdid yourself. You got a problem?"

"I don't guess it's anything. Mona was supposed to be here tonight. Must have been thinking more about her than that bull."

"Need to call her?"

"Naw. Just hate that you came all this way to see me pull a doozy like that."

"Hey, we all have bad days."

"Maybe next weekend, huh?"

Maybe. Zola promised to meet me in Zanesville across the Texas line for a show the next Thursday night. I was still in a muddle about what we should do. Was it my move? Did she expect me to step forward and do something? Perhaps all the answers to my questions would come the next weekend when we got together. I did miss her, more than I probably would have admitted out loud.

For the next four weeks I had a run to make. Four different rodeos, four weekends in a row, so when we got back to Woodbury on Sunday night, I called Tack Butler first thing to have him reset the shoes on Boy. Since my cell phone calls to Rucker had gone unanswered, I carefully listened to my voicemail.

". . . heard you had trouble with the bulls. I cannot understand that, Brad. Call me."

His phone rang four times on that end and finally he came on, "Hello."

"Rucker! I'm sending Gator Bledsoe down there to clean your plow!"

"Wait, things aren't that serious. Those bulls will really buck."

"I scored that black bull around seventeen points. You were talking about sending me twenty-point bulls."

"He must have been off. Who was on him?"

"A pro cowboy, Shoat Krammer."

"Who the hell is he?"

"He won Jackson."

"Oh, well, I can't understand it."

"That crazy longhorn ran away. Never bucked a lick."

"Brad, I'm sorry. They were a little shook up when we loaded them. That was my fault, but they should have bucked, man."

"All you owe me is twenty-five-hundred and a feed bill."

"Oh, my—" And he broke out cussing. I looked at Shoat and shook my head.

"Rucker, you can cuss at the moon. You sold me two buckers. I've got a black kicker and a runaway fighting bull."

"Let me—let me—"

"I don't have time for your crawfishing. I'm leaving and will be on the road for four weeks. You call Gator Bledsoe about what happens next. I'm putting him in charge."

"I don't want you mad at me."

"Mad? Rucker, I am past being mad. I want blood. But if you ever sell me or any of my friends a bull again, he will have to come with your own Good Housekeeping Seal of Approval stamped on his back side."

"Don't go telling everyone. I swear on my mother's Bible. I'll make this deal right." I heard him loud and clear. He obviously didn't have a Bible, since he was using his mama's.

"Send me twenty-five-hundred and the feed bill. Come and get them or I'll ship them to the packers and you can pay me the difference."

He began to moan and whine. "If you knew how little I made on that deal. Oh, Brad, please give me two weeks to make the deal right. Please?"

"Talk to Gator. You've got his number?"

"Yes, but you and I—"

"We don't go back nowhere after this deal, Rucker."

"I'll make it right in two weeks."

"You better." I hung up, still stinging-angry.

"He going to fix it?" Shoat asked, ready to bite into a sandwich fringed in lettuce.

"He will or his bull-selling days are over."

"We got time to try that longhorn again?" Shoat asked between bites.

"Perhaps. We can take him back up there one day this week and buck him. If Gator and I can wave him off you."

Shoat shrugged at the notion that he even needed a clown. But I didn't want him all battered up by the fool bull. I called Gator and we discussed Rucker and his promise. Then I added, "Shoat wants to practice on Dummy one more time before we hit the trail. He thinks there's something we haven't got right with him."

"I agree. We seen that devil buck without anyone on him," Gator said. "I'll call Ule and we'll trailer him up there tomorrow."

"Is tomorrow okay?" I asked Shoat.

"Heavens, yes."

"You're on. Get us a time," I told Gator.

With a little arm-waving, we put the pair of bulls together and herded them into the Gooseneck the next morning. Gator had it set up, so we promised to meet him at Mark's Store and he'd ride up there with us. This proved to be first day in three weeks that the sun had any warmth. Weather up here usually goes back and forth from winter to summer every week during the winter months. Three days of cold, three of sunshine, and the seventh is a tossup. We'd been arctic all the way until this one slipped in with some south wind.

"How they acting?" Gator asked, bailing in with Shoat in the jumpseat behind.

"Acting better," I said, not daring to brag too much.

"What have we got to do to get him to buck?" Gator asked, half turning to question Shoat.

"Don't flank him so tight," Shoat said.

"I thought Art Graves said it wasn't tight enough."

"Jasper Northcutt had a bull that would buck like a tornado if you put a flank rope on him, but if it was tight he wouldn't fire a lick."

"What do you think?" Gator asked me.

"Shoat's the man wants to try him that way. We won't flank him tight."

Ule had opened the end doors to air his arena out, so the midmorning sun shone in a little and it was colder inside than out. We unloaded the bulls and drove them down the alley. Ule had the gates set and they went into the chutes.

Blacky was in front. I'd rather he'd been behind, instead of Dummy, but that was the way they unloaded. Gator fed me the flank rope and I pulled it up, not tight, but snug. Too loose for most buckers to do their best. Meanwhile, Gator pulled Shoat's bull rope for him and we waited for him to get set.

Ule came up the return alleyway, riding a long-headed horse into the arena. I nodded in approval as I climbed over to be the latch man. Good insurance, if we needed it. He rode the gelding to the other end of the big pen in the darker shadowy part. If you looked at the sunshine out the big doors and turned back, it was a long moment before your eyes adjusted to the darkness.

"Ready?" I asked Shoat.

He slid down on Dummy's back and nodded. I jerked the wrap-off to release the gate. On the end of the pull rope, Gator started the gate back slow, then he jerked it when the longhorn turned to look at the gap. Like an explosion, his legs on springs, he went high, then dropped his horns to the right coming down on his front feet and throwing his butt up over Shoat's head. Then he lurched sideways with blinding fury. Shoat looked like ten million dollars riding him, and the Dummy looked to me like four grand at any good bucking bull sale. My heart soared. Counting the seconds off, and admiring the athletic action, I passed six just as Shoat jerked the tail of his rope, kicked his inside leg upward, and rolled off on his feet.

"Hee-yah!" Gator shouted. The confused Dummy spotted the burly steer wrestler whooping and waving his arms, then lowered his head like a freight train. But he breezed past Gator and the gate clanged shut. The first good thing that had happened to me in a while.

When I looked around for Shoat, he was coming back from the stripping chute with the flank rope. "I like that. Let's do it again," he said, a flush of victory shining on his face.

"Might as well," Gator said.

"What about it, Ule? It's your shed."

"Let's do it again. Man, I liked it. You guys are taking all the chances. What did you feed that critter? Hamburger and gunpowder? He bucked like a dandy!"

"Thing I hate the worst is calling Rucker again," I said as Gator brought back Shoat's rope and bell from the arena.

"He should bring a pretty penny if he bucks like that again," Gator said as the three of us prepared the black bull.

"Don't flank him hard, either," Shoat said. "That old boy that owned these bulls must have known his business."

"I'll get his name, but I bet no one knows him or he'd never sold these two to Rucker. Good money he's some rancher who hauls stock around to junior rodeos and hardly charges them."

Gator agreed. "Bet those kids don't halfway appreciate him, either."

I glanced back at the longhorn in the pen behind. Sure wished he weighed about three hundred more pounds. He was too light for the big boys that had the buckouts. They liked bulls they could have down the road week after week and they kept on bucking. A small bull wouldn't have the stamina for the weekly turnout they required. Still, he would find a niche and make some money.

"Hey, get down here," Gator shouted. I hurried over the top and dropped on the arena floor. Shoat looked ready to go, but I wasn't there to undo the gate rope. The knot undone, he nodded and Blacky went skyward with great roar. He made a perfect arc of his back to land on his front hooves then threw himself into a spin the other way. It was twice as fast as the last time. For a moment I was worried for Shoat's safety. But Blacky switched and Shoat impressed me by how he turned off and hit the ground on his feet and running.

At the sight of the horse and riders coming, Blacky headed out the gate like a jersey in a milk cow string. Whew.

"Eighty-six points," Gator said and clapped him on the shoulders.

I went back and took the flank rope off him. Two bulls had sure doubled in value in less than a week, and the longhorn was fertile. I wondered about turning him out with those heifers and bringing him back in midsummer. He probably wouldn't get any taller, but getting wider would help.

"What now?" Gator asked.

"I think a summer on the pasture might really help that Dummy," I said.

"You can put Blacky out, too," Gator said. "I know an old man runs some crosscows that would love him."

"I ain't fertility testing him."

"He'll get calves. Besides, the old man's got other bulls in there."

"Good, we can get them up in August and have them in the prime for the fall."

"How are you pricing them, in case I get a chance to sell them?" Gator asked.

"I'd take three apiece for them now."

"You may have them sold."

"You have a buyer?" I frowned at Gator.

"No, but I think he's only a half-dozen phone calls away."

"Good. Ten percent commission."

"I can handle that."

"Shoot," Shoat said, "I was thinking we'd keep them for practice bulls."

"You'll get enough practice bulls over the next few weeks."

He agreed, and we loaded up our bulls and went for home.

"Rucker?"

"Yeah, that you Brad? Look I ain't had time."

"Forget it. I'm going to sell Dummy for a purebred longhorn. Can you find me papers for him?"

"They used to find racehorse papers all the time. I guess I can."

"We have them settled down. They bucked all right today."

"Oh, thank God."

"Some day tell me how they got that riled up?"

"I will, Brad. I swear I will."

"You can quit worrying now. Good night."

With him still protesting his innocence, I hung up.

Shoat and I were busy making supper. The phone rang—I expected Zola.

"Brad Turner."

"Charlie Striker, Fort Davis, Texas. Rucker said them bulls of mine wouldn't buck. I'm the man sent them to him."

"Well, they bucked today."

"I thought they would. They got so tough down here the kids were turning them out. He said they were wild and flighty? I don't savvy that."

"Not as bad now."

"That longhorn started as a roping calf that we kept as a bull because he was such an athlete. My wife can toll them with a bucket."

"Mr. Striker, how they were handled after they left your place must have been the problem. The truckers were gunshy of them and by the time they got here they were raving mad."

"They never seen a Hot Shot in their life."

"They have now, unfortunately. But they're settling down fine, I'm happy to say." I recalled the blue flash on the end of my wand. Poor West Texas babies didn't even know what it was, and that explained why they never ran from it.

"Rucker acted like you wanted a refund."

"No, sir. I'm happy. There's no problem." I felt like I was eating crow, but I deserved it. Here was a very sincere man, miles away, willing to do the right thing, even if he had to borrow money or what to make a square deal. "Mr. Striker, don't you worry about it. It was misunderstanding and it is all settled. I just got off the phone with Rucker."

"You going to use them?"

"I had them for sale, but I planned to turn them out until fall."

"So you're happy?"

"Yes, thanks for calling. Here's my number, area code 918." And I gave him the rest. "If you ever get any more like them and want to sell them, call me right away. I'd drive out there and haul them back myself."

Shoat served up skillet-fried potatoes with onions and the hamburger steaks on our plates. I hung up the phone and he went to the refrig for the ketchup.

"That was Charlie Striker of Fort Davis, Texas. Man who used to own those two bulls."

"I caught that." Shoat checked over his offerings and then straddled his chair.

"He never used a Hot Shot on his bulls. They didn't know what one was until Rucker's truckers went after them, I guess. Says wife tolls them with a bucket—they ain't ever been choused."

We both sat and laughed, building up until tears ran down our eyes.

"—and he wanted to give you your money back?"

"Yes! Man, was I ready to get off that phone. Striker sounded exactly like my grandfather when I was little. That old man never shirked responsibility in his life and Striker wasn't doing it over two bulls, no matter how bad he needed the money."

"There ain't many men in this world left like that, are there?"

"Nope." I dried my eyes on a napkin. The kid was right—the real ones were a dying breed.

"I know another one. Jasper Northcutt. He's done the same thing."

"You had a good teacher, then."

"I sure did. One of the great ones." Shoat's eyes shone behind his wet lashes.

Chapter 15

"Ladies and gentlemen, rodeo fans, welcome to the greatest show on dirt!" I was aboard Boy making my loop around the arena in the warm Texas sun. Outdoors for Saturday afternoon matinees, South Texas fairs along the Gulf are warm-weather events. You just had to hope that the rain would hold off. The fans were undercover of a roof over the seats, but the competitors and announcer could sure get wet. For outdoor rodeos in this region's late winter, cowboys always bet money it would rain every performance and they usually won.

The sandy ground was in great shape and the top hands knew it well—they had been there for the Thursday and Friday night performances. Shoat made a good horse ride Thursday and scored an eighty, which would win some money. He drew his bull up on Saturday night, so he was working for Johnny and Chester during this one, too.

As I reined in Boy and from the corner of my eye, I saw a woman who looked familiar upstairs—Dale was pointing over the side to show her something. The dark-haired girl nodded. Then she waved at who I suspected was Shoat down below. Mona had come to the Gulf Coast. I only had a second before my spiel and the introductions began, but I wondered how her presence would effect his riding. Last time, I recalled, he lost his concentration. Dang, it was tough being a substitute father worrying about every little detail in someone else's life.

Then the rodeo became the familiar blur. Introduced the dignitaries. The chamber of commerce man rode an old plug like a sack of potatoes. His hat obviously had sat in the closet all year, because the back of the brim was curled. He could have worn the hat backward, pinned up the brim, and been a young Gabby Hayes. He managed with some good chortling to arrive in line with the rancher committee men who were lined across the center. Then they carried out the flag to a rousing fanfare. Then the sponsors' flags were carried in by hard-charging cowgirls, and I knew we were in the Lone Star State seeing these girls really ride.

Things went smoothly. Skip had some new jokes that kept them laughing in the long stops. He could be funny in a Laundromat, a place I hated worse than two-holers that had never been cleaned. I could never enjoy the waste of time sitting in a steamy place that clunked with metal pieces in the dryers, stinking of detergent odors, filled with ugly women wearing sweats with their hair up in plastic curlers.

"Bradberry?" Skip said when a novice bull rider tried unsuccessfully for the third time to get down on a bull. "Is that boy really a bull rider?"

"I think so, Skip."

"Then why don't he slide and ride him already?"

"The bull won't let him."

"I can tell you right now, sonny boy, that bull is going to say no every time you ask him." The crowd was sitting on the edge of their seats, all keyed up, loving it. They laughed at anything that broke the tension.

To my amazement the boy from Waco did ride the bull, and even scored eighty, which put him in fourth place and would probably win some of the day money.

"I guess I'd take that long if I thought I could get the bull's permission to ride him like that," Skip said, head down, making his disgusted chicken walk toward the bleachers.

"Lady," he shouted at someone and jumped on the fence. "You want to ride one of them bulls. You don't? Well, neither do I and that old boy on that gold horse—you see him out there?" He pointed at me with one arm hung over the fence's top rail. "He rode them all until he lost all of his marbles."

Skip jumped down as they loaded another bull.

"Bradberry came down from northern Oklahoma with all them marbles he done won on the schoolyard. He put all them in his mouth every time he got on a bull. Every time he rode one, he'd spit one out till they was all gone."

Then he bent over and looked through the fence at the poor woman. "Oh, you don't believe me? Well, I can prove it."

He came stomping out there in his too-long tennis shoes with his hand out.

"Bradberry, loan me a marble."

"I don't have any, Skip."

"See! Lady, see! I told you he's lost all of his marbles." The crowd laughed. Tip Daniels, a young cowboy out of California, nodded his head for the bounty bull. When that charolais went skyward like a rocket, I saw Daniels's feet fly back. He was thrown face-forward and I heard the clunk when his forehead struck the poll of the bull.

The clowns came rushing. Daniels's limp body hung up on the bull and both bullfighters were trying to jump up and get the tail of his rope. Chester sent his horse in, swinging a rope as the other pickup man, Glen, did the same. They were fighting a tilt-a-whirl out of control. At last one of the clowns hung on to Daniels's shoulders and broke him free. Both fell down. For an instant the bull considered turning back to get them, but the other fighter beat him in the head with his old hat and he changed his mind.

The big white bull fled out of the gate, and the adrenalin immediately drained from everyone.

"Ladies and gentlemen, our hearts and prayer are with that young athlete. We'll certainly want the best for him. And we have the county ambulance boys here, emergency-trained specialists. That brings the curtain down on this performance. Until we meet again, fans, may the good Lord bless and keep you. Good night."

Some of the spectators had begun to climb over the fence to see about the downed cowboy. Johnny asked the reserve deputies to clear everyone from the arena.

"Please give them room, folks," I asked, riding Boy up close enough to see for myself.

Chester came back from the group clustered around Daniels and nodded grimly. "Least he's got good vital signs."

"Took a heck of a whack."

He nodded. "You seen who arrived?" he asked under his breath, pushing his horse in close to Boy.

"Karmann Ghia? Honey-one?"

"No, I didn't see her. But there's a big fat hick in overalls back there who claims he's Pappy Krammer. He drove up here in a big four-door yellow taco car with Arkansas plates."

"He's big?"

"He weighs four hundred, maybe more."

"What's he doing?"

"Acting like he's the kid's manager."

"Hmm. He needs one." I chuckled and shook my head. Then I saw the dazed Daniels stand up, and holding his forehead, shake off the concerned EMTs.

"I'll go get it stitched," he said to them as he held the bandage to his forehead. "But I ain't riding there in no damn meat wagon."

Laughing at his insistence, I shook my head. The only way to kill bull riders was hide their heads from them. Remnants of the crowd gave him a scattered applause. Two pards carried his chaps and bull rope and helped him out of the arena.

A note stuck with duct tape to Boy's gate said that Shoat wouldn't be back until the bull riding events. I was not to worry, but he wouldn't be there to brush Boy and help me get ready for the night performance. At that point I figured Shoat and Mona were off sparking somewhere, so I unsaddled Boy and put him in the pen. Then I went to refill his water pail and as I started back, this big guy came shuffling up the alley-way, wearing overalls, in leather house slippers, his body as big as the Goodyear Blimp. I suspected this was the senior Krammer.

"I know you," he said. "You're Bradberry Turner. Seen you many times."

I hung the bucket on the fence, wiped off my hands on the sides of my Wranglers, and stuck a hand out toward him. He shook mine in his great ham of a hand.

"Skip calls me that, sir. My friends call me Brad."

"Ain't he a hoot? I seen him years ago in Memphis.

He fought bulls back then." He hitched up his overall suspenders. "All right, Brad, I understand my boy's been working for you?"

I shook my head. "He's been staying with me."

"Boy's a sucker. He hung around that damn North-cutt's place and he never got paid, either."

"Pardon?" I frowned at him.

"I mean, that boy needs a guardian. He's been winning a lot of dough, I heard. So I said, Alfred, you better go down there and get that boy his due, what he's got coming to him. See, he's never been in no business." He shoved his hand behind the top pockets and scratched his belly. His personality was beginning to make me itch.

"So I'll be taking care of his money for him from now on. You owe him any?"

"No."

"Well, I guess from now on, you won't be receiving his services."

"Fine, whatever Shoat wants to do."

"Oh, mister, you don't hear good. I'm taking care of him and seeing about his business. That boy ain't old enough or well enough-educated in your people's ways. But I'm here to make sure that if Shoat's owed any of your money, he's going to get it."

"That's fine, but don't get in my way again." I had my finger out and was shaking it in his face. In the recesses of my mind, I knew my anger was past the stopping point, and to escape completely blowing a valve, I stormed away from him.

Stalking past the calf pens, I was by Chester before I realized it.

"You look mad as an old wet hen." He laughed and clapped his hands as if he knew the reason why.

"You talk to that old devil?" I asked, not caring if Alfred Krammer heard me or not.

"Yeah, he's managing Shoat's business now, he says."

"He wanted Shoat's pay for him helping me!" I pointed at my chest.

"Heckuva nice guy."

"Bull manure." That was more than I could take, I headed for the rig, shaking all over with fury. Why, that old bag of wind. No wonder Shoat had his sister handle his money. Poor kid. I about wished for Gator Bledsoe to be there to let some wind out that rascal. Money that *I* owed *Shoat*! The growl came from deep in my throat as I shuddered.

"What happened?" Zola tackled me in a hug.

Taken unaware by her, I turned back and looked to the stables, but saw no sight of that toad in overalls. Then I drew a fresh breath of the warm air, tinged with a fishy smell, that blew in off the Gulf. I hugged her tight and tried to recover my composure.

"Brad Turner, what's wrong?"

I told her all about my encounter with Pappy, and acting all motherly, she led me to the rig. I unlocked it and she took off my hat and patted down my hair, then put it back on with a smile to drive away the anger burning still inside me.

"Sorry, babe," I apologized.

"I wouldn't want you any other way." Then she kissed me soft on the lips, even though we were standing in the front end behind the captains' chairs. People might see us. She usually was more reserved.

"Brad, it's times like this I know how good you really are."

" 'Cause I didn't haul off and hit him?"

She shook her head and looked hard at me. "Because you care so much." She slipped into my arms. "Why did she ever leave you?"

" 'Cause I couldn't get bull riding and winning the world out of my head."

"Was that the real reason?"

"We weren't grown up. We found we liked different things. We weren't meant for each other." I shook my head at the many reasons I had thought of why we had broken up afterward. How would that boy ever get back on track with that old man traipsing along, dogging him at every step? My cheek resting on the top of Zola's head, I wanted to be on some desert island, only the two of us. No problems like Pappy Krammer, rodeos, pleasing committees, crowds—just us. I closed my eyes.

Chapter 16

Late in the evening performance, I noticed that Shoat was back behind the chutes, rosining his bull rope. Knowing he was still around made me feel better. But I was ready to bet on long odds that he would never ride his draw. Too much was going on in his life to concentrate on riding: Mona had shown up there along with his pappy, who could have soured a butter churn.

The crowd had been excited all night. The air felt electrified; that's always a good sign. Better than those shows you can't pull the crowd into—when everything breaks, like the barrier falling apart during the timed events—that's when my job gets hectic. Horses don't buck hard enough, or they simply stall in the chute. Every calf roper misses their calf, or the steer wrestlers bite the dirt one right after the other—those are an announcer's nightmares.

"Let's go down to chute three, to the young man who won the bull riding at Jackson a few weeks ago. Shoat Krammer has drawn a bull we call King Lizard."

"You say that Li-*Zard*," Skip corrected me. "See here? I got me a program and I'm checking on your pro-noncy-ation of things."

"Lizard."

"No, Bradberry, Li-*Zard*!"

"Skip, he's like them things run across the road in West Texas."

"Yeah, them's Li-*Zards,* too."

Shoat nodded for the gate and they swung it back. The big bull surged out, sucked back, and then went into a spin. Shoat Krammer never made the first corner. His feet rocked back. To save his face, he dodged to the side and that let Li-Zard fling him away.

"Boy, that bull was fast," Skip said.

"Fast?" I asked.

"Yeah, you see him lick his feet, then come out?"

"He never—"

"Did so. I seen him!" Skip began walking sideways and pointing at the departing bull.

"How about some applause for the cowboy?" They gave him some, but I saw a very disgusted look on that boy's face, gathering his bell and rope. Shoat knew he could have ridden that one had he been concentrating on the bull and not on other things.

"Figured he could ride him," Chester said to me softly when he rode back from driving Li-Zard out of the arena.

"Me, too," I said and turned back to announce the next rider.

Stacy Brown rode Disaster for eighty-one points. Then in a hail of fireworks, the national sponsor flag-bearers tore in and circled around the walls.

"And you rodeo fans have a safe drive home tonight. We will look for you next year, when pro rodeo returns to your hometown and this arena. Until then, may the good Lord bless and keep you."

I rode out of the pen after the last of the cowgirls, thinking about the week ahead. Plenty of time on my hands—I had until Thursday to get to my next rodeo down the road, a hundred and fifty miles over in Louisiana.

Zola and I had never spoken about what she would be doing. No sign of the kid nor his entourage when I got to Boy's stall. I put the horse inside and took the saddle to the company tack trailer that was kept well-locked and guarded when no one was around. In this world, saddle thieves were more numerous than fleas on a stray dog. And saddles were not cheap to replace.

Where was Zola? On a whim I headed for the rig. I punched open the door.

"If you've got some old hag with you, tell her she can't come in."

"Oh, dearie, sorry, my old lady's home."

"Dang you, Brad Turner." She stood at the head of the steps with her hands on her hips. She even had on an apron. What was I in for? Domestic Zola had obviously shown up.

"What smells so good in here?" I sampled the air. It did smell mouth-watering.

"Fajitas."

"Wonderful!"

"Probably not that wonderful. It's hard to time cooking when an announcer can't shut up and come home."

"If I'd known, I'd been here hours ago," I said, making a quick effort to climb the four stairs.

"Shoat came by and said he was going on with Mona. He would see you next weekend."

"So we're all alone?" I kissed her on the cheek as she used pot holders to move a sizzling skillet to the table.

"Unless you find another stray to take with you."

"Let me wash my hands. I can't wait to try your fajitas."

"Liar."

"Well," I asked calling back to her, "what're we going to do the next few days?"

"You serious?"

"Serious as I can be while drying my hands."

When I came out of the bathroom, she was shaking her head in disbelief.

"I can have you for how many days now?"

"Sunday, Monday," I began counting on my fingers, "Tuesday and Wednesday, need to be in Green Valle on Thursday."

She threw her arms around my neck. "Four days all to myself?"

"Sure." I looked at her blandly like I couldn't understand her excitement.

"We can talk about it while we eat," she said and hustled me into a chair.

The aroma of fried onions, peppers, and beef filled my nostrils. I smiled at her. "You don't have to be a great housewife to impress me."

"It won't hurt," she said and held out the plate of snowy flour tortillas. The tortilla was hot and I quickly dropped it on my plate.

"But you don't mind being pampered, do you, Brad?"

"No."

"Perhaps if I had pampered his majesty this way," she said, talking about her ex, "he wouldn't have ran off and jumped in bed with the damn maid."

I looked into her baby blues and shook my head. "No way. It wasn't you, what you did or anything. He was simply like that, and you are much better pursuing your life without him."

She nodded. "You can still take your life apart, looking for an answer."

"Not about a man who has no more respect for you than to do it in the house you made for you both." I paused holding the filled wrap in both hands. "Quit beating yourself down."

"I want this to work—" She made a face, then went on. "You and me."

A knock on the door sounded and I motioned to her. "Hold that thought."

On my feet, I swung open the door and started down the steps to see who was there. I saw two swarthy men wearing bomber jackets. One had black curly hair, the other straight. Something kicked me in the guts about the situation at hand; for a moment I could not believe what I suspected. They were the muscle looking for Mona and Shoat.

"Howdy, guys. What can I do for you?"

"Where's that Krammer?" Curly asked, only he used the F-word a few times as well.

I stepped down and on the ground. Both of them were burly as football players, no necks, and looked fresh out of some gang movie. In the glare of the fairground security lights, I saw the glint off the butt of a Beretta under the big guy's shoulder.

Curly started up the stairs of the rig.

"He ain't here," I said.

"Thanks, cowboy, we'll look for ourselves." Big Boy pulled the gun, and trained the barrel on my chest.

"Who are you?" Zola screeched when he reached the top step.

"Santa Claus," he said. I knew that he was only

looking for Shoat and meant no harm to her. Not much I could do with Big Boy putting his pistol in front of me.

"Zola, don't argue with him."

Big Boy nodded in approval. In a minute, Curly was back, shaking his head. "He ain't there." He frowned at me. "Where is he at?"

"Haven't seen him in the past few hours."

"You know what's good for you and her, you better keep your mouth shut."

Just like in a movie script a large four-door Caddy arrived. Big Boy ran around the far side, still pointing the Beretta at me and said, "You hear me? You better forget we were here." Curly jumped in the back seat and before he closed the door, tires squalled and the thugs were gone.

"Oh, my God . . ." Zola jumped down the steps and into my arms. "Those guys were out to kill the kid."

Still in a state of shock, I held her in my arms. "They weren't the Clearing House Prize Patrol."

"How can you joke at a time like this?"

"I'm sorry, I'm still weak-kneed. I was worried about your safety."

"My safety. Oh, Brad, you worry about everyone but yourself. Shouldn't we call the police?"

"We better." I looked off in the direction they left. With no license plate numbers, a black Caddy would be hard to locate. All I saw were the red taillights going away.

She brought me the cellular and I considered what I would say. Two thugs came by and interrupted my supper at eleven P.M. At night, looking for Shoat Krammer. One had a pistol. They took nothing. Did nothing but held a gun on me. File a report. I shook my head.

"You calling them?"

"No. It won't do any good."

"But . . ."

I looked her in the eye. "Let's go eat that lovely supper."

"I'm not hungry."

With my arm around her shoulder, I herded her back inside. I guided her gently into the chair and sat down across from her. "I want to eat this delicious food."

"What about Shoat? Will those men kill him?"

"If they find him, they will probably just beat him up again."

"Why?"

"Shoat's a slow learner." Even cool, the fajitas tasted wonderful.

"Aren't you going to warn him? How will we find him?"

"We find 'Honey-one' on a Missouri license plate attached to a Karmann-Ghia, we've found them."

"But there must be hundreds of motels up and down—"

"Them two thugs will have to look, too."

"Except they have a gun."

With a bob of my head in agreement, I swallowed my food. "I have a bigger one."

"A bigger one?" Her blues went wide open. "You're not going to get into a gunfight, Brad."

"My .357 makes bigger holes."

"But shouldn't we let the police—"

"Look, I'm not going gunning. I'm going looking for Shoat. I just hope they don't get in the way."

"The way that one guy swore, I doubt he'll charm a lot of people."

"His vocabulary was rather sparse, save for that one word," I teased.

"Oh, Brad, you can't joke about this."

"I better, because right now I'm mad enough to try to bash both their heads in." With a paper napkin, I wiped my mouth, uncertain the saliva wasn't dripping from it like some mad dog. Why did they have to ruin the most perfect supper in my life?

The whole thing made me reflect. They knew that Shoat stayed at the rig. They must have known who I was. They all said they were looking for him, not for her. Did they even know she was there, too? Strange, what if both of them had been there? The nursery rhyme about the boy stole the pig—"the boy got beat and the pig got eat"—kept cropping into my thoughts. Shoat would get beaten up, all right; those two were real enforcers.

Chapter 17

"The Karmann Ghia is not here," Zola said as I looked up and down the deserted dark street as we left the Flamingo Oasis Motel parking lot. That made the hundred and ninety-ninth motel we had checked. My eyes felt like sandtraps on the Augusta National course. No telling where those two were bunked up.

"I'm tired," I said, disgusted with our search.

"It's only two A.M.," she said and snuggled on my arm. Poor girl was sitting on the console to be close to me. "Next time, I'll buy a truck with a bench seat," she said with a laugh and squirmed to find a comfortable place. "Should we quit searching?"

"We better go back and get some sleep."

She threw her arms over her head, stretched and yawned. With a great ho-hum, she settled back, snuggling my right arm. "Can you drive all right?"

"With you this close? I'm fine."

"Good."

After a few hours shut-eye I managed to get up. I left Zola sleeping and went to check on Boy. I found Chester in the bright morning sun.

"You guys loading up?" I asked.

"Yeah, Johnny wants to go home and get some

fresh stock. These bulls and horses rest better out on the home pasture."

After I related my adventure of the past night to Chester, we both sat squatted down in front of the Boy's stall in the shade of the porch.

"According to Dale, when he got his money in bare-backs, the old man took it."

I shook my head. "Guess he didn't need any, then."

"That old man is obnoxious as hell." Chester frowned. "That boy simply gave it to him. Guess it was easier than arguing with him."

"Nice way to put it."

"We get through in Louisiana, that's the last I'll see of Pappy," Chester promised with a hard glare. "That old bag of wind ain't going from rodeo to rodeo with me."

"Back to my problem. You never saw these guys, huh?"

"Guess not. I don't miss much goes on, you know that. I make it my business. But they must be expert at this stuff, not asking lots of questions and keeping a low profile."

"They knew something. They came for him at my rig last night, and that big guy brandished a Beretta at me. The other went inside to check, to see if I was lying."

"Wish I'd known that." Chester shook his head in disapproval.

"Nothing you could do about it. Next time, I'll meet them with my .357."

"I'll tell Johnny and Glen and the rest of the boys to be on the watch. We can cut them off if we see them."

"I figure if they don't find Shoat and the girl they'll just be back this coming weekend."

"We may give them a real welcome down there. The town sheriff is on that committee. I'll have Johnny call him ahead of time. This ain't some big city where they can run around and break arms. Big shame, though, them thugs after him and his pappy taking all his money. Krammer hasn't got a chance coming or going."

"No, but he should have ridden that bull."

"He rode the horse fine. Then she showed up, and then Pappy—his riding went to hell in a handbasket. What are you going to do?"

"I had planned to go to South Padre and get a tan for a few days. That plan looks scrapped until I find out if the kid is all right."

"Want me to take Boy?"

I considered the offer. It would be an imposition on Chester. Zola said we could stable him at her friend's fancy place. I shook my head. "Thanks, but we've got a place for him. See you Thursday after lunch in Green Valle."

"Sure. Good luck. I'll put out the word to watch for them thugs and Krammer."

After watering and feeding Boy, I went back to the rig. The smell of java filled the kitchen air. Standing at the top of the steps in a T-shirt that advertised some barrel race, Zola greeted me with a can of diet soda in her hand. She didn't drink much coffee. We exchanged a quick kiss and I went to wash my hands.

"Learn anything?"

"Nope. Except the kid gave his winnings to his father and left. Chester hadn't seen those two hanging around the rodeo grounds, nor did he see Shoat take off."

She made a face. "Chester gave his father the check?"

"The old man's his manager now." I poured a cup of coffee.

"I thought you said his sister—"

"All I can tell you, sweet one, is that Krammer has more problems than that little Dutch boy who was sticking his fingers in all them dike holes."

"Where did he go?"

"I couldn't answer that—" The cell phone rang right then and I picked it up. "Hello."

"Brad?"

"Shoat, that you?" I nodded to Zola's frown. "It's him."

"Yes, I wanted you to know that I'm in Woodbury now. Would it be all right if I . . . if we stayed at your place while you're away?"

"We? Sure. You all right?"

"I'm fine. Why?"

"Two thugs came by looking for you last night."

"They bother you?"

"No. But all of us were more than a little worried about you."

"Sorry I'm such a problem for you."

"You talk to Gator?"

"Yeah, we're going to work those calves they brought back from Nebraska."

I looked to the ceiling for celestial help for Gator. Hauling cattle all over the place often created a nightmare of health problems. "Keep your eyes and ears open. Don't mess with those two if they come around. Call 911. We've got good law up there."

"Sure."

"Listen, they know you stay with me now. Be careful."

"Sure—I'll call 911 if anything happens."

"You coming back for the next show?"

"Yes, Mona'll bring me."

"The keys to my pickup are there."

"I won't need them."

"Use 'em if you need it."

"I'll get you paid back somehow."

"Just be careful, and tell Gator the same thing."

"I will. See you." The phone clicked, I looked at the small screen on the phone and pushed the disconnect button.

"Well?" she asked.

"You have a bikini?"

She frowned. "Why?"

"I don't want you walking the Texas beach in a T-shirt and skimpy panties."

"Where are we going?"

"South Padre, soon as we stable Boy at your friends. Will they look after him?"

"Oh, yes." Her arms flew around my neck, smothered me with minty-flavored kisses, and I wanted to shout with glee. Shoat was safe enough with Gator for the time being.

Two full bottles of sunscreen later, we were headed back from our beach stay to pick up the horses. Zola's brown bare feet on the dash and her tanned legs exposed, she sang along with a Faith Hill hit on the CD player. The rig clacked over the seams in the concrete interstate while the sun streamed in on her side and warmed the interior of the coach.

"I had a great time at Padre," she said softly.

I glanced over and nodded, turning my attention back to the road. "Be nice not to have any cares for a while. See the waves roll in, seagulls dip their wings, and those shore birds scurry in and out of the waves."

"Thanks."

"Thanks yourself."

She threw her arms skyward. "Why didn't we meet when we were kids?"

"I didn't have this much style then, and I wanted to be the world champion."

"I would have slept in the back of your pickup in a bedroll."

I laughed out loud at the notion. "You, me, and four other guys gulping down garbage food at those all-night stations. Calling home for more money to pay a fine or an entry fee. No, we were a bathless crew in those days. Drank too much, swore too much, and didn't have much respect for anything but winning that buckle."

Her hand shot over and patted my arm. "Then perhaps both of us saw the other side."

"You, too?"

"Oh, I tried it all. I tied one on after my divorce. I wanted to show him. You know, it is so damn degrading when the man you have loved . . . and you . . . you walk into a bedroom and discover him . . ." She shook her head and sighed. "Makes you feel like you failed."

"It wasn't you."

"I know that now. Thanks to you."

My turn signals on, I swung around a slow-moving pickup with a fifth-wheel trailer. And then it was back in the right lane, Texas pines whizzing past.

"How'd you get back to barrel racing?"

"Oh, I was on a low ebb. I came back to Fort Worth and saw a classmate. She told me she was training barrel horses and I needed to come look at them. I ran them in high school and college. My good horse went cripple and I decided it was time to get on with my life. Big mistake. I can recall how many times I wished I'd still been barrel racing.

"Anyway, she had Thunder. She was riding him for a rich gal out of Plano. The first time I got on him, I got gut cramps, I wanted him so bad."

"Daddy bought him?" I asked.

"Sure, but . . ." She paused.

"What?"

"I sound like some spoiled social princess telling it like this—"

"Not at all—it was you and Thunder, from there on?"

"I wanted to live again. I had a purpose."

"You still do?"

"Yes, though you are becoming distracting." A bright smile crossed her face.

"I can recall some of our first times."

"Oh, you caught me off guard. I figured when I met you, here's a big rodeo announcer with plenty of buckle bunnies to hop in and out of his bed." She shook her head. "After that first night we spent together I really thought that I was a notch on your bedpost."

"Zola? We'd had several dates before—"

"Sorry, I know better now. But you needed to know that's what I thought."

"I knew you sure wanted it kept a secret and I was busting over the fact that I had found you."

She laughed aloud. "Brad Turner, you're a devil in disguise. Say—isn't there some cute little ole divorcee that cleans your house up there in those blue stems?"

"She's married and pregnant, so don't worry. Janie's off till after the baby is born. So my place is a mess right now." That made me think about Shoat and Mona being up there. I didn't figure Mona would do much domestic work.

"I knew the time I was there it was too neat for a man's place."

"You hire a detective to follow me?"

"No, but I sure asked lots of questions." She rolled her blues skyward as if looking for help.

"And?" I asked.

"Found out you broke a few hearts."

"Oh, come on."

"That's not a lie! There's three gals I know about on the circuit that would exchange places with me today."

"Did they say that I lied to them?"

"No. They were put out that you didn't continue on . . ."

"You ever seen one of those cutouts where you put your face through and they snap your picture?" I asked, looking over at her tanned legs that she clutched under her chin.

"Sure."

"Well, it was like that with other gals. I kept seeing Stormy's face on each one of them."

"But you never once saw her face on me?"

"Not once."

She rocked back and forth sideways in the passenger chair. "I figured each time we went out, Well, sister, this time I'm shed of him, but then you'd be back." She blinked at me. "I really tried to shake you out of my mind—and couldn't."

"I just thought you must not be as serious as I am."

"That's only because I was so uncertain about you and—well, everything. But that night, when I drove away from you in Jackson like I did, that ate me up."

"I knew perfectly well with Shoat there, you would avoid me." Glancing over, I saw her chew on her lower lip.

"Yes, but—"

"Zola, if you still need more time to sort things out in your life—"

"Do I have that time?"

"All that you want."

"Oh, thanks. Brad?" She waited for me to look over at her. "I won't ever disappoint you."

I nodded. The next exit off of the highway was ours and I felt a warm wave sweep over my shoulders and relaxed the muscles in my screwed-up back. It washed away all the discomfort and I felt like singing with George Strait about Amarillo in the morning as I swung the rig off the interstate and onto the overpass.

"Brad," she said. "Going east, you see that black Cadillac putting on his brakes."

"Is it them?" I asked, raising up in my seat to try and see off the overpass.

"I don't know, but that car had on its brakes like it had missed the turn off."

"They'll have to go up to the next turnoff to get back here."

Oh, dang, I thought they were long gone. Shoat and Mona were safe in Oklahoma. As for Zola and me, that was another story.

Chapter 18

Zola's friend Judy's place was what I called a fancy horse estate—a big red-brick two-story house with a portico, fresh out of the pages of *Southern Living* magazine. It had acres of lawn, big lush trees, and vinyl fences that must have cost an arm and a leg. The back-to-back row of stables were all steel-constructed to prevent fire danger. Besides the employed hands, Judy also had a full-time trainer, Bart Shields.

"What does Judy's husband do in this world to afford this spread?" I asked, while turning off into their paved driveway. I had not seen any sign of the Cadillac since the interstate.

"Computers or something."

"Enough said. I know enough about them to know they're dangerous." Then I realized something. If those thugs had been shadowing us all the way to Padre and back, I should have seen them in the rearview mirror—but I hadn't.

"What's wrong?" she asked.

"This rig's been bugged."

"Bugged?"

"When you mentioned computers, I began to think how those two could be trailing us since I hadn't noticed them."

"You think they put a radio on us?"

"Something that sends out a signal."

"So they'll know where we are all the time."

I nodded, slowly conspiring how I could locate their bug and turn the whole thing around. If I could find it and plant it on an eighteen-wheeler going the opposite way . . . but first I had to find it. It would be small and not conspicuous. Dang, oh, dang.

"What's the plan?"

"First I need to call Shoat."

"What for?"

"To my notion, they have Mona's vehicle bugged, too. My guess is that they got away and out of range so those thugs couldn't track them. That's why they've stuck with us."

"You really think all this is happening?" She frowned in disbelief at me. I swung the rig up in front of the stables, put it in park, and picked up the cell phone. Mona answered it.

"Mona, this is Brad. Is Shoat there?"

"No, he's helping Gator."

"Good, I'll call him. If I can't get him, have him call me tonight."

I turned to Zola who was waiting in the door. "He's with Gator," I said.

"That figures." She smiled and shook her head.

I punched in Gator's cellular number. It rang a couple of times, no answer. I tried the house and his answering machine came on with his special message. "Stockyard and Bar. Gator ain't here and I can't write, so please leave a legible message at the beep."

"Gator this is Brad. Call me when you sober up."

"He's drunk?" She frowned.

"No, he's out working and never carries that cell phone. He don't like being disturbed on horseback."

"I'm taking a golf cart up to the house to see if Judy's home."

"I'll be here."

"What if they follow us here?"

"They want Mona and Shoat, not you and me. I guess while we were on the beach they were watching us the entire time."

"That makes me mad as—"

"Me, too. And they may be there before long."

"I'll be right back." And then she was off.

"Hi, Brad," the trainer said, sauntering from behind the stables.

"Zola's stolen your golf cart," I said, watching her drive the white contraption toward the house on the paved pathway.

"No, that's for guests." He laughed. "I ride horses, not carts or four-wheelers."

"You know what a bug looks like?" I asked.

"What kind of insect do you mean?"

"No, I mean a radio implant. I think someone equipped this rig with a radio sender and I sure would like to find it."

"How come?"

"A friend of mine has run off with some big guy's woman. They're trying to find him by tailing me."

Bart grinned, took off his ball cap and scratched his honey-colored hair. "Now ain't that something."

"If I can find it, I intend to put it on an eighteen-wheeler and send them to the West Coast."

Bart laughed aloud. "Where do we look?"

"Under the fender wells for starters, only I'm not certain what one looks like."

"Me, neither, but the bossman I'd bet can find it. He knows all about electronics."

"He here?"

"Yes, he's coming back in the cart." He pointed up the pathway.

"Good," I said and straightened. Electronics expert to the rescue.

"Zola said that someone has you bugged." He stepped out of the cart in tan trousers and a chambray shirt. Nice-looking man, ten years older than Judy. "Fred Whitcher."

"Brad Turner. That gadget can find it?" I motioned to the box in his hand.

"It should."

He pulled out an antenna, turned on a switch, and used the dials. Nothing. I looked back toward the road, no sign of the Cadillac. But if they hadn't lost our signal, they would still be cautious enough to stay out of sight. They had done a perfect job of doing that so far.

"I'll try a different frequency," Fred said.

He no more than spun the dials a little and the box began beeping loud and clear. But he shook his head. "That's not yours. That's a ship beacon in the gulf."

Who was I to argue with an expert? He tried another setting and nothing sounded but some static. Maybe I had just read too many Tom Clancy novels.

Then suddenly a sound like a submarine's sonar came out of the box in a two-tone signal. Fred nodded with excitement. He started around the rig and stopped at the rear on the driver's side. I hardly ever used the underneath compartment there. There were hand tools in there if I needed them, a backup PA system, some speakers. Still, I dug out the key for it and shook my head; anyone could open a lock.

"There it is," he said and pointed at a gadget about

six inches square with an antenna sticking out of it, nestled behind two outdoor speakers.

"What's powering it?"

"Your battery. See where they spliced it in the wiring?"

"Can we make it work off my cigarette lighter inside?"

"No problem. It runs on twelve volt." Fred backed outside and turned his locator off. "But why?"

"I'm going to a truck stop and hope they follow me, then I'll pay a trucker to take them to the West Coast."

"Fair enough. I'll need a plug-in adaptor for the lighter. I think I have one at the shop—get in the cart and we'll go up there."

"Thanks, Bart," I said and we drove away.

Fred's shop looked like something else. It was immaculate—with every kind of tool they ever made. Six unfinished captain's chairs sat in a row we passed.

"You make them?" I asked.

"Yes, that's one of my hobbies." He put the locator on a shelf and went to work gathering things in a plastic tray like the ones we used to carry strawberries in.

"These chairs are certainly well done," I said, admiring them.

"You have room for them?"

"Oh, no I couldn't—"

"To be quite frank with you, I'm like the little old lady who makes stuffed dolls. I have too many and no place for them."

"I'd have to come back—" The man had blown my mind, making me to think they would be mine.

"I have to finish the table first, but my company sends trucks all over the United States. I'll have them delivered."

"But you don't even know me."

"My wife knows Zola and they're longtime friends."

The whole thing had me embarrassed. I would never have mentioned the chairs, but they sure impressed me. The moment I saw them I thought how good they would look in place of my straight-backed chairs that came with the trailer. I might even sit in there if I had them.

"Light or dark stain?"

"Light, I guess, but—"

"I have it all—you want a beer? Cold drink?"

"Something diet would be fine."

"We can get one at the house. Let's round up the girls so they can see the setup. You say these guys are gangsters?"

"They're hard-nosed characters." I took a place on the passenger side and we zipped off to the house. "This young bull rider is mixed up with a woman. They beat him up once over in Jackson. Then they showed up last week and I guess they've been trailing me ever since."

"Judy said you two went to South Padre."

"Yes, and thanks for taking care of our horses."

"No problem," he said. "Let's go in—if you have time."

We walked through the French doorways and were greeted by a black poodle. Alert and ears up, he looked quizzically at me until Fred spoke to him and he came over dancing. I petted him and he very mannerly walked with us into the family room.

"Judy, we found the bug," he said to his wife, a tall blonde with a nice figure and a beautiful oval face who was seated at the room's high bar with Zola.

"Was it a bomb?"

"No, a rather large tracking device they wired in a compartment in the RV."

"How did they get in?" Zola asked.

"Locks are no problem to open," he said finding my soda in a refrigerator underneath the bar.

"What now?" Zola asked.

"We're going to fix it so that they follow some trucker to the West Coast, right?"

"Exactly."

"Won't the police stop these guys?" Judy asked.

"They haven't done much they could stop them for."

I agreed and popped the top. We all sat down in the fine family room. At the end of the room stood a sunken fireplace with a circular couch, in front of which sat a large coffee table. The room's floor was polished, red-oak hardwood, with a few expensive Navajo throw rugs here or there. Various sets of stuffed chairs were placed about the room where folks could gather and talk in small groups.

"Can we spend the night?" Zola asked. "Judy invited us."

"Hey, we may overrun their hospitality."

"No way," Fred protested. "Let's you and I go hook up that bug like you want it. You girls find some steaks to grill up and we'll be back in thirty minutes."

"Will do," Judy said and slipped off the bar stool. "I'm so glad that you and Zola are together," she said walking alongside me to the door with the drink in her hand. "That other bastard deserved to be killed."

"Sounded like that to me."

"Oh, she's happy." Judy glanced back to be certain the other two weren't close enough to hear her. "I knew that when she came from Florida after having just met you."

"She wasn't that certain then."

"I was." Then she laughed aloud. "We go way back to high school together. Can you imagine how two good-looking blondes competed with each other?" More laughs. "Welcome to the family, Brad."

"Thanks."

"I swear, those two can tell more funny tales about growing up," Fred said, shaking his head when he caught us at the door. "Peanuts, you stay here," he told the poodle as we climbed into the cart.

"Gorgeous place you all have here," I said absently, admiring the manicured grounds. A place like this took lots of elbow grease, many manhours of work.

"Big dream, isn't it?" Fred said.

I shook my head. Once upon a time I had an even bigger spread in my own grasp. My grandfather's ranch, and I squandered that. Perhaps I didn't deserve another dream.

Chapter 19

"**L**adies and gentlemen—rodeo fans from across the great state of Louisiana. My name's Brad Turner. Is there anyone here tonight ready for rodeo?"

I wondered how far west those two thugs had followed the TKD trucker headed toward Phoenix. He called me from way west of San Antonio on I-10 to say the device was peeping fine. I told him to enjoy his hundred dollars. He said he would.

Gator had finally called me back and I told him the deal. I also suggested that Shoat bring my pickup back unless they could find and disable the radio sender in Mona's car.

When we pulled into Green Valle, I saw Pappy's yellow taco car in the parking lot when we pulled in the rodeo grounds. Zola had brought the horses in her trailer and we stayed in CB range all the way. No sign of the Caddy—my greatest hope was that they went west with the trucker. All I could really do was speculate about that.

Midday, I pulled the rig behind the stables where I usually hooked up, but a young man came over to wave me away. That spot was saved for the announcer he quickly informed me.

"That's me."

"Oh, sorry, Mr. Turner."

"Brad," I corrected him.

"Yes, sir, Brad."

"Keep a close eye on my rig. You see anyone fooling around it, let me know."

"Oh, I sure will."

"Thanks. What was your name?"

"Buddy."

"Nice to meet you, Buddy. You in charge of stalls, too?"

"Got two for you with your name on them."

He showed them to Zola who came leading the pair of horses. I hooked up the electric to the rig and then went to help her get them settled.

"I saw your pickup," she said. "Or one that looks like it, over by Johnny's vehicles."

"Shoat must be here," I said.

"Could mean they didn't find a locator on her sports car."

"Could mean anything. But yes, that, too."

We learned a little later that Shoat came by himself. No explanation, but that suited me. He had pitched in like usual and was helping Chester feed and sort stock. Johnny really liked him.

"He learned how to work somewhere," Johnny said.

"Catching chickens," I said and we both laughed.

"On top of that he knows plenty about handling stock. I reckon Jasper Northcutt taught him a lot of that."

I agreed. Despite all his problems, the boy could be a champion, too—but he had a lot of problems. Number-one problem was his pappy who I despised and avoided. Pappy still found chances to sneak up and spout off his know-it-all to me.

"If you had a silver saddle you'd show up lots better out there."

"I guess when I get rich I might buy one," I said, bending over to clean out Boy's hooves.

"You had a little more flash, you'd get some of those big shows. You got a business agent, Turner?"

"No."

"Well, all them baseball players got them one. They get millions for what they do. You ever need a business agent, contact me. I'd consider handling your business."

"Sure." Contact me? Consider? I was so angry I could have killed him. He went paddling off in his house slippers while I sizzled. Why, the nerve of that dumb hillbilly. I ought to kick his butt up between his shoulder blades.

In a blind rage I went back to the RV. For the next fifteen minutes, I sat in the dinette and let the pent-up anger subside. That man could drive me back to drink. Zola was off shopping and I was glad she hadn't seen me this upset. It would have been a good excuse to take a drink of whiskey and wash him away. Oh, it was tempting, but it passed.

Shoat rode his bareback, but the mare had a slow night and his low seventy score wouldn't place in the three days. Bucked too good for a reride, but it wasn't good enough to win on. The sorrel mare could fire when she wanted to, but who knew what ran through a bucking horse's mind. It wasn't Sissy's day to get high and kick, was all.

Late in the performance, the action was dragging. Skip had tried several of his better routines and even they didn't work to get the crowd up. Team ropers wouldn't nod or the roping steers would turn their heads back to look at the gate man. Barrel racing perked things up some, but the bull riders all had problems getting down.

"I think it's the wrong phase of the moon," Skip said with his mic off as he walked by me, looking at the ground. "Bradberry," he then said over the PA system.

"Yes?"

"You met these two fellows on horses with you?"

"Yes, Chester and Glen, the pickup men."

"No, them's the Lee brothers. Home-lee and Ug-lee."

Just then, someone accidentally let a bull out or a latch came undone, for out of the box came an angry bull without a rider. Head down, he caught the first clown and tossed him up in the air. As the crowd screamed, I reined Boy around to be ready to get out of his way. Chester and Glen rode in swinging their ropes. I recognized the bull as number 356; no doubt he was mean enough to hurt someone.

Chester caught the bull's horns in his loop.

Skip shouted, "I'll bet your horse is really proud of you." It drew a snicker from the crowd.

The bay pickup horse dug in and the bull was swung around. The exit gate boys had the alley open; Chester's horse, hunching under the load, was digging up ground heading for the gate. If the bull didn't run by and exit by himself, then the pickup man needed some gate people ready in back to separate him. If not, in the close quarters, the horse and rider could get mauled.

There was a tense moment or two at this point. Chester went through the out gates, the bull being forced to go, too. After the gates closed, Skip walked around in circles looking disgusted.

"That was my bull."

"That was your bull?"

"Yeah, I was going to show him here at the parish fair."

"You still can."

"No I can't!"

"Why not?"

"Didn't you see him? He's got a green butt."

"That will wash off. They have a rack back there where all those 4-H and FFA kids wash their cattle off."

"Would you wash him off for me?"

"No, he ain't mine to show."

"I see. I'll get this lady over here to wash him off for me." He began talking to a woman in the front row.

The next rider could have saved his plane fare. He was thrown before the timer punched her stopwatch to begin the eight seconds. But by now the "clean the bull's butt" line was working for Skip. He had no volunteers from the front row, but was getting lots of mileage out of the deal.

After five bull riders went home with goose eggs, the sixth man stayed on. No big spectacular effort, but he took his seventy-eight points and won the crowd's applause. Tucker Brown, the last man to ride, had the bounty bull. Tuck could sure enough ride; he'd qualified for Vegas three times and was healthy.

Johnny thought it would be the showdown ride, or a chance for one. Send those fans home on a good note; I really hoped Tuck rode him and gave my spiel about the Casa Grande, Arizona, cowboy's feats to build him up. Mountain Top came out like an explosion. He soared high then ducked right. Brown looked fine, feet in place and his arm working for his balance.

I thought for a long while he might collect the money. Then Mountain Top turned it on. It was like they'd poured nitro in his tank. Brown flew off, but the crowd was on their feet screaming for him. The buzzer blew and the fireworks went off, the national sponsor flags came rushing in, and it was good night, folks.

"Man, oh, man," Skip said shaking his head when we were out in back. "That was a long night."

"Two hours, twenty minutes." That was the total time for the performance. I always check my watch when I ride out of the arena.

"No, I mean it was *real* long."

"What did we do wrong?" I asked.

"Maybe we tried too hard." He shook his head.

"Well, I'm changing the opening tomorrow night. I'll go talk to Johnny and the committee men. We need to wake those folks up."

"Whatcha gonna do?" Skip asked.

"I don't know yet. But I'll work on it."

"Let me know 'cause I sure want to help."

Johnny gathered the committee of eight, and we all met in a small block office under a 150-watt bulb. Not exactly the Waldorf.

"Brad thinks we need to liven up the show. Any of you have any ideas?" Johnny looked around at the faces.

"The stock bucked good," the old man on the committee said. "I hate dem rodeos you go to and the stock it don't buck."

That drew several rounds of approval from the other committees members.

"Is there some local disc jockey plays music these folks like, someone who can really work up a crowd?" I asked.

"Sure that crazy kid on Louie's station. He's a wild man."

"How much would he cost to play Cajun music and give away prizes and have a wild time while folks are getting in their seats."

"Maybe a hundred dollars. Maybe Louie can make him come for nothing."

"I say pay him a hundred. I want free things he can give away. Cash, meals, hats, boots, anything, but give those folks credit for what they donate. Can you trade for that stuff by tomorrow night, and if it works, for Saturday, too?"

"I think so. But what will it do?"

"If I get the two bullfighters and Skip to help them, they can all liven up your crowd—if he's as wild as you say he is."

"If we can get the audience fired up beforehand, they'll tell others and our gate will go up," Johnny said.

It was past midnight when we adjourned. Johnny thought it would work and thanked me. I saw the light on in the rig and knew I was late for supper. A quick look toward the dark sky between the yard lights and then I headed for my whipping.

"Well, howdy," I said and tossed my 10X in the front door.

"Howdy. Chester came by and said you would be late." Zola scooped up my hat and put it on the rack.

"What smells so good?"

"A roasted chicken I've been keeping hot."

"Should be fine." I swept her into my arms and kissed her. Man, I would need to realize that there was someone else to worry about pleasing beside myself. After so long being single, this new position would require some thought on my part.

"What did you do tonight?"

"Oh, hired a Cajun DJ."

"What for?"

"To liven up that crowd."

Seven P.M. on Friday night, the PA came on and the wild man began. Jacques Crusteau, he called himself and from the sounds of him, I judged he had just arrived from Newfoundland, or maybe even France. He had Skip and both bullfighters giving out prizes and kissing women according to what he said for them to do over the PA.

While I was busy getting Boy ready, Louie came by to see me and nodded his head. "They sure having a big time out there."

"Good," I said. "Maybe they will all night long."

"I hope them horses and bulls buck."

"They'll buck," I assured him. Johnny's stock always bucked. Louie was thinking of the days past when the fair association hired an amateur contractor.

"We'll see."

When Jacques called out my name and introduced me, I heard the roar. A boot to Boy and then we were racing into the arena at a hard run around the wall. The fans were ready and I knew we were off to a great night in Louisiana.

The horses bucked higher, and the ropers cut down on the previous night's times. The saddle bronc riding looked like the Vegas finals, team ropers caught both heels, steer wrestlers toppled bulls like they were rag dolls, and even the cowgirls were the prettiest. Especially one on a big dark chestnut horse called Thunder. Shoat had a money bull drawn in the bull riding. Mint Clear was rideable, and we'd already talked some strategy about the bull earlier.

"He'll go hard left and may stay in that spin. But he can pull out and reverse. Watch him," I warned him.

"I'll watch him," Shoat said. "You know, Mona was sure upset when she heard about that bug. I would have never guessed they'd done that to her."

"Is she this guy's girlfriend?"

"No, she's his wife."

"Wife?" I frowned.

"Yeah, she wants to divorce him, but he's too powerful. Got all these lawyers."

"Powerful isn't the word for it. Is she separated from him?"

He shrugged and looked pained at me. "I don't know."

"Well. Ride that bull tonight." I clapped him on the shoulder.

"I'll try, Brad. I swear, I'll try."

"Good. She stay up at the ranch?"

"No—we had an argument. She went home."

"Back to her husband?"

"I don't think so."

I hoped not. Heavens, some people you could help, others were beyond hope. Shoat was fast slipping into the abyss. Why couldn't he be satisfied with one of the dark-eyed Cajun buckle bunnies that were all over the place? I mean, he soon needed to realize that Mona was not free, whether she thought so or not.

All eyes were on chute four, where welded on the white gate was an advertisement for Pierre Devereau's Ford Dealership. Head down and over that bull rope was Shoat on Mint Clear, who was named for the sparkling-water company who bought him.

"Mint Clear, the bull. Shoat Krammer, a newcomer to rodeo's pro ranks, but fans, he can ride. Here's

Krammer." The spotted bull jumped high and sunfished before he ducked left, but the kid was with him. Gouging hide with his spurs, he kept himself in good position and made the ride look easy. The judges gave him an eighty-two, which I thought was two points short, but it was a money ride and Shoat sailed his hat at the crowd.

"Son, don't be so generous. You ain't won enough money yet to buy a new one of these," Skip scolded him and brought Shoat's hat back to him.

Chester and Glen both nodded in approval at me. Mint Clear went out the drain like he was supposed to. We were down to the bounty bull and the youngster who drew him had not ridden anything in two years, at least not at a rodeo where I announced. Either his daddy had money or he had a sugar tit to finance him. Paying hundred-dollar-a-weekend entry fees and not winning any money was a tough row to hoe.

"Sprig Casey's drawn the bull to ride—White Ghost." I told the crowd the story of how many trips the White Ghost had been out without anyone claiming the five thousand dollars riding him.

"We're down to the final question for five thousand dollars, can Casey ride that bull?"

Shouts of "yes" and "no" came from all over. I nodded. "That's the final answer, Casey."

Casey rode great for two seconds. The way that bull was leaping and bucking, I figured he'd be an ambulance passenger soon enough, and about the count of six, White Ghost threw him clear of his horns and hooves. No one could ride that bounty bull. "Good night, folks," I said in a hail of fireworks and hard-riding cowgirls holding flags circling the arena.

I rode Boy up the alleyway when a lanky fellow came over the fence. "Brad Turner?"

"Sure." I reined Boy up.

"I'm Jim Hendden, also known as Jacques Crusteau." His trademark French accent was gone. "Hey, that was a great idea you had, man. I had more fun tonight than I've ever had in my life. They want me back next year."

"You sure helped the crowd, and I thank you." We shook hands and I started on my way. On foot, the old man was coming up the alleyway toward me.

"Man, oh, man, everyone is talking about the rodeo tonight."

"I guess those horses and bulls really bucked?"

"My God, man, they're talking about really helping us out, now. Buying ads and everything!"

"Wonderful."

He used his hand to shield his eyes from the yard lights and looked up at me. "You done that for us. I told them. They need to know how much I appreciate you." Then he dropped his hand, blinked his eyes, and grinned real big. "Man, did they buck." We both laughed.

"Hey," Zola called out and caught up with me. I dismounted and loosened the cinch on Boy.

"I've sure been propositioned a lot getting here."

"By who?" She looked around with a frown.

"One was that boy DJ who enjoyed himself with the pre rodeo festivities, and the other was that old man on the fair board, Louie, who got some new sponsors tonight."

"You should be an agent."

I stopped and gave her a dirty look. "That's what Shoat's father is."

"Who would have him?"

"I'm not sure, but I wish he was miles away. Shoat came within a hair of not riding that bull tonight. That bull should have been a regular day at the office for that boy."

"Where's Mona?"

"That's another story you won't believe. Let's go out to eat and I'll tell you all about it."

"At twenty to eleven at night? Well, considering I'm starving, I'll take you up on it, Mr. Turner."

I took her hand. It felt simply natural in my grasp. Shoat and his problems could wait; the lady and I were having a late meal.

Chapter 20

"Shoat should be getting his entry fee paid for him," Pappy announced to me.

"Oh?" I said when he confronted me in the middle of the parking lot. He hadn't bothered to shave in several days and must have slept in the overalls. How I missed seeing him coming my way was beyond me. But he must have planned to waylay me ahead of time and I never saw his approach.

"Mr. Krammer, you need to talk to the contractor or someone with more power than I have. I only work here."

"I've heard they pay the entry fees of the top-notch cowboys to get them to come here."

I shook my head. "Not my area of expertise."

He shoved his hand down inside his overalls and scratched his privates. "Well, someone knows. They can pay other stars', they can pay him."

"I don't think this committee pays anyone's fees."

"I bet that's a lie. I've learned a lot about this rodeo business. I'm getting him a national sponsor, too."

"That should work."

"It will. You just watch me, fancy boy."

I didn't bother to tell him you needed to be a big-name rider to even be considered, but why argue?

He pulled his hand out and wagged his finger at me. "You can't buy him off loaning him your pickup, either."

"Buy him off?" I must have frowned.

"Yeah, I know what you're doing. Make that boy dependent on you so you can take his winnings."

"Get out of my way!"

"I may be from the sticks, but I ain't dumb!" he shouted after me.

Unable to control myself a moment longer, I turned and said, "No, you aren't dumb, you're just plain stupid."

"Smarter than you are!"

His words stung me. The rage inside my chest felt like a boiler threatening to explode. All the old man needed to do was say three words to me and I was on fire. I had to stop getting so mad or avoid him.

"Morning," Chester said, leading a horse out of a stall next to Boy.

"How are we going to get rid of that bag of wind?"

"You mean Pappy? Well, I'm working on it," Chester said in confidence.

"Not fast enough."

"That's the truth. Man, he's a sight."

"Sight? He's a pile of dung that needs to be pitched over the side."

"Oh, by the way, Johnny said the committee is having a get-together at noontime and you're invited."

"Where?"

"You better ask Dale. She'll know. Your horses been fed and watered."

"Did Shoat feed Boy and Thunder?" I asked, looking over in the stall and seeing some grain in the feed bucket and the water one full.

"Yes, that boy's a good hand. He said to tell you that he planned to take your pickup back home."

"What's he going to do then?" I asked, concerned that he'd have no transportation once he got there.

"He's running errands for me right now. He promised Johnny he would help us load tonight."

"I'll find him. Need to talk over driving up to Fort Worth next."

"He went after a load of feed just a few minutes ago."

"I better find out about lunch today, too."

A rap on her rig's door brought Dale to it.

"Hi, Brad."

"Where's the lunch at?"

"It's at the main office, up by the gate. Bring Zola. She'll charm those old boys. Suppose to be a barbecue."

"Fine—noontime?"

"Yes. And, Brad, I hope you and her get together."

"So do I." And off I went to find my barrel racer.

Kids were washing their calf entries on the racks. The slick black animals were soaked down and sudsy as their owners scrubbed away. Next came the blow dry and the combing to get them ready for the show ring. Gator and I did the same thing with herefords. Grandpa furnished the cattle on a loan. We even signed the loan papers. Of course, if they lost money after the premium sale, we had to work that out on the ranch. One year, we even took our steers to the Tulsa District Fair, and at the carnival I wasted all my money trying to win some doe-eyed girl from Venita a panda bear. I was a sucker for a cute pair of jeans back then. Luckily, we got enough money for our cattle at the auction so we didn't have to build any fence for gramps to pay off our debt that year.

It still stabbed me, thinking about those rolling hills of grass that used to belong to my family. Would I ever get over that loss and erase it from my mind? I still hear those red-tailed hawks scolding me as I loped a good-blooded horse out of Leo or Hancock blood lines across the windswept country. I still see white faces raised up and watching me when I rode past fat calves bucking and playing. The thud of the square baler making another leaf of hay. Gramps always bought International square balers. He wasn't that way about tractor brands, but he was convinced the red ones were the only hay machines that would hold up.

The last one he bought brought four hundred at the auction. A steal, but few folks used them since the big systems in round and square baling replaced the work of teenage boys; you couldn't find youngsters today to haul hay at any price. As obsolete as draft horses, they went by the wayside. Gramps sent off his last team of rusty-colored Belgiums when I was in first grade. They had done little in years and were near thirty, so old that their faces had turned gray.

I can recall black-and-white photos of all the draft horses with my father standing on top of a hay rack driving the team. He had a clear-cut grin, youth and enthusiasm written all over his face. Perhaps had he and Mom not been killed in the car wreck, the cushion of his generation would have saved the ranch from dispersal. I shook my head, feeling the lead ball in my stomach.

"What's up cowboy?" Zola asked when I opened the rig door.

"We have a luncheon appointment."

"Oh, should I wear my Dior dress?"

"No. Wranglers will do."

"You sure looked serious coming back," she said as she sidled up to me.

"It's nothing. You know you're the sunshine in my night," I said, feeling like a sailor who had just discovered land on the horizon; I rested my cheek on the top of her head.

"Is it dark in your world?"

"You've swept the darkness away."

"Will you fall back into night if I make some more rodeos?"

With my hands on her upper arms, I held her out to look in her blues. "No, I want you to be happy. Make the runs you need."

"Great." She shook her head and wet her lips. "I didn't want to tell you—"

"Why? Hey, we both need some slack in our lives."

"It's been so dreamlike." She looked at the ceiling and shook her head as if to escape her sadness. "I didn't want to bust the balloon."

"Our thing better be more than that."

She hugged me tight. "It is. It is."

The luncheon, accompanied by a Cajun band, proved to be tasty. The brisket was spicy and covered with hot sauce, but tender. The okra and tomato mix went well with the rice and red beans. French bread, wine, and beer helped make the lunch a celebration. The president announced that he and Johnny had signed a new five-year contract and that made everyone applaud.

"Now if we can agree with Mr. Turner on him coming back here for five more years . . ." he said and looked hard in my direction.

"You keep having these good meals, I'll sure be here," I said and waved my hat at them.

"Well, you won't starve for a while, anyway," Zola said at my elbow.

"Mr. Turner, my name is Barreau. They tell me you do commercials, for a fee, of course. Would you do one for me?"

"When?"

"Monday. We can talk later about the money and the rest, no?"

"Fine," I agreed.

"You come to my house on Sunday. We will have dinner at one o'clock. Your wife can come too, no?"

"You going to be here?" I asked her.

"I would love to come," Zola gushed to Barreau.

"Good, I'll make a map."

"Fine."

Johnny drifted by and nodded his head in approval. "Your Cajun preshow deal made this one work."

"Got lucky. Some of my ideas work. Others don't. All they worried about was whether the stock would buck."

Johnny chuckled. "That was their main concern until you turned it around. They have five new major sponsors for next year's show. All from one night's work."

"Wait until tonight. The word's just got out that we're having a real show."

"What else can we do?"

"Have a wild animal race."

"What's that?"

"Saddle up a mule, a cow, or anything else that they can ride—even an ostrich. First one across the line wins. Get the local youth in it and offer a good prize to the winner. Print the riders' names in the local paper."

"Where did you get that idea?"

"You ever go to the McAlister Prison rodeo?"

"No." Johnny shook his head.

"They used to open that rodeo with prisoners seated in galvanized bath tubs on the wildest assortment of animals. I think it would appeal to these folks, but I'd use real saddles for the kids."

"I'll plant the idea in their heads."

I nodded. Johnny could have the credit for the notion. We worked together and anything that pleased crowds meant we had work. A five-year contract was comforting when you were at home wondering what you would do next year. Zola and I finally excused ourselves, and I went back to the rig to lounge around until show time.

The country music of Doug Kershaw was on the stereo. The Weather Channel on the TV was muted so I could glance up to watch the approaching storms in California. I tried to balance my checkbook, and called Gator's cell phone twice.

"He's not got it on?"

"Must be riding. He never takes it with him on horseback."

"Why not?"

"Gator's got more superstitions than a voodoo princess."

"Really?" she asked while drying the dishes.

"Hey, I can do dishes," I said and then realized she was about done.

"I want you to miss me when I'm not here."

With a smile, I nodded. "I will Zola. I really will."

"Ladies and gentlemen, rodeo fans, welcome to the parish fair and pro rodeo. Are you having fun?"

The roar went up and I reined up Boy in the center of the arena. "Then let's pay off our friend from Hot Sauce Radio, Jacques Crusteau, with a great big hand." I pointed my hat at the booth and he took a bow to their enthusiastic applause. "Next year we're going to get him out here on a horse. How's that?" They cheered and we were off with a full house. Before I rode in, word came to me out back that all the seats were sold.

The mare who couldn't buck for Shoat came out on fire this time and went up in the clouds. The rider took an eighty-two on her. A pleased Johnny nodded. Between bucking horses, Skip was doing a polka in the stands with some rather large gal to some Cajun music Swing was playing for him. It was going to be a great night. I hoped that the concession stand's roof held up under the fans who were swarming on top of it.

Enthusiasm is contagious. These folks were surely infected and my job was to keep them happy. We went from money rides in barebacks to steer wrestlers throwing caution to the wind. Previous times were bested. Saddle bronco entries were a little light from turnouts. After two riders, Skip drove around in a chariot pulled by a Welsh pony and raced around the arena sword fighting against someone called the "Dark Invader" in his chariot. They clashed swords and rode hard and the fight sure sounded real. Of course when they quit sword fighting and the clanging went on, the crowd realized it was all on a soundtrack, which amused them greatly.

Skip stopped his horse in the center of the arena, jumped down from his rig, and pushed down on a fake detonator plunger. The Invader's backside exploded, and he went out the alley in smoke with the crowd laughing. Took up enough time and we went back to saddle broncs. No one who went home that night ever noticed that there were only five saddle bronc riders. If Johnny had bucked those five horses in a row to get to the next event, the audience would have felt cheated. "They didn't have any riders at the rodeo," would have been on their lips for a year. A man once said that Buffalo Bill was the world's greatest showman. He certainly was a model for the later-day Western movies and rodeos. He never wrote a book on how he pulled off all his tricks or I would own it, but I suspect we probably borrowed indirectly from him tonight.

While I was settled up in the corner on Boy, calling out the calf ropers and their times, Chester came along side me. I flipped off the mic.

"The cowboy that drew the bounty bull is out of the competition. So Shoat's going to ride the bounty bull last."

I nodded and went back to announcing the ropers. "That cowboy was Jim McNeely. Shame that calf kicked. Cost him some money. His time is eleven flat."

We were soon down to the bull riding and with nine riders including Shoat, it would make a good enough final act for the show. A finals' qualifier came within a tenth of a second riding a top bull. The fans paid him off, then the bulls tossed two more riders toward the lights.

"They got birds' nests built in their hats up there," Skip said. "They may become astronauts."

The rest were nothing to write home about. We were down to the bounty bull, a great red cross named Regulator that weighed in at over 1,400 pounds. With a *69* branded on his right hip, he originally came from an amateur contractor in Colorado. A true finals bull, he'd only been ridden twice in the three years Johnny owned him. Once, the flank wasn't tight enough and the other time, the cowboy got some lucky moves. Regulator bucked into his hand or he'd never been there at the whistle.

The five thousand bonus could only be won by the rider who actually drew him, so Shoat wasn't eligible to win it. But he could ride him to the whistle, and give the crowd a thrill anyway. I introduced him and told them all about the bull's feats. The gate came open and Regulator did not disappoint. He went high, threw his hips up higher, and danced on his front legs long enough to throw most riders down on his polished horns. Then, in a twist that would have made a gymnastic star ache, he corkscrewed to the left. I saw Shoat touch him on the shoulder with his free hand, his outside spur pounding the big bull, who next flew into a great vortex, then reversed. The crowd was on its feet, the shouts deafening. Then at the buzzer, still sitting on his back as the bull went sky high, Shoat jerked his tail and threw his left leg over the bull's back. He landed on his feet and threw his hat at the crowd.

"You wanted him to win? Well, he made it look easy. The bad news is he touched the bull with his free hand, and that cost him. But you'll see lots more of that young man, rodeo fans. His name's Shoat Krammer and he's a rising star!" The fireworks went off overhead and the sponsors' flag girls charged into the arena. "May the good Lord bless and keep you until next year, rodeo fans."

Chester rode up beside me in the alleyway. "That boy can ride, can't he?"

"He's a natural," I said and shook my head. How

would I ever get him on a steady schedule of that style of riding? All he needed was a chance, away from other distractions. Deep inside me, the resolve to get him there filled me with a newfound determination.

Chapter 21

Will Rogers Coliseum in Fort Worth is the place an Oklahoma country boy loves to drive into with a thirty-two-foot-long rig and a horse trailer on behind. Coming down from Okie City isn't half bad on I-35, but the approach from the east bisects Dallas. I took the northern route, skirting Big D. Zola called earlier and said that she decided to make some smaller rodeos that week. The way to win is to be at shows with less competition. We had parted with a long kiss, but the parting grew tougher and tougher each time. I was past the point of thinking why the two of us shouldn't get together. My new concerns were about a rich girl getting along on a rodeo announcer's meager existence.

How our two lives could ever come together as one had troubled me the entire drive across East Texas. A gloomy late winter day, the clouds hung low. On the cellular, Gator told me earlier on the phone that it was spitting sleet at home. He had a bull buyer who wanted to see those two bulls buck when we got back. Shoat was driving my pickup behind me—since the Fort Worth Rodeo started on Tuesday and we had no time to go home without turning around and coming back.

The groundsman directed me where to park, and

Shoat was there when I climbed down and stretched my stiff back, pulling on a nylon windbreaker.

"Give me the key, I'll plug you in," Shoat offered.

"We both can," I said, wondering if the water hookup hose would freeze and whether I should use the reservoir in the rig instead. I decided to try the hose on their faucet. Shoat reeled out the electric cord while I unspooled the white hose.

"I'm sorry about Pappy bugging you. He can be overbearing."

"Hey, he's your father."

"Don't excuse him. He gets these big ideas. Like I'm going to make millions of dollars and I'm going to need a financial advisor."

I nodded and listened, twisting the brass coupling to the faucet.

"I asked him to go home last night until I make some more money."

"You give him your mount money?"

"Yeah, I did, so he had money to get there."

"Man, he's been pretty expensive, hasn't he?"

Shoat nodded. "But he's gone home, so he shouldn't bother you or any of the crew."

"You can't help your relatives."

"I know, but I want to make it in this business—"

"And you don't need any baggage to hold you back."

Shoat smiled that big, wide, handsome grin. "I'll get you paid back, too."

"Maybe sooner than you think. Gator has a buyer interested in the bulls when we get back."

"He's a pretty good salesman, isn't he?"

"If Gator had ever settled down and gone into any kind of sales, I figure he'd be rich by now."

"He said he went to college."

I nodded, recalling my pleading for him to finish his last year at OSU. He was hauling an above-average dogging horse, and the prize money kept growing. After three years of part-time jobs, scraping up money, using duct tape on the holes in our boots, Gator was ready for the world, whether it was ready for him or not. He could have played football on a scholarship, but he wasn't cut out to be a football player despite his high-school success. He was a steer wrestler, through and through, and so I completed the fourth year at OSU without him.

He passed through Stillwater every few weeks, offering me rent money, entrance fees, trying to coax me away to join him. It was a real strain on our lifetime friendship. Only thing like it happened in the sixth grade, when he gave me a black eye over something that I forgot.

When I got home with my shiner Gramps said, "You go apologize to Gator."

"Me? Apologize to that bully?"

"Yes, 'cause Gator never would have hit if you didn't have it coming."

Though my grandfather had been gone for over a decade, I could still remember lots of things he taught me. We lived in a womanless house, but it never lacked being a real home. We both cleaned house, did dishes, took turns cooking and doing the wash. That's what prepared me for my bachelorhood.

Maybe I didn't know what a real woman about the place would be like. Stormy sure was not Betty Crocker. She burned water. I cooked whatever food we had at home—she thought KFC was cuisine, as long as she didn't have to mess with it. I even had to show her how to use the machines at the laundromat one time when we were too broke to send them to the cleaners. She didn't speak to me for a day over that indignation—sitting in a steamy Laundromat with a dozen chatty housewives in sweats with their hair in pink curlers.

She was so vain—she was afraid those women had a disease, and she'd end up dressing and looking like them. It was all my fault that we were in there and had little money. Plus she complained that I was trying to mold her into being a dutiful housewife who would be happy cooking, cleaning, and making beds. I told her I didn't see one female in there I wanted to hop into bed with besides her.

That caused her to say I was out looking for someone else to take to bed. My, but we had the most interesting ride from Santa Fe to Wyoming along the front range of the Rockies on the interstate. On the limited budget, her shouting was broken only when we stopped to eat the snacks we bought at the truck stops.

Going through Colorado Springs, she saw some big hotel along the highway and wanted me to pull over there. Her plan was go in and eat in the hotel's fancy restaurant, sign the tab with a fictitious name and room number, then get out of there and be on our way. She claimed they'd never catch us and we would have some real food for a change.

"Better yet," I told her, so disgusted that I was about ready to shove her out the door at sixty-five miles per hour, "get that .38 out from under the seat and the next truck stop we'll rob them at gunpoint."

She looked aghast at me. "That would be robbery."

"What in the hell did you think signing a phony name is?"

"They'd never miss it." She shook her head as if she could not believe me.

"Neither would Conoco or some other big oil company."

"You are talking prison time, Brad Turner."

"Only if they catch us."

"Stupid!"

"So's stealing a hotel meal."

We didn't talk from the north city limits of Colorado Springs to Casper, which included the hour when I took her to a famous bar and restaurant in Cheyenne off the interstate and spent my last ten on two hamburgers and fries.

Gator had showed up to compete at Casper and he loaned me some money. A week later in Rock Springs, she got up in the middle of the night, left my gear on the curb outside the motel room, and drove off in my pickup.

How did my thoughts get that far off track, I wondered, hooking up the RV. Shoat had already leveled the rig with the electric jacks from inside and we were parked. Chester said Johnny had sent some of his bucking stock to help out the main stock contractor for this big show. Chester brought them over, showing up while we were making sandwiches.

"Guess you're here all week?" he asked Shoat.

"Yeah."

"Good, can you help me?" Chester took off his felt hat and ran his fingers through his curly blond hair.

"Be glad to," Shoat said.

"Wash your hands and make a sandwich," I said to Chester.

You never have to bribe a road cowboy to eat. They can get up from one meal, go to the next place, and start eating all over again. That comes from the lean days, like the ones my ex and I shared on the interstate.

All that recall put me back to thinking about Zola. She came from a bigger house than any I knew about. Woodbury, Oklahoma had a small country club, an even smaller society, and I didn't play golf worth a flip. Zola never mentioned golf, but more than likely she played the game. Well, she could play it, if she wanted to; I'd go to the sale barn with Gator. But at some rodeos, the announcer was expected to play in their tournament.

One big committee man wanted me to be his partner at their golf tournament. He called me six months ahead to tell me we were playing together. I soon learned all about him. This guy never came in out of the money. He told me how he won the local bass tournaments, won the local bowling events, had a whole caseload of softball trophies his team had won.

That rodeo has a different announcer these days. I know the guy who does their show well and warned him when he called me with suspicion in his voice. "How come you aren't doing their show?"

"Simple—don't ever play golf with the rodeo committee president unless you're as good as Jack Nicklaus, at least if you want to keep that job."

"Thanks."

So the guy's either a par golfer or he drives the beer wagon—the cart loaded with coolers full of beer and liquor that keeps everyone lubricated.

In the RV, Chester, Shoat, and I ate real ham sandwiches with sliced tomatoes, lettuce, and mayo. They drank beer. I had a diet soft drink for our late lunch—or perhaps supper, depending on how things went.

"Can you buy beer on Sunday in Texas?" Shoat asked.

We all looked at each other. Not drinking any longer, I didn't know. "Think you have to be twenty-one."

"Figures," Shoat said.

"You check the bulls and horses for me," Chester said. "I'll borrow Brad's pickup and replenish our stock."

Shoat stood up and dug into his jeans's front pocket to throw a twenty on the table. "That's my part."

"Save your money. Johnny sent some money along," Chester said between bites.

Shoat shoved it back down in his pants and sat down to finish his lunch. My mind wandered away for a moment. With a wife, I wouldn't be having these guys over for mens-only lunches, hanging out with the boys, having our discussions about the performance, which bulls were bucking, and who got thrown off which horse. Those times when you unwound. I can recall Stormy's insistence: "You'd rather be with your damned old crowd of busted-up, beer-swilling, lying cowboys than me."

"Not really," I said back to her, "but they've all got a place in my heart." By that time I had drank enough brew it really didn't matter, her sharp tongue couldn't hurt me—nothing could.

"Mine certainly comes after them, that's for sure." And she went into another fuss.

I needed to be glad I still wasn't married to Stormy. Looking out the side window, I waved at a familiar face going by the front of the rig—Zack Martin, a bronc rider, who waved back. Then it struck me like a sledgehammer. Why Zola didn't want to compete here—because it put her back close to her father. Why did that strike me looking out the windshield of the rig? It sure wasn't the guy who went by. He was just another competitor. For what other reason wouldn't she want to run in her own backyard? She had a good enough horse. Thunder could take the competition on here as well as elsewhere. Dang, I'd sure ask her when she called me.

Chapter 22

"Pappy ain't coming to Fort Worth," Chester said as we drove around in my pickup looking for a beer stop.

"Shoat said he went home."

"He ain't going home, either, unless he walks."

"How come?"

"Glen and I took the drive line out of that ancient taco car of his and we fixed it so you can't fit one back."

"I'll keep your secret." Then I spotted the "quickie" and turned in.

We finally found a "choke and puke," that's a cowboy's term for those speedy marts that sell beer, food, and gasoline. Their specialty on the wall menu listed brown-crusted potatoes and fried chicken hind parts served in a paper dish. In those stops, the clerk would always shake his head and tell you someone else had already gotten all the white meat before you got there, when actually, they never had any breast meat to fry. Made the chain a lot more money to serve only hind parts; it's called corporate profits. The bottom line.

Chester bought a case of beer. I took a six-pack of diet and we were on our way back to the rig.

"Shoat going to come out of it?" Chester asked, cracking open a can.

"I think so."

"He say if Mona was coming here?"

"No. He don't say anything about her."

"Just as well." Then Chester chuckled and wiped his mouth on the back of his hand. "I'd bet them peckerwoods are damn mad at you sending them on a wild-goose chase to the coast after an eighteen-wheeler." He laughed some more.

"You just remember they're armed and dangerous."

"Hey. I ain't no hero."

"Don't become one, either."

"You figure they'll come back?"

"I have a notion that if Mona's husband wants her home, they'll find her soon enough."

"Oh!" He slapped his forehead and upset his felt hat. "She's married."

"I got that much out of him."

"Where did he find her?" He reset his hat and drained the first can. It made a crinkling sound when it hit down by his boots.

"If I was judging, I'd say she found him."

Chester nodded and drew out another beer from the cardboard carton. He ripped it open as we pulled back onto the grounds. Shoat was shouting and waving us toward the barn where the stock was penned.

"What's wrong?" Chester said, bailing out before I turned the key off.

"Whiskey Mad's got the colic."

"Damn!" Chester swore and the two rushed through the door. I reached in, took out my cell phone, and dialed the office.

"Front office."

"You have a vet on call?"

"Yes, sir. Doc Murphy."

"Send him down to barn three right away, we have a colicky horse."

"Who should he see?"

"Chester White or Brad Turner. We'll be right here."

I snapped the phone shut. When I passed through the doorway, I heard that familiar strained grunt of a colicky horse. You've ever heard that long moan you don't forget it. All my experience was with ranch and roping horses. I'd walked several infected animals all night long to keep them from lying down, rolling, and twisting a gut. Somehow that's what they want to do—roll to escape the pain in their belly, but that just twists their intestines and cuts off circulation.

A big gray mare I was double proud of came down with colic from eating green oat hay. Gramps and I used a hose to give her an enema. We did what we could figure out to ease her discomfort. I walked her all night. At dawn, Gramps called an older cowboy, Ward Tipton, who lived down the road. He came and looked the mare over and nodded real serious-like about her condition.

"Should have called me last night." Ward shook his head again and I figured the worst for the gray.

"Didn't want to wake you," Gramps said.

"Get me a tablespoon, boy."

I rushed off and quickly returned. Ward took a small bottle from his pocket, carefully put a few drops on the spoon, then handed me the bottle.

He turned to the gray, opened her mouth, and put the contents of the spoon on her tongue like he was wiping it off. Then Ward looked at the house and nodded.

"You two got any coffee?"

"What about the mare?"

"If she ain't better by the time you all get some coffee built and I have a cup, we'll give her some more."

I read the label on the bottle: DR. BELL'S VETERINARY MEDICAL WONDER. "What is it?"

"You can't buy it in this country. Have to have someone smuggle it out of Canada for me. Pretty priceless stuff."

I turned as the mare grunted. She stretched her neck out and then wallowed her tongue around in her open mouth like she didn't like the taste.

"Unsnap the lead, she'll be fine." Ward motioned for me to go to the house.

To disobey him would be disrespectful, but I had been up all night walking her. To leave her to roll made me sick and half angry.

"Come on, Brad," he insisted. With a shake of my head and big knot in my stomach, I went to the house after him.

Gramps had already put the pot on the stove. We drew up chairs at the wooden table. Gramps dug out the canned milk and sugar for Ward. We took ours black and unsweetened to show how tough we were. I swear, the habits you get into. Gramps saucered and cooled his when he was at home, but said it was bad manners to do the like in public. I just drank mine from the rim of the cup when it cooled barely enough not to scald my tongue.

This time it took forever to get that cool. My mind and concerns were on the gray out in the yard. The crows flying over the house cawing sounded like they were taunting me. At last, my first cup down, I went to pour another and refill theirs. When I looked out the kitchen window, instead of the gray being under the pecan tree, she was nowhere in sight.

"Mare's gone." I shot out into the cool air of the summer morning and saw her grazing her way toward the stock tank.

"She's eating," I said in shocked disbelief. I looked back at the two old men on the porch.

"She'll be fine. But I'll leave this bottle here, just in case," Ward said.

With a nod, I agreed. Next time I'd have a bottle of Dr. Bell's Veterinary Medical Wonder. Gramps knew a man that went to Canada to hunt and had him bring us back some. I never was certain how many years in prison you could get for bringing it into the U.S., but it sure cured lots of good horses and saved them from a painful death.

Standing there under those big lights in the framework ceiling high overhead, I wished for one more dose for the big bay saddle bronc. The vet slid the big door open and drove his pickup down the alleyway.

"What's happening?" he asked. The coughing bay stretched his neck and acted wobbly on his feet.

"Whiskey must have drank too much of his own stuff," Chester said. "I thought they were fine when I unloaded them a few hours ago."

"Something sure gave him the bellyache," the vet said and shook his head. "He's a bucking horse, isn't he?"

"Doc, he is and he ain't halter broke."

"And you're . . . ?"

"Chester. That's Brad, and that's Shoat."

We nodded as we stood outside the pen, each of us wondering how we would handle the big horse. He weighed at least twelve hundred pounds of head-slinging fury. Things were sure fixing to get Western in Fort Worth's barn number three.

"We need to oil him," Doc said. He was a man in his late forties, short with a handsome face and intense blue eyes, his short sideburns had begun to whiten. He wore an LBJ Stetson and white coveralls. Under that he had on a necktie, so I didn't know if we had interrupted his going out or what, but he was giving the bronc a very hard once over.

"Is he wild?"

"Sure is, Doc."

Chester looked over and nodded at me. To treat him, we both knew that meant inserting a tube down the horse's gullet and treating him with mineral oil. A serious project with a tame horse. Unlike a saddle horse turned bronc, Whiskey came into this world wild and no one had ever conquered him.

"Of all the horses to colic," Chester said warily, shaking his head.

"We can make a squeeze out of panels," I said, looking around at the unused worksheets stacked to the side. Shoat and I went after some.

"I don't dare give him too much sedative," Doc said.

"Lord, Doc, that pony's worth between ten and twelve thousand dollars. Let's do all we can for him," Chester said, undoing the gate.

"I will. That's my job." He went off to his pickup to get his instruments and medicine.

No doubt Chester was bearing all the responsibility for the horse's ailment on his broad shoulders. Johnny would be upset, but even he couldn't have prevented the case of colic if he'd been there. I kept thinking about the gray mare and her cure. But I hadn't had any of that patented medicine in years, didn't even know if they still sold it in Canada.

When Shoat and I'd packed the panels back, the next chore was to get Whiskey out of the pen where he was with a dozen buckers. He might have a bad bellyache, but when Chester tried to cut him out, he headed right into the other horses. Shoat crossed over through the next pen to get ahead, while I slipped in to help Chester.

"Reckon I made the doc mad?" Chester asked under his breath.

"How's that?

He glanced back, then in a low voice said, "When I said he needed to save this one."

"Naw, vets get that kinda talk all the time when someone's animal is sick."

"Hope so." The horses crowded in the corner turned and looked over us for an escape route. Whiskey, who'd been in the rear, had turned and was ready to bolt over us. Despite our arm waving, Whiskey batted his eyes shut and knocked us both aside, as the others charged through the gap he made. I scrambled to stay out of the way of their hooves and held myself tight to the fence while they ran by us.

Chester picked himself up and dusted off his pants seat as I looked at the herd.

"Bring him back 'here!" Shoat shouted. "We can gate cut the other horses out of here and leave him."

"Good," Chester said. "He's the only guy with any sense."

So, waving my arms and threatening to step in front of them, we cut out the other horses into the next pen one by one. At last, the sick pony was by himself worrying the fence by walking back and forth, trying to rejoin his comrades. That rasping moan in his throat made me sick to my stomach. Shoat and I hooked two portable panels together and, carrying the sections, we advanced on the bay gelding.

"Whoa," we both said as soothing as we could. Chester cut off Whiskey's escape to the rear and we kept closing in.

"Watch that he don't kick the fire out of you," Chester warned me as the world around Whiskey grew smaller. Shoat slammed his end into the fence and braced both feet on the panel. Doc appeared on the far side and used a rope to secure it. We had the bronc trapped between two twelve-foot panels and the main pipe fencing.

Chester helped me close the gap behind Whiskey as we tried to avoid the wild horse's hind feet repeatedly kicking the panel. I had to watch my fingers while Chester used his belt to secure the panel to the pen.

"Here." Doc tossed him some more rope.

"Got it."

Despite the barn's cool interior, when we finally had him in the squeeze, I sliced the sweat off my forehead with the side of my finger and we were all sucking breath. Whiskey slowed his struggling to only an occasional kick of a back hoof.

"Need to get some ropes to put over the top to contain him," Chester said.

"They in your tack box?" Shoat asked, and when he got the nod he hurried off to get them.

Chester and I studied the situation. The horse would need to be driven up and then squeezed still more for us to ever doctor him.

"Bet you'd rather work on them gaited horses than one of these?" Chester said to the vet.

He shook his head. "They're all a challenge. The worst ones to work on are those that give up."

"You mean won't fight?"

"Yep. They just lose their spirit."

"Still it would be a lot easier to work on a broke one."

Doc laughed. "Don't apologize, he's all we have tonight."

"Yes," I said, and smiled at the short man. The sun had set outside and only then had I realized Zola would be trying to call me. Oh, she'd have some cute remark about my absence. But we could talk later.

After Shoat returned with an armload of lariats, we gradually managed to get the bay pinned between the panel and the pipe fence. Then we roped over the top so Whiskey couldn't rear up if he had the energy. After a half-dozen tries, Chester managed to get Doc's chain on his upper lip. He twisted it tight and we had him. Chester gripped the handles of the twitch. Shoat and I were both on the fence, attempting to hold the horse's head while Doc administered the mineral oil. It was a slow process that Whiskey violently disproved of despite our constant assurance it would make him feel better.

After the oil, Doc gave him two shots, one to tranquilize the horse, and the other to ease the muscles in his gut.

"What now?" Chester asked.

"I'll check on him in a few hours. We won't know much until daylight. Even then, the damage that might have occurred to him internally won't show."

"Should we leave him in this trap?"

Doc nodded. "He must be some bucker."

"He used to get high as the lights when he came out."

"He will again," he reassured Chester. "Where will you be at?"

"I have a motel room, but I'll stay here tonight. I've got a bunk in the trailer that Flying Star Rodeo Company parked in the lot."

"If you can't get him there," I told the vet, "that class-A RV out there is mine."

"Well, all we can do now is hope the medicine works."

We all agreed. Doc backed his truck out and left. Chester went for the beer. Shoat closed the big sliding door after the vet. He caught the can Chester pitched at him. It spewed some when he popped the top, but he quickly lapped up the foam.

"Better call Johnny," Chester said.

"He'll understand." I clapped him on the shoulder for reassurance, then unlocked the rig. Failure is never easy to accept, even when it's beyond your control, like the captain of a ship run aground by an unavoidable storm. You still look for ways you could have avoided it, despite the futility of the search.

"I guess he'll have to." Chester shook his head as if the weight of the world had fallen upon his broad shoulders.

Twenty-four hours would tell a lot.

"Hello." It was Zola on the other end. Busy turning the steaks on the electric grill, I tucked the cell phone between my cheek and my shoulder and finished the job.

"What's new?" I asked.

"Oh, I tipped a barrel."

"Sorry."

"But my score stayed up and I'm winning first up here."

"Wonderful. Is it cold?"

"In Rapid City, or in the motel room by myself?"

"Wherever."

"Sure it's cold. Hot in Texas?"

"No, but it's been above freezing all day. Cloudy. One of Johnny's saddle broncs colicked this evening and kept the three of us busy."

"I wondered where you were when I called earlier. Is the horse going to make it?"

"We'll know more in the morning."

"Shoat there?"

"Yeah. He said, hi."

"Me, too," Chester said raising a beer as they watched the TV.

"Hear him?"

"Sure. You guys be careful. Those Texas cowgirls may grab you. Are you coming home Sunday?"

"Yes, I plan on it."

"I'll be there Monday night—if that's . . ." She hesitated asking.

"Yes. You come on, and drive careful. I miss you."

"Me, too. See you then." I shut off the cellular and wondered how we'd ever make it. Dang, we stayed worlds apart. But that might just be the glue that worked; I hoped so.

"She doing good?" Chester asked.

"Winning a first," I said, checking on the meat.

"She's going to make it to the finals this year, isn't she?"

"She hopes to."

"Need a campaign to get you voted in to announce them." Chester stood up and waved his beer can at Shoat. "You and me better get started before the ballots come out."

"What do you think about that?" Shoat asked.

"I'd be flattered. A man would be a fool not to be, but I'm not going around kissing babies to get the vote."

"That's what friends are for," Chester said and sauntered off to use the bathroom.

"You ever announced the finals?" Shoat asked, checking on my cooking.

"No, only the circuit ones."

"Chester's got a good idea. You're our favorite announcer."

"Lots of good boys working behind the microphone in this business."

"Yeah, but we like you." He pounded me on the shoulder, then swapped turns with Chester in the bathroom.

First time he ever touched me. Guess I had really gained his confidence. The boy had a wide aura that kept people at arm's length. Shoat was not a back slapper, nor did he throw his arm over your shoulder to tell you a secret. He always stayed his distance; I felt that perhaps I was in his inner circle—or maybe the beer had relaxed his rigid posture. No reason to wonder how he acted after I saw where he came from and what his background must have been like. His Pappy wouldn't have built trust in anyone. Thank heavens he wasn't in Fort Worth—yet. But the rodeo wasn't over, either. Did Mona know he was there? Lots could still happen.

Chapter 23

The dead wagon came for Whiskey about noon. A horse lying on his side, his legs stiff with rigor mortis resembling sticks with cups on the end—it looked so out of place. For an animal that spent ninety-nine percent of the time on his feet, including when he slept they don't even look horselike on their side. The groundsman came with a yellow industrial tractor and pulled him to the sliding door. He didn't want animal-rights people passing by to see Whiskey, so he closed the doors until the rendering plant truck arrived.

A black driver slid the door out, letting the midday light in the barn. Then he pulled out the cable and looked at the three of us.

"Gonna be fifty dollars. They done told you?"

Chester agreed and handed him two twenties and a ten. The man put them in a big wallet with a chain leading to his belt loop, then got out a receipt book from his shirt pocket, wrote "dead bay horse disposal—fifty dollars," and he scribbled his name. Then he went about his undertaker duties, hoisting Whiskey's still body up and into the truck bed, which was already filled with dead cows.

"Johnny would have buried him with a backhoe at home," Chester said.

"Nothing else we could do here," I assured him.

"It would have taken three ricks of wood to cremate him. I've cut the wood and done that before at home," Shoat said with a shake of his head.

"Yeah, but the good ones always die. You couldn't kill the sorry buckers with a pailfull of arsenic," Chester complained.

"Well, as long as the rodeo secretary knows and they have another horse drawn in his place."

"I already told her that he was sick and couldn't go out. Doc did the right thing, putting him down," Chester said. "He wasn't improving and his spirit was gone."

"Thank you, fellows," the driver said and pulled off his heavy gloves.

"Hope we don't need you again."

"We all gots to die," he said. "Animals, too."

So the white diesel hearse pulled away and we left the big doors open since the corpse was gone.

"Wasn't much of a funeral."

"You're right."

"Someone's come looking for you," Chester said to Shoat.

Without looking, I recognized the roar of the powerful engine. Mona had arrived in Fort Worth. Damn, oh, damn, we got rid of Pappy and we had her back. I looked all over to be sure there wasn't a big Fleetwood behind her.

"See you guys later," Shoat said and went off to talk to her through the car window. He had not gotten into her vehicle, and it sounded like they were having a serious discussion. When I reached the rig door to unlock it, the sharp squeal of car tires made me turn around to see Shoat standing there, left behind.

"When she leaves, she don't waste no time," Chester said as he waved good-bye at me and headed for his motel room. It had been a long hard night and now that it was over, he planned to get some shut-eye. After tonight's rodeo, the pickup-man-turned-stock-contractor intended, no doubt, to do a lot of belt-buckle polishing on some Texas cowgirls. Chester was a lover, fighter, and a wild horse rider and a dang good hand at all three.

"She upset?" I asked waiting for Shoat before I went inside.

"I told her she needed to settle with him. We argued about it at the ranch."

"None of my business."

"Yeah, well, I guess it is now. I told her to give him his car and cut it off. She said it was her car and that wasn't my concern." Shoat shrugged with a scowl on his face. "Made me mad that those thugs got after you."

"Don't worry about me. I can fight my own wars."

"It wasn't your war, it was mine."

"So—she drove all this way to see you?"

"I guess." Shoat shrugged. "You have much trouble with women?"

"The first one I ever loved I divorced—or she divorced me. Don't ask me for a lot of sound advice." We both laughed.

"You in there?" A familiar woman's voice asked as someone rapped on the door.

"Mona back?" I asked Shoat.

He pushed open the door and standing at the bottom of the stairs was Gloria Hines. She swept the brown curls back from in her face and smiled.

"Long time no see, *kimo sabe.*" She grabbed the rail and swung up the stairs.

"Shoat, meet Gloria Hines," I said.

He nodded and stood back to let her in. She wore a ruffled yellow blouse and a matching pair of Rockies, all form-fit and poured full.

"Thought you were coming to Jackson," I said.

"Oh, well, I had truck troubles and I never got out of Florida. And I forgot your cell phone number."

I handed her a card.

She looked at it. "I was one digit off; some SOB was mad after I called him twice."

"He never saw you. Have a chair."

"Hey, I need to go check on the stock. I'll leave you two," Shoat said.

"Nice to meet you, Shoat. You're with a heckuva guy." She smiled and winked at him. When flirts came, Gloria had the match won.

"Nice kid. Who is he?" she said when he was gone.

"Just a stray I picked up."

She slid in the other captain's chair. "I know I didn't make Jackson—and I should have found your number. My ex—" She dropped her head and shook it.

"You getting back with him?"

"Gods, no! I now know I don't ever want him again." Her brown eyes flew open wide, and her too-long lashes flickered. "You knew?"

"Rodeo's a small game." I'd played my hunch about what she wasn't saying.

"I went back to see him and . . ."

"I know. I did the same thing—once."

"Dumb, wasn't it? It didn't work then. It don't work now." The face she made was one of plain exasperation.

I agreed.

"What do you think about us?" She shrugged her

shoulders, folded her upper lip inside, and spilled her long hands in her lap.

"I've been seeing someone."

"Can't play, can you? Stupid me."

"No, you're not stupid—you're like me; you can't believe something that you originally wanted so bad has turned out so poorly."

"That's it!"

"I'm sorry."

"Hey, if it don't work out for you this time, I'll *still* be around. And who knows? By then you might want an old maid."

We both laughed. My roiling stomach eased some, not having known how she would take my honesty. Honesty to Zola and to myself. I wasn't making one-night stands anymore. Maybe I was growing up.

The cell phone rang. I picked it up.

"Brad Turner."

"Wendell Johns. I understand that you're in Fort Worth. I got your number from a business card my daughter left. Are you available for lunch tomorrow?"

"I could be. Where and when?"

"Noon at the Wrangler Club."

"Meet you there, then?"

"Excellent. I shall look forward to meeting you."

I hung up.

"Business?" she asked.

I nodded and rose from the chair. She shook her head, stood up, and then kissed me. "That's for the good times. Good luck, too."

"I'll need it."

"Ha! It's my loss." She bounded down the stairs, jumped into a pickup, and waved at me as she drove away.

"She wasn't here long," Shoat said drifting back.

"I told her about Zola."

"Guess I'd have fled, too." He laughed.

"You ever been to the Wrangler Club?" I stared after her Florida plates.

"That a big cowboy honky-tonk?"

"No, it's a private oilman's club up there in the sky."

"Wow, you going there?"

"Tomorrow, my friend, to meet Zola's daddy."

"What do you do in those places?"

"Put your Justins under the table and do whatever you want."

"I know you shouldn't pick your nose." He grinned big and chuckled. "But I mean, using the right forks and the rest would surely mess me up."

"Just act like you've been in lots better places and it will always work."

"What if you ain't been? Then what?"

"How will they know? Just act like it's McDonald's."

"That the truth?"

"Absolute."

"I ever get invited to one of them fancy places, I'll do that."

"You will, Shoat, you will get invited someday."

"You keep expecting such big things out of me."

"You're only going to jump as high as you let yourself."

He nodded his head. "I see that."

The rest of the day, I wondered what Daddy War-bucks wanted with me. The father-in-law-to-be speech. Dang, was I ready for that? I might be all left hands as bad as Shoat—who knows until the time comes.

Take the private elevator to the twenty-second floor and step off into that world of big shots. I had ridden lots of them with men who were worth billions. In the same car were men who had lost as much and were holding on by their fingernails to that fragile place in the upper crust, hoping some gusher would come in to save them.

First night of the rodeo went well. I kept wondering what Wendell had on his mind. I wasn't some little boy asking for a teenager's hand. I first met Stormy's folks when we drove through Chandler going to the Fiesta Del Sol in Tucson. Her daddy, Tony, had a heating and air-conditioning company, big Spanish-style house, and an in-ground swimming pool. I was very impressed by the pool business, but I soon found out that everyone in the Valley of the Sun had one. Like a bathroom in a new house in Oklahoma—everyone had them now.

Her dad drank a lot. I did, too, back then, so we swilled his good bourbon and ice cubes in crystal glasses and had a high old time. He even wanted me to think about taking over his affairs when I got through rodeoing.

"A guy with a college education—hell, you could run this with one hand tied behind your back. I came out here from Chicago twenty-five years ago. I graduated from an industrial school. Huh? Too dumb for the college business, they taught me sheet metal and the heating business. Hey, two months later, this dumb dago was in business for himself.

"Look around you, you ever see so many houses going up? When I came here it was the same thing. It was like falling into a bucket of shit and coming out smelling like roses, huh?"

He clapped me on the shoulder. "College boy. Hey, you could be the AC king of the whole Phoenix area. Don't worry, I'll show you how."

We went for refills as great ole pals. The last time I drove up to his house he came outside waving his hairy arms at me. "Get out of here you . . ." Lots of cuss words. "You broke my baby's heart, you stupid, dumb cowboy!"

Tony never said, "She broke your heart because I spoiled her to death when she was growing up." So when I left the raging Italian in the street, I bought my own bottle of Jack Daniels and drank it with ice cubes in a plastic cup in a pastel-green motel room with fake pink flamingos around a swimming pool half as big as Tony's.

Something bad happens in your life and it burns forever in your mind. All her mother could say, every time she had a chance, was that we needed to get remarried in the Catholic church before the baby was born. We never had any kids.

Have you ever parked a pickup in a parking garage made for Japanese coupes? You can get two of those in where my rig has to sit. Three, if you put the last one in the truck bed. I wore a tan suede sports coat for the meeting with Zola's dad, tan slacks, white shirt, and my Sunday-go-to-meeting full-quilled ropers, and a tan-tinted 10X Resistol on my head. I told the man at the Wrangler Club's private elevator my name. He dropped his finger down the list until he found me.

"Go ahead, sir, and have a nice lunch today."

I thanked him, went in the elevator and was whisked skyward in seconds. When I stepped off, I faced a huge Charlie Russell bronze of the buffalo goring the Indian hunter and his horse. It was twice life-size.

"May I help you, sir?" the maître d' asked, taking my hat.

"Wendell Johns."

"He's waiting for you, sir. This way." He handed the hat to an assistant and led me down the stairs to the second level. I felt I drew several eyebrows as I crossed the room. A gray-haired man stood up.

"Brad?"

"Mr. Johns?"

"Wendell," he corrected me and we shook hands. "Have a seat. Will you have a drink?"

"Ice tea is fine."

"Very well. Iced tea, Charles," he said to a waiter and the man was off like a shot.

"Some view of the city from up here."

"Yes, there is. Did the rodeo go well last night?"

"Yes, it did." My iced tea arrived and the waiter offered me sweetener and I shook my head, thanking him.

"I'm curious." He smiled with a handsome enough face, but with one that could hide anything—and might be right now. "You've been in oil?"

"No, oil was in me." I waved off that reply. "Actually I did some work in oil and got caught in the big price break."

He nodded like he knew about it. "And you paid it off."

"Wiped me out. But yes, I paid my debts off."

"Any plans to return to the business?"

"No. A boy once burned doesn't play with matches."

"Charles, bring us a salad and some nice club steaks. I like mine medium, of course." He looked at me.

"Medium rare is fine."

"Dressing?" he asked.

"Ranch, house, whatever."

There I sat looking out the tinted glass at the skyline of Fort Worth, talking to a man who could probably buy or sell the county I lived in at home. Did he want me in the AC business, too? Or perhaps in petroleum?

"You're probably wondering why I so boldly invited you to lunch?" He swept up the napkin Charles had placed in his lap and wiped the corners of his mouth. "I want to be a grandfather." He controlled a laugh and nodded his head. "She's thirty-one and shows no sign of slowing down this pursuit of hers. Can you lasso her? Get her to settle down and—well, you know what I mean."

"I'm kind of a Sunday roper myself. Not too great with a rope."

"You were married before?"

"Long time ago."

"She was, too." He leaned back in the seat and tented his fingers on his chest. "I didn't come here to bribe you. I came here to see if you thought there was anyway to make her settle down long enough—"

"To have grandchildren?" I asked, seeing a steel light in his blue eyes. This man could do anything he wanted to do. Buy anything imaginable. And he came asking for something I wasn't certain I could deliver.

Over our lunch, we talked about some mutual people we knew in petroleum. The man was sharp; he knew my bad experience had burned me to the core and he never again broached the subject of my return to the oil business.

"So, bucking bulls. Do you get involved in buying them?" he asked.

"I trade in a few."

"It may be a fool's game, but I've heard about men making some money at it."

"It's as risky as any venture I know of. Yes, you can trade in the good ones. There's always a demand."

"Then would you consider a partnership?"

"In bucking bulls?"

"Yes. We can call it the JT Cattle Company."

"How would it work?"

"I supply the money for the bulls and expenses. You supply the pasture, place to keep them, and do the contracting, buying and selling."

"I'd have to think on it." The offer knocked me down. He was saying carte blanche that we'd be partners. Perhaps the altitude was making my head swim. It was an opportunity of a lifetime.

"What happens if she says good-bye to me?"

"Brad, you and I will be in the bull business, period."

I wiped the sweat off my upper lip on my napkin. How I ever thought of it, I'll never know. The room felt hot and the curved leather chair with the brass tacks I sat in felt more like a wood stove.

"You need a string of bulls to readily sell them. Then you take them to these big bull ridings and get a rep—that's the basic steps."

"That's why we're going in the business. You know bulls."

"It's a fad, like ostriches," I said to warn him.

"But they always need good ones for rodeos and bull-riding competitions, right?"

"Yes."

"You can always sell a diamond. Glass is harder."

"Refill your glass, sir?" the waiter asked.

I blinked at him. For a moment I was so engrossed in the newfound notion. "Oh, yes, please," I finally managed.

"What do you think, Brad?"

"You'd do this on a handshake?"

"Yes."

"We aren't in-laws." I looked for a flicker of his blue eyes.

"A mutual friend told me about you selling the ranch. The one you inherited?"

"What does that mean?"

"You have a fine reputation for being responsible. Men who planned to steal from you can't be curbed by written agreements."

"A reputation—glad I have something."

"You do. And a good one." He bent over and pulled out a blank signature card from his briefcase. "Sign it and we're in business."

While I signed my name, he came out with a loose-leaf checkbook. "Glad you agreed to JT Cattle Company because that's the way the checks are printed."

"Fine. May I use your cell phone? Mine's in the truck."

"Who are you calling, if I may ask?" He handed it over.

"Gator Bledsoe. My man in Oklahoma. And tell him two bulls aren't for sale yet."

"Oh, we have two?"

I nodded as the phone rang. When he clicked it on, I could hear the auctioneer in the background.

"How they selling today?" I asked.

"Oh, some are off a dollar. Brad, that you?"

"Those bulls aren't for sale. Got a new deal."

"What's that, pard?"

"The JT Cattle Company of Fort Worth."

"Never heard of them."

"You will, pard. They have a branch in Woodbury."

"You find an oil well down there?"

"You could say that. Yes."

"Hey, I've got to bid on this lot. Call me back, I want all the news."

"Later."

"They good bulls?" Wendell asked.

"Good enough to start with."

"Now. My daughter—"

"Let it work or not work between us. I want it to work very much. If it doesn't, then it wasn't mean to be. Sorry I can't promise you the moon, but you never can tell."

I swilled down the sixth glass of ice tea. This time, I was thankful that at least I was sober when I talked to the father.

We rose and shook hands.

"To the bull business," he said. "You belong to AA?"

"No, sir, I simply don't drink."

He nodded like he understood.

I started to leave with the checkbook under my arm, then I turned back as he stood to fill out the luncheon check and sign it.

"One more thing, Wendell. I think if we both stop pressuring her, we both might win."

He nodded very slowly that he got my message. "I understand."

No way that I could tell the man his daughter was in Rapid City and not there in Fort Worth because of his pressure. She'd be in Woodbury on Monday. Would she get mad if I mentioned the bull business?

Fly off the handle and say he had bought me off? I
sure hoped not. I'd give it all up if that happened.
Dang, life left you hanging with your feet barely tread-
ing the floor so often. I needed to get back to the
rodeo grounds—I had another performance to do.

Chapter 24

"**D**amn you—"
It was Shoat's voice from outside the barn.
I rushed to the walk through door to see him staving
off two thugs we ran to the West Coast. The first fork
I could find was in my grasp; I charged, jabbing Curly
in the butt with it. Lucky for him it was a manure
fork, but he jumped skyward when the tines struck
him in the seat of his pants.

When he whirled around, I smashed him over the
head with the implement. He wilted and went to his
knees. Shoat was down on the ground and the big one
came running at me. I drew back the fork and tried
my best baseball swing at him. The fork caught his
shoulder and spun him sideways, knocking him to the
ground. I rushed over just as he scrambled to his feet
in his shiny black loafers, and applied the fork to his
hind parts.

His scream was earsplitting, but he jumped to his
feet nevertheless. The big Caddy screeched up, and
both men dove inside the rear door, one on top of
the other. When the big car reached the main street,
the rear door still hung open and came within inches
of smashing a fireplug as the Caddy went squealing
around the corner.

"You all right?" I asked, out of breath and leaning
on my fork.

"Yeah," Shoat said, getting up rubbing his jaw and smiling. "Them guys sure got forked."

"I'd had a real fork, they'd have been fondue."

Chester came galloping up on a big bay pickup horse, which he held in a tight rein. "What happened? I was putting my stock away and they said I'd better get over here. There was a fight going on at barn three?"

"We were just pitching some thugs around," I said and Shoat laughed aloud. Then we had to tell Chester the whole story.

"What did they want?" he asked with a frown when we finished.

"Mona's here in town," I said.

Shoat nodded, then he held his palms up. "She ain't with me."

"You're getting smarter," Chester said. "You should have given up on her a long time ago. I'll get this horse put up and we can go honky-tonking. Brad, you want to go?"

"No, thanks, guys," I begged off.

Chester shook his head as Shoat led Chester's horse toward the barn. "That boy maybe learning."

"I think so, too."

In a flash, Chester and Shoat were off to go boot scooting and I was watching the red taillights of my pickup recede into the night. Those boys' heads would hurt come morning, but, oh, the memories of the good times. I wanted to call Gator and talk to him more about our new bull venture, since I needed a partner to handle the deals while I was away rodeoing. It was eleven o'clock when I checked my watch under the streetlights, and one of the uniformed security force came hurrying over.

"Mr. Turner? Was there a fight here?"

"They're gone."

"Both sides?"

"Except for me."

"Did they hurt you?" Busy securing a pencil and pad from his pocket, he looked ready to take down the facts.

"No, I used a pitchfork on them."

"Really?" he asked, dropping his pad and pencil to his side and blinking at me.

"Yes. They left in a black, late-model Fleetwood. Missouri license plates."

"You see them very good? I mean, could you pick them out of a lineup?"

"Perhaps." I wondered to myself if I remembered them well enough to do that.

"I'll get an all-points out on the Cadillac. You have a general description of the men?"

"Both were about six feet tall, bull-necked, like football players. Dressed in black suit clothes, black shoes. I'd say late twenties."

"You catch a name?"

"No."

"Any other witnesses."

"I think that's about it."

"I'll report it to the Fort Worth Police. They may want to talk to you in the morning."

"Fine. Not before nine A.M., though."

He smiled. "Yes, sir. You're in the big RV by barn three, right?"

"That's me."

I looked at the yard light shining on the deserted street. Everyone else was gone. I just hoped those two thugs stayed away. At the rig, I climbed inside and turned on the lights. Then I walked back and removed the .357 from the dresser drawer. I was not afraid—I didn't feel that threatened—but I wasn't taking another whipping, either.

After checking the revolver's cylinders, I put it on the nightstand by my bed. With a deep sigh, I dialed Gator's home number.

A sleepy voice answered, "Yeah?"

"You ever want to become a stock contractor?"

"Huh?"

"This is Brad. You awake?"

"Yeah. Where are you—what time is it?"

"Eleven o'clock—no, it's eleven-thirty. We've got us a partner with deep pockets."

"Who's he?"

"Wendell Johns."

"He legit?"

"Yes. If Zola doesn't have a conniption, her daddy wants to buy a string of bulls."

"Zola's daddy?"

"Yes. I met with him today."

"You getting in his family?"

"That's not a condition."

"Tell me more."

"We need to find some good bulls. Need a couple of trailers to haul them. Need to make some contacts and hire them out, so that we can eventually take them to the big finals in Vegas."

"Whew, it feels like I'm dreaming. I'm half awake here, wondering what my old pard's been drinking."

"I'm not drinking."

"No, I know that, but I ain't had half enough time to think how we're going to handle it."

"You'll figure that out. Don't sell those two bulls,

Blackie and Dummy. That's a start And start calling around. We don't need average bulls. We need haints."

"There's a guy in Nebraska—"

"There's guys all over. We're only going after the best. Johns wants a top string."

Gator whistled through his teeth. "He's got that much money?"

"He says he does."

"I better find out where the next bull sales are."

"Yes, and look into stock contractor sell-outs, too. They won't come easy."

After I hung up, I went and took a diet soda out of the refrigerator, popped the top, and considered whether Zola would be mad over my accepting the bull deal. It wasn't a conspiracy on my part—and if Wendell wanted out of the deal, I'd let him go. But somehow if we could find a string of real buckers, then Gator and I might have a good moneymaker.

Could Gator Bledsoe and I put the pieces together? We knew as much as most operators. Money obviously wouldn't stand in our way. When I closed my eyes, I tried to think of all the details I needed to go over with Johns. Handing me a bank account was fine, but I'd never be satisfied spending it without going over every expenditure with him. I'd make sure to do just that.

My gritty eyelids opened to the glaring light again. I stared at the red-and-white can on the table top. Zola's reaction really ground at my guts. I didn't want to lose her, bad as I wanted the chance to prove myself in this bull deal. Still perplexed, I tossed the aluminum can in the recycle bin. Time for bed—this all could be straightened in the morning. I hoped.

Chapter 25

"How could you?"

I didn't want to open my eyes. It was daylight outside the drawn shades of the rig and the irate voice in my ear was Zola's. My mind was not in gear. I bit my tongue to keep from telling her, It had been easy. Instead, I let her fume and fuss on her end of the phone line.

"Brad Turner, are you there?" she demanded, out of breath.

"Yes."

"Then answer me!"

"What would you like to know?"

"You and my father—behind my back! You're in the bull business now?"

"Well, we have two bulls—"

"Two bulls already? Did he have you up all night buying them? He's a slave driver. Oh, Brad, if only you'd asked me."

"Asked you what?"

"How impossible he is to work for!"

"Sounded like a businessman to me who wanted to get in the bucking bull business."

"No! No! He wants in my life. Don't you understand? He's never happy until he runs everything."

"Running the bull business?"

"No, your life, damn it!"

"Easy, easy. He's not buying my soul. We're partners."

"You'll see."

"I didn't hire on to be his errand boy."

"He'll have you under his thumb, I'm telling you. Tell him no. Send back the money—oh, Brad, please?"

"Zola, will you listen—"

"No!" The phone went dead. Tossing back the covers, I threw my legs off the bed and considered the worst-case scenario. She'd call me back in ten minutes and talk sense or else she'd never talk to me again. That hurt, but I was not some teenaged boy who could be torn away from a deal that would further my career.

With a hard yawn, I wondered what it would be— ten minutes or never? I padded barefooted up front and started a pot of coffee in the white plastic machine. Shoat raised up on the couch and shook his head gingerly, like it hurt.

"Morning already, huh?"

I gave a solemn nod. "And it hasn't kicked off that good."

"Trouble?"

"Made a deal yesterday that has Zola all upset."

"Women can sure be a problem." He mopped his face in his palms and then he shook his head as if to dismiss the idea. "Can't live with them or without them."

"Guess we're experts on that," I said, still perplexed about Zola's anger. There had to be a way to convince her—but she knew her father better than I did.

"I'm taking a shower," Shoat asked.

"Go ahead. I'll rustle something up for breakfast."

He nodded and disappeared into the bathroom. The refrigerator light popped on when I opened the door and highlighted the bacon and the egg carton. I took them out and turned on the burner. A Teflon-lined skillet soon covered the blue flames and I stripped out the slices from the package.

There had to be some way to reason out Zola's reaction. Why was she so against the idea? A super bull deal could be profitable and also further my career. Rich people invested their money in lots of different ways. They bought sports teams, cutting horses, racehorses, show cattle, and lots more. If her old daddy wanted bucking bulls, why couldn't he be the one to finance the deals? I had the eggs whipped into a froth and the skillet sprayed with cooking oil when the cellular rang on the counter.

"Brad?"

"Gator, what's up?"

"Found us three bulls to look at in Nebraska."

"They good ones?"

"A pro contractor carried them last year. He couldn't meet this guy's price."

"Must be high." I cradled the phone on my shoulder and added the eggs to the skillet.

"He wants us to come look at them."

"What's the price range?" Where was the plastic spatula? I rifled drawers in the cabinet, finally discovering it.

"I think ten grand a piece."

"I'll call the man today." With a fork, I turned the browning bacon in the sizzling grease in the second pan.

"What should I tell the seller?"

"Tell him we're considering. There a place up there to buck them out?"

"I'll find out. Hey, I need to run up to Kansas and look at them wheat pasture calves today, so I won't be back until late."

"Drive careful. We can talk in the morning."

"Fine. Zola there?"

"Off barrel racing."

"Oh."

"See you." No sense my explaining the situation to Gator over the phone.

Wendell Johns's receptionist answered the private number he gave to me.

"Is Mr. Johns available? Brad Turner here."

"I'll see, Mr. Turner."

Wendell came on the line. "Hello, Brad, how's the rodeo going?"

"Smooth so far. I haven't fallen off my horse."

He laughed on the other end. "What's on your mind?"

"There's three bulls up in Nebraska. Owner says they're good, but they have a hefty price tag."

"Too much?"

"No, not if they're good."

"Let's go look at them. We can be up there in thirty minutes in my jet, if we can find an airport close by."

"When are you free?"

"Friday?"

"Can we put down in northern Oklahoma and pick up my man?"

"Sure."

"How many passengers can we fly?"

"Half-dozen."

"Good. If they have a place, we can buck the bulls.

I'll get some guys from our end here to ride them. It's always good to have someone with the skills to try them."

"What will they cost?"

He caught me off guard. I planned to load some bull riders in his jet and call it a favor to them. "A hundred-dollar bill would make them grin."

"Cheap enough. You're the man with the expertise. I would have thought they'd wanted a big fee."

"Rodeo's a close-knit family. Not many of us can command superstar prices for a job. Besides that, this will be an adventure for most of the guys."

"Looks like the weather up there will be all right. I just checked on my computer. Fly out of Alliance at eight A.M.?"

"My crew will be there."

"Hangar three."

I managed to turn the scrambled eggs, though they were a little brown. Shoat was dressed and making toast. "We'll be there."

"Friday at eight or you'll call."

"Yes. Have a good day."

"Sounds like fun. You do the same."

The phone clicked and I turned to Shoat. "You ever rode a private jet plane?"

"I ain't flown in nothing."

"After Friday, you won't say that again. I've got to call Gator."

"Jet-plane ride? Where to?" Shoat made a face.

"Nebraska."

"What's up there?"

"A couple bulls to ride."

I dialed Gator's number. "Hey, the man wants to fly up there in his jet. We'll pick you up a little after eight out at the Woodbury airport. Line up the bulls at a place to buck them. I'll bring the riders. You'll need to get a van at the airport to meet us."

"Whew," Gator gushed. "You've got a meal ticket. We have time for Grady to interview the jet pilot? He'll want it on the front page of the *Gazette*."

I laughed, amused. Grady Moore ran the weekly newspaper and he always was looking for something exciting to put on the front page. "No, tell him next time."

"He'll be there with his camera anyway." Gator broke into laughing hard.

"Don't drive off the road going to Kansas," I warned him.

"I might—"

"Friday, unless I call you."

"I may have the high-school band out there," Gator managed to tease. "I'll get it done somehow and put it on your message service if I can't get you."

"Great. Be careful."

"I will." He hung up, still laughing at his plot.

"Line up another bull rider to go along," I said to Shoat. "I'll get a bullfighter."

"Man, you mean he's taking a jet plane up there? Getting Gator on the way and then going to Nebraska?"

"We'll be back for lunch, too."

"Holy cow, Brad, that amazes me!"

The phone rang. I looked at the ceiling for heaven's intervention. If it was Zola, I hoped she'd reconsidered. With a heart filled with dread I punched it on.

Sniff. "Brad?"

"Yes?"

"I know this bull business must intrigue the heck out of you. But, he's such—"

"Zola, how can it hurt us?"

"Oh, he'll have you doing this and that. Soon he'll have more of you—"

"Zola, listen. I'm not marrying him." With a frown, I shook my head at her hardheadedness.

"He gets into everything I do."

"Maybe, because he's your father."

"I'm not a teenager. I'm thirty-one years old."

"Dang, I thought you were eighteen."

"Don't patronize me."

"Where are you?"

"South of Denver, headed for Arizona."

"Slow down. There's plenty of room in our lives for this bull deal. Besides, I like him."

"I was afraid of that. I never wanted you to meet him."

"Why?"

"Because you were mine and not his."

"Zola, drive careful please. This cowboy is yours and he's worried you're stretching yourself too much."

"I will go slower. I've plenty of time."

"Good. Call me this afternoon."

"I will—I miss you."

"Miss you, too. Keep your mind on that white line."

"I will, Brad, I promise."

With a click, I closed my eyes. *Dear Lord, protect her. Hold her in Your hand.*

By the time I finally sat down, my eggs and bacon had turned cold. I dressed them with salsa from a jar that Shoat had placed on the table. Slowly chewing each bite, I tried to think of all the arrangements I needed to make.

We'd have to hustle Friday morning to get around and out to Alliance north of Fort Worth by eight.

Strange how life went. Trails that you rode forked

when you least expected them to. A new opportunity arose that only the day before you never anticipated. Still I needed to steel myself; rich folks could get tired of their frivolous games as easily as they got into them. My new venture was like the bucking stock a competitor drew at a rodeo. You might not have the best one, but you needed to ride him to the maximum of your ability. That was the way I planned to operate the bull business—as good as I knew how. Then let the cow chips fall where they might plop. If those bulls were duds—it would be a lesson for my new partner. But I'd been to big deals before that turned out to be one of those stories where only the mouse crawled out.

On TV, the weather girl talked about the East Coast, and when she went to her partner, he showed that the temperature in Grand Island, Nebraska, was a high of only ten degrees. It drew a shiver under my shirt; Shoat, in his jumper, nodded, grim-faced.

"We better dress warm," he said. "I'll go feed and water Boy. Anything else?"

"That's enough. You ever quit me, I'll have to hire help."

"Hey, I appreciate it."

"Shoat, you want wings, you fly. Hear me?"

"I will."

Over my third cup of coffee, I looked out the front windshield, drapes swept back. Sunshine glinted off the leafless trees, vehicles, and trailers around the rig. It would warm into the sixties by afternoon. The notion of Nebraska's deep freeze made me shiver. Whew. Why, the elms were already trying to leaf out down here.

A black-and-white pulled up and a full-faced officer

climbed out and came to the rig, accompanied by a woman officer.

"Morning," they said and introduced themselves. They accepted my offer to come inside and took down all I knew about last night's fight. I never offered to let them talk to Shoat, who was down at barn three tending to Boy and no doubt helping Chester. They finally thanked me and left.

Then Gail Roach, a short brunette out of the rodeo's publicity staff, brought a reporter over.

"Brad, this is Neada Hocolm," she announced. "She wants to interview you for the paper."

Neada looked to be sixteen. But when I studied the thin girl in a wind suit at a closer distance, I actually realized that she was older. Her face was too narrow to be pretty, but her brown eyes were large and she used makeup well.

"Have a chair," I said as I quickly collected up my breakfast dishes. "Coffee?"

She shook her head and arranged her long narrow spiral pad and pen on the table before shrugging out of her blue windbreaker.

"I must say your entrance into the rodeo each night is different than most announcers. Have you always done it that way?"

"Three years ago, I found Golden Boy and tried it out."

"Here?"

"No, in Jackson. Some arenas don't have the spots and lighting."

"I understand. Golden Boy is the palomino you ride?"

"He's a registered quarter horse."

"Where did he come from?"

I began to tell her about my gift and her bony fingers scribbled the words on her pad.

"He was some gift," she said, impressed. "I came to get a story about you. But I think our readers would love this, too."

"Well, Boy is theirs, too."

"You mean he belongs to the fans?"

"Of course, all of us belong to them. We all work to perform. The cowboys and cowgirls, stock contractors, bucking stock, announcers—we all belong to the people who buy the tickets. Sure, rodeo sponsors help, but they only come along if the fans come and enjoy themselves."

"I listened and realized you must have a mic on the horse. The drum of his hooves—his effort is all on the PA, too, isn't it?"

"Wow, not many folks figure that out. Yes, he's wired for sound."

"It sure gives fans in the stands the sensations that they are riding him around the arena."

"I should let you talk to my regular sound man. He suggested the mic and added it to the opening."

"What's his name?"

"Swing Michaels. We were afraid we could get messed up trying to talk while riding hard at the same time. So the sound effects of Boy were added to the entry."

"Will you announce this year in Vegas?"

"That's up to the finals' qualifiers voting."

"Politics?"

"Don't that make the whole world go 'round?"

She smiled at me and shook her head. "No wife?"

"No, are you interested?"

She blushed and we both laughed.

"It wouldn't be a very great life. You move every weekend. Sometimes I don't get back home for weeks, and I have to depend on friends to do my chores."

"I take it there's no woman in your life?"

"Let's not put that in the paper." I reached over and put my hand on hers. She nodded. "There's one. We're trying to work out all this shuffling, so it fits the both of us."

I couldn't even talk about Zola and not get a knot in my belly. Whew, I had a bad case that must be growing worse. We chatted more about the rodeo until Shoat came back; he snatched his hat off for her as she stood to leave.

"She wants some pictures of Boy. He's the star today. Why don't you show her over there," I asked Shoat.

"Thanks, Brad," she said and zipped up her wind suit. I watched them stroll toward the barn.

By three o'clock that afternoon, my crew for Nebraska was all lined up; Randy Holt, one of the Fort Worth Rodeo bullfighters; Greg Nance, a pro rider who was staying over until Saturday, joined the team, and Shoat and Chester, who didn't want to miss the plane ride for the world. Gator had confirmed the deal. Counting him, that made six of us. From the barn, I phoned Wendell to let him know the size of my force. He suggested that we have two vans since the pilot and copilot would probably want to go along to see the action, too.

"May need a bus," I said as a joke and we agreed on the time again.

I left word on Gator's answering service to rent two vans for the crew. Shoat and I were trimming the ends of Boy's mane when the phone rang. It was Zola.

"I'm in Albuquerque," she announced.

"You staying the night?"

"Yes. You know Mader Lane?"

"Yes."

"I'm staying out at her place. She's got a nice barn, and Thunder is doing just fine."

"Good. I'll feel better about that."

"Brad—I miss you."

"Me, too."

"Hey, do you think we can ever work this out?"

"We will, Zola, we will."

"I can be in Oklahoma by Monday night."

"Drive slower, I'll be there."

"But for how long?"

"I have the next weekend off."

"Great! See you Monday night."

"You drive careful, hear me?"

"Yes—" There was a long pause. "Brad, I love you."

"Me, too, Zola. Me, too."

Chapter 26

Dressed for the arctic with their war bags all piled around them, my crew prepared in the forty-degree air to board Johns's corporate jet. The pilot, Mark Simms, and his copilot, Lacy Killian, were busy stowing the cowboys' gear in the compartments. Wendell wore a fur-collared goosedown coat and an expensive black felt hat with a diamond stick pin in the hatband. I had brought along my red-brown insulated coveralls to put on when we landed and my sweat-stained working hat.

Wendell used a pocket-sized digital camera to take shots of the event. Satisfied that his bags were stowed Randy Holt, the bullfighter, went up the steps. Wendell explained the camera's ability to Shoat and Randy while I ducked to enter the plane's cabin. I took the right front seat across from Wendell after discussing the pickup of Gator at Woodbury International.

"You reckon Gator will be there?" Chester asked.

"He might have a brass band waiting," I said, teasing, but really not knowing what to expect.

The takeoff went smooth and we zoomed out of Alliance with a quick view of the big race-car track under us. We dropped down in what seemed like only minutes and swooped into the small municipal airport north of Woodbury. When Simms pulled the jet up to the passenger depot, I saw the red uniforms of the Woodbury High School band. They were playing some Sousa march music. Grady took several flash pictures of the copilot and Gator before they hurried aboard and the door was shut. Wendell had taken more shots with the digital camera, a huge smile plastered on his face.

"Some homecoming," Wendell said, shaking Gator's hand.

"We sure don't get many real jets at Woodbury," Gator said.

"Oh, your plane is going to be the centerpiece on the front page of the Woodbury weekly tomorrow," I said to Wendell as Simms swung the jet around and we were off to Nebraska.

Still chuckling, Wendell shook his head. "How did he get the band out for that?"

"Listen," Gator said. "They've been getting donations out of me for years. I told Mr. Pollack, the band director, it was my time to collect. Besides, them kids need out of class every once in a while for a break."

Wendell was still laughing when we soared off to Nebraska. A little after eight-thirty, we climbed off the aircraft and ducked into the small airport reception area. Snow was piled all around the runways and field. The north wind wanted to rip apart my coveralls.

A tall rancher in a green-quilted coat met us. Jim Swenson stood well over six feet tall and shook our hands. Clean-shaven, he looked to be in his forties; his fair-complected face was red from the biting wind. He went around and met the crew.

"We'll be going out to Slewcowski's arena. It's about five miles from here. The bulls are out there already and we shouldn't hold you here long," he said.

"Oh, we've got those vans warmed up outside for you, too."

"Thanks," I said as Wendell and I headed for the front door after him.

"What, no band?" Wendell asked over his shoulder and everyone laughed.

"We ain't got Gator up here to arrange for it," the bullfighter said.

We set off to the arena.

The three bulls had enough size. We examined them in the indoor pens under some dull incandescent lights. Swenson listed them as three and four years old. He handed us printouts on the bulls.

The one branded with a 7 on his right hip, he called Midnight Last. A crossbred bull, he was the shortest of the three, with plenty of scars on his hide despite the winter hair. I noticed on the sheet that he was a spinner. Usually went right, and it was best to use a left-hand gate for him. He had been the top bull of the year in a Midwest amateur rodeo association two years before and went unridden. The pro boys had ridden him some the past summer. Ten trips out, and two were first and second place rides. The rest were buckoffs, but I didn't recognize those names as top hands.

The next bull was tall with a simmental white face. They called him Big Ox and he wore a 56 brand. Billie Brett had scored ninety-two points on him his first time out at a pro rodeo. They'd underlined that stat with red on the sheet. However that was the first trip, and the rest of the time he'd had buckdowns, except for a third place at a county fair late in the summer. It was an eighty score. I figured hauling the big bull might have worn him out. He'd bear watching. These bulls hadn't been bucked in several months and looked feed-yard slick. I would have liked a photo of them when they finished the season. They'd sure mended, but some bulls hauled and maintained their condition; others didn't.

The third bull wore a set of tipped horns, and he acted like he could use them. A little more ear, the brindle-hided bovine looked like he'd be a lot more comfortable in Texas than Nebraska. His *X13* brand served as his handle. He had five scores over eighty on his sheet and three buckdowns in his summer campaign. Made me smile. These bulls had been out about ten times. Even at eight seconds a ride, they'd worked a minute and half total, give or take, throwing riders. Tough life.

The help had the first bull, Midnight Last, chuted. Shoat put his rope on him. Swenson threaded a flank rope around the animal while Gator pulled his rope tight.

"He'll fall to the right and spin. You'll have to distract him out of it at the end," Swenson directed the bullfighter as I studied the arena through the bars under the dull lights. With no heat on inside, our breath made little clouds.

"What do you think?" Wendell asked quietly.

"My first thought? Overpriced. These bulls have not been used much."

"Oh?"

I shook my head. "He must have hauled them to these rodeos, rather than have the contractor pull them mixed with his stock. They never bucked twice in a weekend. Say, out on Thursday and again on Saturday."

"What does that all mean?"

"They haven't been really campaigned with."

Wendell nodded as Shoat prepared to ride. They jerked the gate and Midnight tossed him hard to the right, and as expected, took up a spin. It was a furious move and Shoat rode him like a snap clothespin on a sheet. At six seconds, he jerked his rope, threw up his leg and rolled off like it was another day at the office. The girl upstairs looking at her stopwatch blew her whistle.

I shook my head slightly to Wendell. "That won't get twenty points at a pro bull show."

"You mean?"

"Each judge has twenty-five points to award a bull, the same to the rider. We need twenty-one to twenty-three point bulls before we buy."

Wendell nodded. He rubbed his leather gloved hands together. Gator joined us. He leaned on the fence. "Sorry guys, that one ain't no real tornado."

"Hey, we haven't seen them all," I said. "I told Wendell we'd have to look at lots of them to get the string we want."

Wendell nodded to Gator. "Are there any good bulls in Florida to go look at?"

"If so, I'll find some," he promised and turned back as Swenson standing behind the chute told the bullfighter how Big Ox would go.

"What about this one?" Wendell asked. "Big Ox?"

"I'm worried he's a big baby. Be hard to haul, maybe. He's sure not seasoned."

"I wondered about that, too," Gator agreed. "You get these bulls on the road and you can haul the guts out of them."

Wendell nodded, so I didn't bother to explain that not only did a bull need to buck, he had to be up to traveling. Greg Nance was getting ready and Shoat was pulling his rope for him. The competitor from Tennessee could ride the tough ones as well as Shoat. A few years older than the kid, he was seasoned enough to ride the tall bull—unless he put on a great show.

The dull lights from overhead glared in the dusty air and made it feel no warmer than a meat locker. The two men readied themselves at the gate as Chester joined us. Nance nodded and the white-faced bull launched sky-high and made a far jump into the arena. His butt over his head, he danced into another towering leap and that time loosened Nance enough that Randy ran in, shouting at the bull to distract him. The bull went sideways for Randy and flung Nance away. Nance picked himself up and hurried to the fence, but the bull went out of the pen like a docile cow.

"He score enough?" Swenson shouted at me.

"Good bull," I said, and my cohorts agreed.

"Wonder how long he'd hold up doing that?" Chester asked.

I nodded. "That's my concern. He's been babied."

They had the last toro in the chute, and I was wondering whether I wanted the first two at any price. Shoat was getting ready for X13.

"Tell him to watch them horns," I said as Gator started over there.

"I will."

"What's he asking for them?" Simms asked, jamming the webs of his fingers into his gloves.

"Ten thousand apiece."

"Man, bulls are high."

"Only the cream of the crop are that high," I said in a low voice.

It had been a long trip for the listing and no doubt

expensive in terms of the jet. I could tell Gator was not overly impressed with the choices, either. Shoat took a deep seat and nodded. The bull called X13 exploded like a rocket. He went higher and dove sideways. Here was a bull on fire and by his second toss, Shoat left his back and flew in the other direction. I could see the admiration in the boy's eyes as he stood unsteady for a second in his boots and watched the bull go two more bucks. Then when X13 came around looking for something to bulldoze, Shoat threw his hat in the angry critter's face. X13 gave him two mad head tosses and snorted at Randy before he shot out of the pen.

"That's a twenty-plus bull," I said to Wendell.

"Well. What do you think?" Swenson asked, coming over to the fence where we all stood.

"Five thousand for the last one," I said.

"No, I can't take that for him."

"He's the best one," I said, "but there's lots of other bull buyers."

"What would you give for all three?"

"Midnight Last is worth about twelve hundred for me to make any money on him. I'm afraid of the simmental. He won't stand any hard hauling. The last bull would do, but he's not a finals bull yet. It would take two years of hard hauling to earn him a reputation. I figure it's fifty-fifty in two years, if he still has that much fire left in him."

"I would take twelve grand for him alone," Swenson counteroffered.

I shook my head. "Sixty-five hundred."

"You came a long ways. That simmental will be bucking just as hard a year from now."

"You want to guarantee that?"

He shook his head. "Bob Ray will pay more than that for him."

That was a ploy to get me committed. Bob Ray bought lots of bulls, but he was smart. I doubted he would be fooled.

"You can call Gator if you want to sell the X13 bull. We sure thank you for your time."

We were back in the vans headed for the airport when Shoat spoke up. "He's pretty proud of them bulls."

"You think they were high-priced?" I asked.

"Lord, yes. Why, those bulls must have been eating so much corn silage and getting fat that they couldn't buck any harder than that."

"I liked the last one."

"He was good, but like Jasper Northcutt used to say about them feed-yard bulls, if he needs that much gas in his tank to buck, I can't afford him."

"Northcutt is a small contractor that Shoat used to work for," I explained to Wendell.

"Well, I sure thank everyone," he said from the front seat. "It was educational for me."

"For all of us. Next time we're going to look at bulls in South Texas or Florida during the winter," I promised them.

Chapter 27

Shoat drew an ordinary bull in Friday night's performance. Scored seventy-six points, too far down to win anything. His best hope was getting into the short-go on Saturday night with the top twelve. We were down to the last match. Hayden Smithson had drawn a bull called Noodles. Since Saturday night would be a sellout and also a televised event, I told those who could not get in to watch the short-go on their sets at home the following week. Smithson was the only one who could knock Shoat out of his place in the final go.

The barrel man Jinx Malone staged a fight with a teddy bear that had the kids laughing. Twice the gatemen were ready, but Smithson needed to repull his rope. Noodles, a big charolais, was a handful but a sure top-money ride if you could straddle him for eight. Smithson finally nodded and the white bull blew up. The bull's bell clapping like a fire truck, Noodles mixed it up for the cowboy. At the four-second mark Smithson's feet flew up and I knew then that Shoat would be in the final round.

"Ladies and gentlemen, give that Oklahoma cowboy your applause. He came and tried the tough one. No disgrace to be bucked down by that bull. That white bull's as hard and tough to ride as they come. You need to let him know you appreciated his effort, Fort Worth."

Soon, the flag bearers came in two by two and split on both sides to circle the pen. Boy hunched up under me as I said, "Good night," and the fireworks overhead sent trails of red sparklers down upon us.

In the alleyway, I leaned over and shook hands with several officials.

"Good show tonight, Brad."

"Yeah, nice job."

The compliments were always appreciated and I always acted polite and grateful. I signed a few programs for some kids on the fence. Chester came and straddled the top rail, shaking his head. "Shoat left with Mona. Said for you not to wait up."

"He know that he's in the short-go tomorrow?"

"I think so. Damn, that girl is poison."

"Maybe worse than that for him."

Chester agreed, swung a long jean-clad leg over the fence, and dropped to his feet. He waved over his shoulder. "Thanks, I sure enjoyed the trip today."

"Hey, it was enlightening." I rode Boy back to his stall and began unsaddling him. It had been a long day after a short night. Maybe I had jet lag. I turned with the saddle in my hand and almost mowed down a woman in a fur jacket.

"Excuse me," I said close to being embarrassed.

A small smile crossed her full lips. Then under the yellow light my heart stopped. Stormy? No, it couldn't be her. But there was my ex, standing in front of me, blocking my way. She wore a gold blouse that housed her ample bustline and a long black skirt that was split up the side. A necklace of gold blocks in a keystone cut lay around her neck. Her hair was curly and in her face. She pushed it back and to the right.

"Hey there, Brad. Doing well?"

"Yes. You live here?"

"Not at the coliseum," she said.

"I meant in the area."

She nodded as if in deep concentration about something unsaid. "You never remarried?"

"No." I resented her asking me that. One thing for certain, the reason I hadn't remarried was not because I'd been so forlorn over losing her.

"You don't drink anymore?" She looked at the ground and shook her head like she could not fathom my sobriety.

"You hire a detective?" I shifted the saddle in my hands. It grew heavy, but I wasn't about to admit anything to her. Not one snitch of any satisfaction for her in any way. I'd spent seven years hating her guts for what she did to me.

"You're a big rodeo announcer now. My, my, your life is an open book. And I heard your grandfather died. Sorry—I liked him."

"So what are you doing here?"

"I live up at Plano. You should come by. I have horses. Some good barrel prospects."

"You riding them?"

"Of course."

"I meant are you riding them on the circuit?"

"No . . ."

"I see."

"You don't see a damn thing. You didn't see anything back when we were together and you don't see now."

"So what are you doing?" I asked, ignoring her trying to bait me into an argument. "Married again?"

"Divorced," she said in a small voice that shocked me.

"You're good at that—" I didn't see the slap coming. It burned into my face and I felt the hot flash of lightning go up from my jaw through my cheek.

"I didn't mean to—I'm sorry—I came to talk to you." Tears began to gather in her thick lashes and she shrank back.

Holding the saddle with extended arms I began, "We could always find a reason to fight. I never had that experience with anyone else in my life."

She shook her head as if that wasn't the point. "I have a son from my second marriage. He's five, and I told him I knew that cowboy on the palomino in the rodeo. A real one who'd come and ride with him. He has a pony. Would you?"

"Don't have much time left. Maybe in the morning. Could you draw me a map? I doubt I could haul Boy out there."

"You could ride one of our horses."

"Draw me a map, and I'll do that for your boy. But I'll need to get back here right after lunch."

She smiled. "I promise my best behavior." Then she crossed her heart. "Cheyenne will like that. Really, he was so excited when you rode in and I said I knew you."

I simply nodded.

"Thanks," she said sweetly, shoved a crudely drawn map in my shirt pocket and turned to leave. I watched her shuffle through the fresh shavings and for a minute I wanted to change my mind. But no, I would go meet her son. For him, not for her—I'd do that much.

So I rose early, checked on Boy, and drove north to Plano in my pickup. I hoped Shoat would drive the pickup home for me when the rodeo was over. No telling what his plans were—he hadn't showed up at the rig overnight, so I suspected he was still with Mona.

The map was clear enough and I pulled into the circle drive between two towering red-brick posts at ten after eight. The dwelling looked big enough to house an army. Wide second-story dormers signified many rooms behind them, and the five-car garage looked like overkill.

A bobtailed blue heeler and two pointer bird dogs came running around to bark at the intruder. But soon enough they acted glad to see me and danced all over as I stepped out of the door and put my Justins on the concrete driveway. Stormy had herself a real castle, one of those slick magazine models full of every gadget they made last year. The landscape even had a new look.

"Brad, this is Cheyenne. Cheyenne, this is Mr. Turner."

The silver braces on his legs caught my eye as he waded over to me. He swept off his cowboy hat and stuck out his hand. "Pleased to met you. I love your horse."

"Sorry I couldn't bring Boy. Your mama says you have a pony."

"His name's Wildfire."

"Good name."

"Chy, why don't you take him back there and show him his horse to ride."

"I will," the little fellow agreed and started with effort for the gate. I wanted to scoop him up and carry him, but I saw her closed lips and the small shake of her head.

"Let him walk," she said under her breath, reading my first impulse to carry him.

"Mr. Turner, you get to ride Sam Elliot."

"I bet I like him."

He stopped and looked up at me. "He's not your gold horse."

"I bet I can ride him just fine."

"I hope so. I do like your palomino horse."

"He's a good one. Next year, you come to the rodeo. You can ride him before the show."

"Can I?" The kid was sure excited about the prospect.

"Sure can."

"There's Sam." He pointed. "That's Wildfire." He undid his reins and led the pony beside some stairs. "I can make it fine." He went around and made his way up on the stoop. Wildfire waited with the patience of much training. I checked the cinch and stepped up on the big bay gelding.

"Who taught Wildfire to stand there?" I asked the boy, checking the big horse.

"My mother did."

I waved at her and she motioned for us to go on. With Wildfire's jog to match the bay's stride, we took the disced-up trail. The boy could ride, braces and all; he was a horseman and had obviously spent many hours in the saddle. We rode over the hill and through some cedar groves and finally back in sight of the house.

Accompanied by the three dogs that found plenty to point and chase, we talked about team ropers and how Cheyenne intended to be a good one. I never doubted the little guy's determination, or the time someone had spent with him, teaching him. He was good as anyone could be with those braces. It wasn't easy for my ex to tell me not to carry him; she had the same problem. She knew. Damn, all the bad things I said about her over the years, she at least had treated her son right. I bit my tongue and let the upset in my guts pass.

"Let's race," he said.

"You race all the time?"

"Sure."

"You ever fall off?"

He looked up at me and nodded, his freckle-sprayed face and his green eyes shining. "But I always get up."

"Race, then!" I shouted and let him have a head start. The slick pony ran flat-out for the gate which opened into the pasture. Cheyenne bent over him and urged him on. I let the bay single-foot after him until, at last, he reached the backyard and waved his cowboy hat for me to come on.

He handed the reins to his mother and waded off toward the house. She was standing there when I loped Sam in. I dropped out of the saddle and undid the latigos.

"He's some cowboy," I said and turned. "His father never rode with him?"

"No."

"I told him next year he could ride Boy. Bring him down there."

"How will I live with him this year?"

"We all need things to look forward to." I wet my lips and gazed across the brown, rolling Texas countryside.

"I looked forward to seeing you."

"Me, too, I guess," I said with a sigh. "Though we never did make a good match."

"I take it there's someone in your life?"

"Someone, yes. But the offer to Cheyenne is still good."

"I want him to have a father. He needs a man."

I dropped my gaze to the dead grass, then looked up at her. "He needs the good care you have given him. You making certain that he walked and rode, that he'd be self-sufficient. That's powerful medicine. Even if you don't find someone who's willing to share his life with the two of you, Cheyenne will be fine. He's the biggest little man I've ever met." I shook my head to clear it. "He'll make you proud some day."

"He needs a man."

"Hire a cowboy to be around the place, then."

"You don't think he needs a father?"

"I think he still has one—somewhere."

"He won't ever do anything for him—oh, damn it, Brad Turner, why did you come out here, anyway?"

"To meet your son and ride with him."

She bowed her head, shamed. "You've done that and I thank you."

"No, it was my privilege. Bring him to the rodeo next year."

"I will." She threw her head back and fought the thick curls away from her face. "God bless you, Brad Turner."

To those words I could only nod, ignoring her silvery wet eyes while I took my leave.

Chapter 28

Where was Shoat? I crossed the grounds for the barn with him on my mind. Inside, I found Boy and he nickered to me. Shoat hadn't been there to brush him, so I led him out to do a quick cleanup and saddle him. Chester came in with my saddle in his arms.

"You seen the kid?" I asked.

"Nope. You go look for him?"

"No, I went up to Plano and rode with a little boy in braces this morning."

"Teeth braces?"

"No, leg braces—but he can ride. Tough little man."

"Really?"

"It's a long story." I told him about my ex, how I'd resented her for so long, and all about Cheyenne.

"Sounds to me she's done a heckuva job," Chester said and I agreed.

With Boy saddled and ready, I put him back in the stall to go catch a sandwich in the rig before I rode him over to the coliseum. It was down to the wire. Finals night in Fort Worth and we were ready. Sellout crowd to whoop and holler, it would be a fun night to be an announcer.

The diet soda and the sandwich I fixed would fill a void inside of me. Chester came by and fixed himself one, too, at my invitation. He had three head of Johnny's stock going out in the last performance.

"Wish Shoat was here," Chester complained, putting squirt mayonnaise on his bread with both hands.

"I do, too. But he's a big boy."

"Lordy, we jimmed that taco car and figured he'd have a real chance not to be all compromised by his relatives. Then she had to show up." He dressed some ham up with mustard and added cheese slices like he owned the factory. *Don't complain,* I told myself, *you invited him to supper.* There was no way to fill that giant up, anyway. He added enough lettuce to make a chef salad and, satisfied with his mammoth production, sat down with a beer across from me.

"Why're we worrying about him?" he asked, then took a large hunk out of the sandwich.

"Guess we like him."

"Damn pup," Chester swore, and shook his head, holding the monster sandwich in both hands. "I swear I thought he was shed of her."

"She can sure mess up his mind." Maybe this time, he'd survive. Just when he managed to get his head screwed on right, somehow she distracted him so badly, that he couldn't ride a sawhorse.

"Guess we'll see," Chester said between mouthfuls.

Though unspoken between us, I knew we both felt the same—the bull ride would be a disaster. What a waste and shame. The notion tempered my enthusiasm for the night's show. All the things I enjoyed, full house, top competitors, the best stock from five rodeo companies—made me shudder, because I knew the most talented rookie in pro rodeo was headed for a goose egg.

Where was he? I ought to go use the toe of my

Justin on him. Then I settled back. Shoat Krammer would either learn, or be a falling star sputtering out in the sky. You couldn't beat a competitive spirit into someone. He either wanted to grasp that brass ring and fly or sit back and watch the merry-go-round spin without him. Somehow I couldn't believe that Shoat didn't have the ambition to be in that big winner's circle. Better quit worrying about him and get ready myself.

"See you later," I said getting up. "You can lock her up when you leave."

Chester swallowed his beer and waved what was left of his sandwich at me. "I'll do it. Gracias for the meal. Sure been fun, going to Nebraska like it was a bus ride across town. Hope you and Gator do real well in the bull business."

"Keep an eye open for us."

"Hey, sure will," he said after me. I headed for the barn. Inside, I took Boy out of his stall as someone drove up. I heard a car door slam. When Mona stepped through the door, her eyes flashed with anger.

"Where is he?" she demanded.

I adjusted the stirrup and prepared to mount. "You asking about Shoat? I thought he was with you."

"He in your RV?" she asked.

"No. When did you see him last?"

"Couple of hours ago. He left me in a bar."

"Guess he had business," I said and stepped in the stirrup, and swung into the saddle. With the rein in hand, I checked Boy. "I haven't seen him since he left with you."

"You don't like me, do you?" she said as she lit a long, thin cigarette.

"I wish you would find someone else to bother besides him."

"Bother him!? Mister, I'm the one's been paying his entry fees. I've got a big interest in him, too."

"Every time he's around you, he doesn't concentrate on his business enough to win."

"That's bullshit! He won in Jackson."

"He also got the tar beat of him. Your friends did that."

"They ain't my friends." Then she swore under her breath.

"Weren't his, either."

"Well, Mr. High Pockets, he's mine."

"Maybe, maybe not. Don't look to me like you have him right now." I pushed Boy for the open tall doors.

"I will!" she screamed after me.

Outside, a cool north wind swept my face. Where was Shoat? Did those thugs have him? I hoped not. But there was no way to be certain. Dang, another deal to worry over. Saturday night and I planned hard to enjoy everything. Behind me was a haughty woman and somewhere in the greater Fort Worth area was a cowboy who needed to be getting his backside down to the rodeo grounds.

What else would happen? I rode past the security guard with a smile and said, "Evening."

"It's the last night," he reminded me, and I bobbed my head going in. Boy did a sidestep up the alleyway. Like a great-muscled cat, he was ready to eat up the world. You couldn't fool him, he knew when the time came for us to head back for the bluestem hills. He was one in a million, perhaps ten million. I needed a reserve, but I could always borrow one of Johnny's paint horses. No, I wouldn't go looking for his replacement. Might be like they said about calf ropers carrying a second loop—you never missed roping a calf the first time until you carried a second loop.

Whew, cowboys are a suspicious lot. Why, there must be more superstitious beliefs among cowboys than any other segment of society. I'd heard all my life it was bad luck to eat peanuts at a rodeo. Saw country star Reba McEntire say the same thing on TV. She was raised up rodeoing. And don't put your hat on a bed. That's worse than breaking a mirror. I knew bronc riders would never wear a yellow shirt in competition or who would slide out the passenger side of a pickup from behind the steering wheel. Gator believed that shining your boots was irrevocable bad business. Perhaps I'd done all those things as depressed as I felt, riding up the alleyway to put Boy up until I needed him.

Dismounting, I loosened the cinch and stuck him in with the pickup men's horses. The funny man was checking his sound in the arena. With the two-way radio, I called the sound folks upstairs.

"Sure, that you Brad?"

"Right. You get through with Cecil, I'll test my mics."

"Sure, switch on the horse one now."

Boy made a snort which carried over the sound system. The clown let out a yelp. "Man, I thought he was right behind me," he said with a laugh. "It'll work. Thanks, guys."

I put on the headgear, turned on the switch. "Test, one, two, three. Sound all right?"

"Yes."

"Let's try my backup."

"Sure thing."

"Test, one, two, three. It works." I put it in my saddlebags in case the headset went out. I was covering all the bases—some day, none of them would work and humble me.

"I'm doing the dead cowboy routine," Cecil said, going by in his rainbow outfit. "But you know it."

"I hope so," I said and smiled at him. "Like we did in Utah last year?"

"That's the one," he said over his shoulder.

My recollection of the act—two guys in whites like medics carry this cowboy on a stretcher into the arena. Cecil hollering, "Wait! Wait. Hold the rodeo. There's a man injured down here." Then he asks the stretcher guys a lot of questions, finally says he knows first aid and can doctor this cowboy. After he undresses the guy by reaching under the blanket and tossing out his clothing, the guy jumps up in his red-and-white polka dot boxer shorts and chases them out of the arena. Kids loved it and the crowd got into it, too.

So I went upstairs to check the list of contestants and bucking stock with Ruth, who was the assistant secretary. She was a little chunky in her jeans and a frilly white blouse, but we went back a long ways to the days we both competed. Her full cheeks always shined a little red and her mouth was ready to kiss. Still attractive, she talked big.

"I haven't heard from Krammer." She looked a little peeved.

I shook my head to dismiss her worry. "He'll be here."

"Buck said you would know where he was."

"Shoat will be here unless he's broken his leg." I hoped he would show up even if he had.

"Oh, and be sure to mention this dealership." She handed me a sheet with a letterhead and typing on it. "Somehow, we left him off your list the last two nights. I'm sure he'll be here tonight."

"Sorry."

"Not your fault, but they make deals up in the office

and never tell us, then we catch the flak. I swear we didn't have a word about him before they came down here all headed up about it."

"I'll please him tonight."

She smiled. "You'd please anyone. You still single?"

"You still married?"

She curled her lip. "Yeah, but I'd quit him . . ."

"Liar," I whispered with a wink and she laughed out loud.

"Don't forget the dealership."

"I won't."

The primary stock contractor, Cy Montgomery, met me on the steps. A small man, sixtyish, in a light tan Western-cut suit and tie, he smiled. "Guess I owe you a meal. You missed the cookout."

"Wasn't on purpose. Had to run look at some bulls."

"I heard you were busy. Food wasn't that good, anyway. You ever come to South Texas, you come by and stay at the ranch house. I'd like to discuss you doing a few more rodeos for me."

"Don't know when that would be, Cy, but we can talk on the phone." I started to give him my card.

"I know your number. Next fall, come down and stay a few days. We've got some big trophy bucks down there that need culling."

"Now that might be a deal."

"I'm not doing anything right away—" A cowboy cut through us on his way up the narrow stairs with an "excuse me" and we both told him, "Hi."

"But," Montgomery continued. "I'm not any younger. Miles are getting to me." His steel-blue eyes looked hard at me. "You have the sense to keep an outfit together and the rep, too. You do some thinking on it."

"I will." We shook hands. I was amazed that such a legend would think of me to ramrod his outfit. Wendell Johns's deal had been an ego boost, but he was an outsider to this business. Cy Montgomery was a landmark in pro rodeo; to even be considered as his replacement was flattering to the core.

"I'll call you," he promised and I was off to Boy. Strange how when one thing breaks, a damful of opportunities floods you. Oh, well, I still had a last performance in Fort Worth to do.

The TV cameras were posted around the arena. I'd been over the list of contestants and had enough information on each man for my part. In case my brain slipped a gear, I had the stats on the bucking stock and how the money was figured on some index cards.

"Can Salty Barr ride the Devil Horse?" a television reporter asked me as I readied Boy. I paused and nodded to him. We'd done a few impromptu interviews before other performances.

"Like the cowboys say, there's never been a horse hasn't been rode and never a cowboy hasn't been throwed. That sums up the match. Little doubt the Devil Horse is a tough-enough draw for the veteran cowboy. You hardly ever get a goose egg in the saddle bronc riding with these top boys, but that pony has sure sent some of the best into orbit."

"Who do you like in the bull riding?"

"Matt has a good shot on the Sidewinder bull. Jerry Jones should ride his draw, Leonardo, and if he has his head screwed on, Shoat Krammer can ride Drifter."

"Krammer comes in last?"

"He can ride that bull."

"But he's a rookie."

"You're saying rookies are inconsistent?"

"Yes and—"

"When it's all over, you come tell me. We'll know if the rookie can ride or not."

"He's a friend of yours? This Krammer?"

"Sometimes."

"Turner, I'm going to use that as a pitch for the ten o'clock broadcast. Can a rookie ride the toughest ones. Thanks."

I nodded, then thanked him and the camera man with the lens still in my face.

The production outfit taping the performance wanted some sound bites from me. With twenty minutes left, I went down behind the chutes and sat on the cowboy bench, that area back of the chutes which was still empty of competitors.

The TV commentator came over in his makeup and cowboy hat on the back of his head. We sat side by side and they turned on the bright lights.

"Why is Fort Worth Rodeo so special?" he asked and he pointed the mic at me.

"Look out in front to start with. There, the world's great roper sits on his horse like an archangel and looks over this place and all the fans. That Cherokee grin set on his mouth and those bright eyes twinkling, you can almost hear his slow drawl. The entire world laughed and loved him. He could have been elected president if he'd wanted. His humor and sayings are still with us today."

"You talking about that statue of Will Rogers?"

"Yes. They only made one of him. But he's a lesson we could all study from. He taught us life could be funny, it didn't need to be profane or smutty. Will even taught us to laugh at ourselves."

"They say cowboys are close to God."

I nodded, gathering my thoughts. "Most of us consider the wind his breath and the circling hawks his angels. When we work out on our ranches, there isn't a man-made structure in this world as fine as the cathedral we ride through.

"Cowboys and ranch folks live so close to life and death, the seasons, the droughts, the rainstorms and the rainbows that bow over and touch them. Yes, cowboys ride real close to God."

He nodded in approval as we had finished the bites he wanted. "We need a final curtain closing." He aimed his mic at me again.

"Well, pard, this brings down the curtain on another great Fort Worth pro rodeo. We can stand here on the banks of the Trinity, look northward, and still see the ghostly streams of those thousands of longhorns on the trail to Kansas and the railroad yards at Abilene. See the likes of the Charlie Goodnight, John Blockers, cowboys of every color and denomination, the vaqueros and their sombreros on dancing ponies snapping their bull whips over those cattles' backs. The wagging canvas tops of the chuck wagons as they rocked from side to side on the ruts, powered by half-broke mules, as ready to runaway as the wild cattle in those herds.

"Tonight, we close another chapter in this long-running history of the cowboy here in Fort Worth. May the Good Lord bless and keep you until next year."

"Thanks, Brad. As always, you can find the words."

I nodded thanks and excused myself, headed for Boy. Maybe I was a dreamer. I always appreciated how writers, newscasters, and others put words together. I didn't need to think long, because as an announcer you never have much time. Practice helps, but some folks never find their own. For that instinctive skill I was grateful. It sure saved my life many times.

I stepped in the stirrup and swung the blue-with-gold-fringe chaps over Boy's butt. No sign of Shoat yet. Somewhere under the Arizona stars, Thunder and my woman were getting ready to run the barrels. I liked the sound even as I said it in my head: *my woman.*

Chapter 29

"Ladies and gentlemen—three time Pro Circuit Finals announcer, from Woodbury, Oklahoma—let's give a great Fort Worth welcome to your friend and mine, Brad Turner!"

The gate opened and the powerful muscles between my knees burst into the spotlight. The drum of Boy's hooves on the arena dirt, the creak of leather, and his huffing breath came across the PA system as we made our laps around the arena. Saturday night, Fort Worth, Texas, and I could sense the anticipation of the capacity crowd clapping and cheering loudly. Boy slid on his heels for ten feet.

"Are you ready to rodeo tonight in Fort Worth?"

They shook the rafters and their enthusiasm fed me. "Well, big and little rodeo fans, we have the best of the best here tonight, and this performance is especially planned for you. The contestants fought all week long to make the short go-around. Three hundred and seventy of the best have been here, and out of each event we have invited back the top guns. Twelve competitors from each specialty that have shown how good they are, and we've cut out for them the toughest stock that money can buy to compete on. So sit back and enjoy the toughest sport played on dirt. Fort Worth, let's rodeo!"

Preliminaries went by fast: dignitaries, a prayer, the national anthem. They tore open the bucking gate and we flew through the bareback riding. Team ropers had to be in the six-second range to even get a peek at any money. Steer wrestling flashed by as well and soon enough, the calf roping events were running. After a short run down the arena, a roper would flank a calf, have him half tied before he hit the dirt, then throw his hands skyward to stop the clock. Some amazing performances, but the night was flying by.

We were soon down to bull riding. I'd read over the skipped ad three times and recognized the president of the dealership in his box seat. I saw Ruth upstairs, nodding in approval.

Then I saw Shoat climb up on chute four. Chester was with him and I announced the first man out. Childers rode two seconds before the big crossbred bull sent him flying. Two more good ones missed the buzzer. The bulls must have been sick, the funny man complained, they were throwing up cowboys in epidemic proportions. Two high seventy scores, and we were down to the last rider, the final chance to take home first place in the short-go: Shoat Krammer.

"Here's a Texas cowboy getting ready in chute four. Kinda like the owner of a big football team around here, he came down from those Arkansas hills." It drew some laughter. "And he's drawn a finals bull. I say if we whoop and holler enough, you can encourage him enough to stay on this bull for eight seconds. When they crack that gate let's scream, stomp, and holler at them.

"Here he is on Drifter."

The crowd, taking my cue, was ready when the bull flew out. It danced on his front feet, then slung himself hard to the left. Shoat held his seat and even moved up on his hand. The bull began to bellow even louder than the crowd's screams and shouts. The bell under his belly rang like one on a frantic goat being chased by a coyote. The power of Drifter's twisting jumps became evident when he threw himself back the other way with all the fury of a whirlpool in a mighty river.

Then the buzzer rang above all the noise. Shoat waited until the bull went left to pull his string and kick off. Clowns wanted their chance and they were at Drifter's head, taking the furious bovine away from Shoat's tracks. Out of breath, he climbed a few pipes up and hung over it to get his wind.

"Ladies and gentlemen, scores are coming in. It looks like it is—yes! Eighty-eight points!"

Shoat took his bull rope from the clowns, slapped their high-held hands and waved his hat at the cheering crowd. He nodded to me. I had little doubt he was back on track.

"I can promise you one thing, rodeo fans, you'll be seeing more of that young man."

The curtain came down in a shower of red fireworks spilling over me and the impatient Boy and we rode out after the sponsor flags. Good night, Fort Worth.

Chapter 30

After the rodeo, I only saw Shoat in passing and then lost him in the confusion. I figured he had things to do. So I went back to the barn. I locked my saddle up in the storage under the RV, put Boy in the stall, and was about to finish up when Chester arrived to put up his horse.

"You seen Shoat?"

"Only for a minute. Guess he's big enough to take care of himself."

"Oh, yeah, but I kinda figured he'd come around to see us."

"You talk to him?" I asked.

"Yeah, sure did. He said he seen what was happening and he wanted to make you and me proud of him."

"I sure was."

"Me, too. Man, he rode that big bull tonight like he did in Jackson."

"He mention them thugs being around?"

"Nope."

"It all beats me. Did he say if he planned to drive my pickup back?"

Chester shook his head. "All he told me was that he wanted you and me to be proud of him."

"I'm not half as worried about that now as I am getting the pickup back home."

"Aw, he won't forget."

I hoped not. It was a good seven-hour drive back for it if he didn't. I decided to tell the security man to watch for it, anyway. No need in it being stripped before Gator could bring me back for it.

At the RV, I checked my voicemail. First message: "Guess what? I won a first out here. I'm winging your way, cowboy. Kisses."

I collapsed on the couch and replayed it to hear her voice. My mixed world; Zola out there on the Colorado River; Shoat, heaven knew where; and even worse, I was facing a seven-hour drive home. At that point, home was where I wanted to be more than anything I could think of.

I closed my eyes, and could see myself riding a good horse across the hills to check on a cow close to calving, or on a water gap some angry bull had destroyed. On such days I could be free—free of worries, free of a conscience that ate my soul because that hunk of dirt, grass, and fences wasn't mine any longer. I yearned for that freedom again—like the red-tail hawk soaring on his silent wings, the rocking chair gait between my knees, without a spotlight, and the eternal wind sweeping my whiskerless face.

If I had it to do over, perhaps I wouldn't make all those bad decisions. In my daydreams, I spurred that Hancock horse after a big black-eared jackrabbit. To the drum of hard hooves on the ground, I'd went over the hill, led by the rabbit's zigzag antics to entice us in the chase. At last he would reach a ridge, yards in the lead, rearing up to search for the stragglers and thumb his whiskered nose at our efforts before he went racing away. I'd pull the gelding down to a walk to cool him and we'd go on in a head-swinging gait on our conquest to find that cow or fence break.

Perhaps Zola and I could take such rides together, take the time to experience moments I treasured. I could hear her say, "You're silly." I doubted she'd do that. Could I find the way back to those times? Perhaps not, but I still intended to look for them—with her. Together, yes together.

Soon I would embark on another journey—if she was willing. Lord, Lord help me.

Late Saturday afternoon, I unloaded Boy out of the trailer at home. I put him in the big corral so he could roll and limber his legs. His mane flashing in the low-hanging sun, he ran the pen like we were at work again. I enjoyed watching him; then I headed for the mobile home.

Gator must have piled all the mail and newspapers on my dining-room table. There was the weekly newspaper spread out with Gator waving from the jet's ramp at the camera, and a picture of the band on the airport porch in their bucket hats.

GATOR GOES JET! was the headline and I started laughing. Only Gator Bledsoe could have pulled that off. No one else in the county would have gotten away with it. But all our lives, Gator had set off so many pranks and managed to stay alive and out of jail.

I found a diet soda in the refrig, but the shelves were bare. All the food was in the rig. So I decided since I had no truck and there wasn't anything but a pizza place open on Sunday night in Woodbury, I better go out there and find myself some supper.

Cellular rang. "About time you got home."

"What's happening?" I asked Gator.

"We still in the bull business?"

"Sure."

"Good, we've got four to go look at below Fort Smith this week. Shoat there?"

"No, he's still in Fort Worth I think."

"What's he doing?"

"Gator, I don't know, but he's supposed to drive my pickup back."

"He making the payments?" He laughed.

"He could. He won the short-go in bulls down there."

"Whew! You done him some good."

"Sure, and he's probably back with Mona by now."

"Aw, give the boy a chance."

"I have."

"He'll make you proud yet."

"I'm busting my buttons already. I just hope we don't have to go bring the pickup back."

"We won't."

"Come by in the morning. I'll buy breakfast. I'd hate to drive up to the café in the bus. They might think the Greyhound service was back again."

"Yeah, I recall us coming home on the bus when that truck engine blew up in Nebraska, that first time we competed at Cheyenne. We were real whizzes in those days. Tails between our legs, we came home on that bus like two chicken-eating coyotes."

"Sure, and that bus driver unloading our saddles out from underneath, made a big deal out of it in front of everyone in town. All we lacked was our picture in the paper and the high-school band."

"Hey, I guess we came up in this old world since those days, anyway."

"You have. You can make the front page now and look important," I said, over his hollering. I told him six-thirty was fine, I'd be ready.

*   *   *

Gator showed up at six while I was in the shower. Dripping wet, wrapped in a towel, I unlocked the door for him. He helped himself to my fresh coffee, spread the latest issue of the *Farm Talk* magazine across my kitchen table, and straddled a chair to sit down and read.

"Calves are up a dollar and a half."

"Sounds good," I said from the bathroom while shaving.

"I need to have another bunch of calves to sell."

"You having financial troubles?"

"Naw. I'm just not getting ahead. My long-term plans were to buy some more land this year. Don't look like I'm gonna buy a cow pie."

"And?"

"Makes me mad. I work hard, make some good deal and bang, I'm out money for this and money for that. Latest thing was a rear tractor tire for my big one. You'd die if you knew what one of them cost."

"Lots," I said, drying my face.

"Lots won't even buy one."

"You bought it, though?"

"Had to have it to feed cattle with."

From the closet, I put on a fresh-ironed long-sleeve shirt, snapped up the front, pulled on some starched jeans, and went out to find my belt. Farming was always one episode after the other. You had to engage in what I called "inventive financing."

"I got a feeling Shoat's coming back today. That, or we're going after my pickup."

"Shoat wouldn't do that to you."

"Me? You mean to you, cause you'd have to drive me down there."

"Hey." He folded the tabloid magazine back. "There's a guy down in Oklahoma that raises turnips."

"Turnips? Maybe we can plant this place with them. He making any money?"

"Don't say, but he says sheep get fat on them. They're Scottish turnips."

"Big as bagpipes?" I asked sitting down to put on my socks.

"Can't tell. He says you can grow lots of them per acre."

"Yeah, but how does he harvest them?" Bent over, I pulled on my working ropers. They were a little scuffed and still had some bloodstains on the toes from working Gator's "cheap" cattle the past fall.

"He don't say in here."

"Count me out if you have to pull them."

"Well, dang, how would you unroot them?"

"I remember digging Irish potatoes with a small horse."

"Yeah, we borrowed that pony off that old man on Slater Creek. We sure got rich on that project."

"We'd have made more money if we'd weeded them. Those weeds would have made more potatoes."

Gator bobbed his head, still engrossed in the tabloid. "We gave that widow woman half a truckload for free. Maybe we could have found more poor folk to give them to if we'd had a bigger crop."

"You ready to go or do you want to gripe about that potato deal more?"

"Oh, I'm ready. I never begrudged her them potatoes, just telling you that sometimes you're too good to folks."

"Like Shoat?" I asked, going out the door.

"I like him, but he ain't real dependable. Not bringing your truck back, for example."

"He may bring it back today."

"That's another thing. They didn't give you that truck."

"Gator! Get it off your chest."

"Did we make a bad judgment on that boy?" he asked, hesitating before he climbed in his side.

"No, he's just having problems."

"Problems are fine, but he don't need to have them over a forty-thousand-dollar truck that don't belong to him."

"He'll bring back the truck or—"

"I know. We'll go get it."

He cranked up the diesel engine and we growled off to town. The usual flurry of customers filled the barstools, and everyone looked up to see the two troublemakers arrive. We came by the title honestly when we were growing up.

"Whatcha doing for the cover picture this week, Gator?" Wick Stamps asked.

"Mooning some range cows," Gator said and scowled at the wisecracking man in overalls.

"Why, that ain't nothing new, you been doing that for years," Stamps said, and drew his share of laughs.

We took a booth and Vi, a grandmother in her sixties, brought us two mugs of coffee.

"Don't mind them, Gator," she said. "They're all mad cause you scooped them out of the checkers-game picture Grady planned to run in the paper. The headline was to say, 'World Champion Checkers Super Bowl in Town.' "

"Guess I kinged that deal," Gator said loud enough for all to hear. "I'll have scrambled, biscuits and gravy, hash browns, and sausage patties."

"Cheese-ham omelet and the rest," I said.

"Good to have some tippers finally come in here," Vi said and went off with her small pad in her hand.

"Tippers? Why, Vi, I leave you a tip every day," Wick said.

"Ha," she said over her shoulder standing at the high window to the kitchen. Snapping the order on the wheel, she spun it around for the cook. "You ever left more than your dirty dishes, I'd faint."

"These bulls at Fort Smith—they worth going to see about?" I asked Gator to get out of the usual morning bickering.

"He says they're tough."

"Figured out a time when he can show us. How's those other two? Blacky and Dummy?"

"Settled down and they do handle all right, if you're easy."

"Good, we can work around that."

Vi brought our breakfast and while we ate, we went over more plans. I needed some grasser calves to go on my place before the price went sky-high. Usually there is a time right before the grass greens that you can still buy some weaned thin stuff to put on grass for the summer. My place would handle three dozen. Wormed and worked, they'd put on some weight. No get-rich project, but another iron in the fire. They should cover a few truck payments and the land taxes.

Coming back to my place, when we turned down my lane off the county road, I could see some vehicles in my yard. "We've got company."

"That's your pickup!" Gator said and stomped on the accelerator. "Who's that Cadillac belong to?"

"Oh, shit! That means trouble!"

Curly had Shoat by the arms from behind, and Big

Guy was pounding him in the gut. Gator jumped out
of his truck before it stopped. I was looking all over
for his cellular. The truck bumped into the Caddy, but
I still hadn't located the cell phone. My hand shot
down beside the console and I felt it in my hand.

Gator took Big Boy by the arm, jerked him around,
and gave him a vicious smash to the face. The fight
was on as I punched in 911.

It rang twice. "County emergency. Do you have
an emergency?"

"Damn right, I do. Brad Turner, I live on County
Road 546 east of Woodbury and there are some thugs
out here beating up my friends; correct that, my
friends are now beating up the thugs. Send a couple
deputies out here. I'm pressing charges."

By this time, Shoat, with his shirt half torn off his
back, was backing Curly up with a barrage of fists
thrown like a windmill. Dawg had hold of Curly's
pants leg and was shredding them. Mona was
screaming.

"This is a serious-sounding altercation. Are there
any firearms?"

"Yes. Get someone out here. There may be a
killing!"

The operator went over it again. "Is this a police
matter? Do you have a medical emergency? Are there
any life threatening injuries—"

"Lady, this is an extreme emergency! Send them
now!" I punched the phone off and scooted out. Curly
was a good match for Shoat. That was until Dawg
came over and bit into his ankle. The guy went to
screaming like a girl when the canine teeth ripped his
pants leg off to the knee. Dawg had to shake the first
mouthful of wool material off his teeth before he

could dive in for more. Dawg caught the guy under the right hind pocket and the bite left Curly in his red boxer shorts, when he jumped for the top of the corral and tried to belly over it, screaming, "I give up! Call that freaking dog off me!"

"I ain't half through with you!" Gator shouted and jerked him down. The thug balled up on the ground and went to whimpering.

"Dawg! Get in the truck!"

Disappointed that his fun was over, the red heeler wagged his butt, since he had no tail. He looked up at Gator as if to ask if he could have one more bite of those pants and reluctantly, he obeyed his master. He bounded back into the truckbed and soon looked over the edge, ready for the next big fight.

"I called the high sheriff," I said to Gator, when I could hear the whine of the siren coming off the state highway.

"You order an ambulance?" he asked.

"No."

"How about the fire truck?"

"No." Peeved that they were coming, I looked east at the sound and the dust.

"That's the Willow Creek Volunteer Fire department coming from that way." He tossed his head toward the sound.

I frowned at him. "Why're they coming?"

"Lord would only know. Them boys ain't lost a foundation in ten years."

"Let's make a deal," Curly said.

"You've had your deal with me. Pointing a gun at me and threatening me. Assaulting Shoat and Gator here."

"Yes, and trying to kick my dog, mister," Gator

began. "Kicking a good dog in Oklahoma is real serious business. Could get you nine to fifteen years."

The two squad cars arrived, light bars flashing, sirens winding to a halt. With a .357 held in both hands, stationed on top of the open car door, Deputy Carl Means took a bead on us. "Everyone stay right there."

Carl never was the brightest of the Means boys. His daddy made some money in oil and was a party faithful. He gave the campaign limit to anyone running for office on the ticket, so when Carl needed an occupation, they gave him a badge. Three years younger than me, he'd gone to college every fall for six years. Somehow he never stayed for the whole semester, so his daddy got him a deputy commission.

Sam Good, the older deputy, climbed out of his white car and leaned his elbows on the hood of Means's car to survey the situation. He'd been the law back when Gator and I were, according to him, the number-one troublemakers in the county. Twice, he had been elected sheriff in years past, and though he'd worked for the state drug task force, I figured he was getting close to retirement from this job.

"Who's the fighter and the fightee?" he asked in a slow drawl.

"Should I check them for weapons?" Means asked.

"In due time. What the hell's going on, Turner?" Good paused to frown with a look of disgust just as the fire department hose truck came to a screeching halt beyond his vehicle. Then he shook his gray head further at the captain of the Willow Creek volunteers, who in his knee-high rubber boots came tromping over and out of breath asked, "Where's the fire?"

"In the damn ambulance, I guess," Good said as the yellow unit came down the drive way in a screaming cloud of dust.

Gator tossed his thumb to the west. "And just guess what's going to be on the front page of this week's paper." It was Grady's car right on the tailgate of the meat wagon.

Chapter 31

The two thugs, their hands cuffed behind them, were in Deputy Means's back seat. The fire truck was gone and the ambulance left screaming on a run to Carstead. Life was finally returning to normal at my house. In a fresh shirt, Shoat was talking serious to Mona over by her sports car. Gator was sitting on his tailgate drinking a can of beer and shaking his head. Chief Deputy Good was scratching Dawg's ears, and the fool red heeler was beside himself over the attention.

"Those two—they'll probably pay a hefty fine and get off," Good said to caution us for the truth.

"Get the bond up high enough," Gator said.

"Oh, we will. I'll have Al haul that Caddy in. They aren't dumb enough to have anything in it. They have a Missouri permit for their guns. You want to charge them with threatening you?" He looked at me.

"I want them to stay in Kansas City."

"I think they will when Judge Ponder gets through with them."

"Sorry about all the ruckus," I said.

"No problem." Sam shook his head to dismiss my concern. "Most excitement we've had in three months."

I turned when I heard the sports car's powerful engine start, and saw Mona wave at Shoat. He walked over to join us as the Karmann Ghia crawled out the driveway and headed for the road.

"Mona leaving?" I asked.

"Yes, sir. Until she divorces him, I told her not to come around me."

Gator raised his beer in a toast. "Now that's a good idea."

I agreed.

"She said she told you that she paid my entry fees." Shoat shook his head. "I paid her back every dime. I ain't one of them Arkansas Krammers."

"Yes, you are. But you're the good branch of that tree."

I looked up at another cloud of dust on the country road.

"Who's that?" Gator asked.

"Zola," I said and smiled.

"Well, we better take them in. Al's wrecker's coming for the Cadillac. You three don't get in any more fights today." Good pushed off the tailgate and waved for Means to go ahead with his prisoners.

"What's happened here?" Zola said, jumping out of her pickup and frowning at everything.

"Let me tell you, girl. We had a big drug bust here," Gator said and went out to hug her. He came over with her under his arm. "You ever met Brad Turner, world-famous rodeo announcer? Oh, girl, I could tell you tales about him that would chill your blood."

"Gator, I want to hear all of them." She kissed him on the cheek and ran over to hug me. "You all right?"

"I'm fine. With a fighting force like this, who wouldn't be?" I was looking down in her smiling face with my arms around her.

"Man, I hate those Western movies where the guy gets all kissy-faced with the girl in the end. Shoat, you can have a beer now that the sheriff's deputies are gone." Gator handed him one. "Let's you and me run up to the Kansas line and check on some of my calves. We're not needed here."

I was busy kissing Zola—no, they weren't needed there. Not for days.

It was early summer at the Dodge City Rodeo, on a Saturday night after the last hurrah. Zola and I had made some serious plans for our future together after the week we spent together at my place. If by Labor Day, she didn't stand a chance of making the top fifteen, she'd join me for my fall rodeos. We'd see how we got along on the road and at the ranch, being together all the time. The bucking-bull business, I thought, was kind of a catalyst to get her and her father talking again. The times the two of us were with him, the tension had eased. Gator and I were still chasing prospects for our partner's string of super bulls. The search was expensive and elusive.

Wendell still wanted to get in the business. But that night in Dodge City, bucking bulls were the furthest thing from my mind as I rode Boy down the alleyway between the stock pens under the yard lights. The sounds of the stock being loaded and their bawling rang in my ears; I was headed for a parting I dreaded. It seemed like only yesterday when I introduced him for the first time in Jackson.

I dismounted at the back gate and Shoat opened it for me.

"Been a good one," he said and grinned.

"You did good here."

"Oh, I guess."

"No, you did real good. You're headed for the big times, Shoat Krammer."

A shake of his head and a bite of his lower lip, he tilted his face to the side. "Brad, I won't ever forget Jackson and all the things that you've done for me since then."

"Aw, that's water under the bridge." I clapped him on the shoulder. The pride inside of me over his success could have filled a section of wheat—but no need to get sentimental over it here.

"I won't ever forget it." His eyes narrowed when he looked at me.

"You keep riding them rough ones. I want to be there when you win the big gold buckle."

"Why, Brad, you'd better be there doing the announcing."

"Damn it, Shoat, you coming or not?" his impatient traveling pard called out. "We've got five hundred miles still to drive tonight."

"I'm coming. See ya," he said and hurried off under the stark lights to climb in the club cab of the waiting pickup. He had some good running buddies—Taylor, Marks, and Denton; they'd show him more of the ropes.

Chester rode up the alleyway on a lathered horse from sorting the bulls to load out. He stopped the hard-breathing big gelding beside me.

"Damn it, Brad, that boy's going to make one helluva champion, ain't he?"

"I think so. He's what the bossman calls a natural."

No other series has this much historical action!

THE TRAILSMAN

To order call: 1-800-788-6262